The
Runaway
Sisters

ALSO BY ANN BENNETT

The Orphan House

ANN BENNETT

The
Runaway
Sisters

bookouture

Published by Bookouture in 2020

An imprint of Storyfire Ltd.
Carmelite House
50 Victoria Embankment
London EC4Y 0DZ

www.bookouture.com

ISBN: 978-1-83888-234-1
eBook ISBN: 978-1-83888-233-4

For all my sisters: Mary, Kath, Maggie, Dot and Lizzie, with love.

Chapter One

Helen

As the lane climbed towards the open moor it became narrower and steeper. The high Devon banks on either side closed in, thick with bracken and dripping greenery. Helen drove slowly, but in places the way ahead became so confined that she had to slow the car to walking pace to avoid scraping it on the sharp rocks, obscured by ferns and foliage.

It seemed to Helen that this tiny lane, with its tortured twists and turns as it laboured up the foothills towards Dartmoor, somehow reflected her own mood, even more so as the dark clouds ahead closed in on her and she drew closer to Black Moor Hall.

At last she entered a stretch of dense woodland, where a moorland stream rushed downhill in a gully beside the road, and the entrance to the house came into view. Black wrought-iron gates rusting with age stood between tall, granite pillars. She pulled off the lane, stopped the car on the little bridge that crossed the stream and got out to open the gates. As she did so, she glanced down at her phone lying on the passenger seat. A text was flashing on the screen.

Sorry, going to be a bit late. Something's come up. See you later. Laura.

Helen sighed, inching the car through the gates. Predictable; typical even. But it didn't matter really; it would give her a chance to wander around the place alone and get her thoughts together. She needed time to reflect.

She drove along the rough track, through the spinney of evergreens, and as she rounded the final bend, the old house hove into view. It was a grey, overcast day, with mists rolling in from the high moor. The house looked even more forbidding than usual with its sombre granite gables and square bay windows either side of the imposing entrance. Helen pulled the car up on the circular drive and, suppressing a shudder, fumbled in her handbag for the keys.

As she paused on the threshold, she realised that she couldn't remember a time in recent years when she'd been inside the house alone. As she closed the heavy front door behind her and ventured through the porch into the vast entrance hall, she felt the chill wrap itself around her.

She paused in the galleried hallway, half-expecting her mother's voice to ring out from the kitchen.

'You're late again, Helen… Well, don't just stand there, come on in and peel the potatoes. Good God! What on earth are you wearing?'

But the house was still and silent – as it had never been before. She wandered through into the dining room, with its dark marble fireplace and huge bay window overlooking the rolling moor, vast and open, rising gently upwards to the crags of Black Tor in the distance. She'd half-expected to see her mother sitting in the corner by the window, pedalling away furiously on an old-fashioned treadle sewing machine, running up curtains, clothes, or patchwork quilts, or kneeling before the fire in her gardening trousers, working the wooden bellows to get the flames going. But the room was as still as the grave, ornaments and knick-knacks gone, the bookcases emptied of their books, which waited in tea chests to be taken to the second-hand bookshop in Ashburton.

Sighing, Helen walked over to the fireplace and peered at the framed photographs that still stood on the mantelpiece. She and

Laura must have somehow forgotten to pack them away when they had cleared this room yesterday. In pride of place in the middle was the one of her mother and father at their wedding, outside that whitewashed church in Darjeeling, the hill-station in India where they had first met. *Daisy and Arthur's wedding, October 1945*, the inscription underneath the photograph read. Her father, short and balding, a good fifteen years older than her mother, was smiling from ear to ear, but her mother looked wistful and a little surprised, in a white lacy dress and veil, her hair swept back from her face. Beside it was the one of Daisy collecting her medical degree in 1955, holding up her certificate, a triumphant look on her face. Next to that stood the picture of Laura and Helen, probably aged thirteen and three respectively, standing together on the front step of the house in London in white dresses, then there was Laura in cap and gown receiving her degree; Laura and Paul getting married, and several others of their two children.

There were no further pictures of herself, she noted with a wry smile, because she had neither got married nor finished her degree. Looking at the photos on the mantelpiece now, she realised that the display was a snapshot of all the things her mother was proud of.

She ran a finger through the dust on the dining room table and checked the label tied to its leg. *Scorpio Antiques, High Street, Totnes* was written there in her own handwriting. The shop belonged to her friend, Jago, and it was where she'd worked for several years.

She wandered across the hall and into the living room, with its bay window and Daisy's reclining armchair. She pictured her mother slumped in it in the weeks before her stroke, watching daytime television, a sure sign that something was very wrong. Normally Daisy would have scoffed at the idea – she'd been so dynamic, so full of energy.

Helen walked through to the kitchen where she'd found her mother sprawled on the floor in front of the Aga a month ago. It was fate that had brought Helen to the house that day. She'd been on the dual carriageway, coming back from a shopping trip in Exeter, when she'd seen the turn-off to Black Moor Hall and taken it on a whim.

Now, Helen put the kettle on the hob and peered out of the window. It looked out over the back lawn, to the garden hedge and over the wild, neglected farmland beyond. Daisy had forbidden Helen to venture in that direction as she was growing up. A couple of fields away beyond an overgrown wood, in a hollow in the hills, stood a derelict farmhouse, surrounded by tumbledown barns. The buildings were smothered in ivy. Ferns and buddleia sprouted from the caved-in roofs.

'It's dangerous down there,' Daisy had said when Helen had asked about what was over the hedge. 'It's out of bounds. There's plenty of space to explore on the other side of the house. The whole moor, in fact. You've absolutely no reason to go onto that land.'

Helen had obeyed her for years, but on many occasions when looking out of her bedroom window, she had been surprised to see Daisy herself wandering through the tall grass of the forbidden field, heading in the direction of the old farmhouse. She would return later, walking slowly, her head bowed, lost in thought. Helen had not dared to ask her mother about it, or even mention that she'd seen her. Daisy wasn't that sort of mother. But she recalled being mystified, as well as feeling hurt at being excluded on seeing her mother wandering in that field alone.

She'd only ventured there once in her life, through the dense wood, to stare down at the old farm nestled in the valley. She'd done it as an act of rebellion against her mother. She'd trespassed on forbidden ground. An act that had had lasting repercussions for their relationship.

She cast her eye around the kitchen to check that she and Laura hadn't missed anything yesterday. Cardboard boxes were stacked in the middle of the room, containing all Daisy's cooking equipment and china. It wasn't likely they would have – the photographs on the mantelpiece were a slip-up, but otherwise Laura had been ruthless.

'What about this?' Helen had mused, holding a silk print of a Sikh warrior up to show her sister. 'Don't you think we should keep them? Mum must have had them since she was in India. She might be upset if we get rid of them.'

Laura had given her that look – the one with the raised eyebrow – that said it all. She didn't even need to speak, and Helen had automatically taken the prints off the wall and stowed them away in a tea chest, along with all the other memorabilia.

'Look at this lovely cushion,' she'd said as they were clearing the sitting room. 'Don't you remember Mum doing this tapestry herself? She worked on it, night after night. It took her ages.'

'Yes, I do remember. But, sadly, we can't keep everything. There's just too much. It's such a shame, I know.'

It had been awkward between Helen and Laura at first. They'd hardly spoken for years. It wasn't a rift exactly, but they had always been so different. Laura, with her ambition, her fast-paced legal career, her big house in a fashionable suburb of Exeter, and now her other roles. She was a mother to two equally successful thirty-somethings, and consort to her husband Paul, who'd recently given up his job in the City to become an MP. Helen thought of her own life now. She had no real career, other than helping Jago in his antiques business, she had no qualifications and no children. She'd always found life so difficult. She supposed life in Totnes was pleasant enough though. She had friends, she enjoyed her yoga lessons once a week, meetings with the Green Action Group and dabbling in her art. But it had been so hard to find her place in the world. It felt, now, as if she hadn't got much to look back on. Just a series of broken relationships and missed opportunities. She bit her thumbnail absently as she thought about it.

She wandered upstairs and stood in the doorway of her childhood bedroom. Weak winter sunlight streamed in through the window. This was where she'd slept since they'd moved to the house when she was nine, until she left, aged eighteen. The white walls were bare, with paler patches where her pictures had been taken down. She sat down on her old brass bed and a host of memories came flooding back. She could almost feel multiple versions of herself lying right there on the bed beside her. So clear were the memories that she had a sensation of vertigo, as if she was looking down from a great height as the years unravelled beneath her. Here she was, lying on the bed as an anguished nine-year-old, staring up at the cracks in the ceiling, wondering why on earth her mother had insisted on tearing her away from her school and her home in London, from everything she'd ever known, and bringing her to live here in the middle of nowhere.

The sound of a car engine and the scrunch of tyres on the drive broke into her memories. She crossed the landing to the front bedroom and peered out of the window. There was Laura's BMW parking up, sleek and new, beside her own small and battered Renault. The door opened and out got Laura, mobile phone clamped to her ear, dressed in designer boots and jeans and a casual sweater, her blonde hair tied back in a ponytail. Helen watched her sister cross the front drive and mount the steps of the house. A pang of envy went through her.

Helen heard Laura's voice in the hall as she finished her conversation. She went to the top of the stairs.

'Oh, there you are,' said Laura, looking up. 'Sorry about that. Some work thing. A client needed some urgent advice on a deal.'

'I thought you'd retired,' Helen replied.

'I have… well, semi anyway,' Laura said, coming up the stairs. 'I'm just a consultant now. But this client asked specifically for me to take care of this deal. I really couldn't say no. He brings in a lot of income for the firm.'

Laura was at the top of the stairs now and, with a waft of Chanel No 5, gave Helen a peremptory peck on the cheek.

'All set, then? Have you started yet?' she asked breezily.

'Of course not. I wasn't going to start without you. It's Mum's bedroom, after all. I wouldn't want to do that on my own.'

'Why ever not?'

'Well, it's so personal. Lots of memories, that sort of thing.'

Laura gave her a sympathetic glance and, picking up a couple of empty cardboard boxes, strode in front of her and into their mother's bedroom. Helen followed, a feeling of dread in the pit of her stomach. She hadn't been in there since Daisy went into the care home, weeks ago. Mrs Starr, the cleaning lady, would have been in to strip the bed and clean the room, but it still felt odd venturing into Daisy's personal space. This was somewhere else that had been out of bounds when she'd been young.

'Come on, then. Let's start with the dressing table, shall we?' said Laura.

They systematically went through Daisy's hairbrushes, her perfume bottles, her scarves and her jewellery. Then they emptied her chests of drawers and wardrobe of clothes.

'She did have an awful lot of old rubbish,' said Laura, holding up an Aran sweater with holes in the sleeves.

'She knitted that herself, I think. She used to wear it for gardening,' Helen said, picturing Daisy pruning the roses around the drive, weeding the flowerbeds in all weathers, pushing the lawnmower vigorously across the lawn.

'Well, let's face it,' said Laura briskly, 'no one else is going to want it, are they? Full of holes like that. And Mum isn't going to need it any more, is she? When I spoke to the doctors at the care home they gave me the impression she wasn't doing very well. I know you don't want to believe it, Helen, but she really won't be coming back here. Another one for the clothes bank.' She screwed the sweater up and dropped it into a bin bag. Helen winced, seeing another precious item consigned like this. How different they were. How could Laura be so practical about all this, when everything they associated with their mother was being discarded for ever?

*

The morning wore on and after a couple of hours they had finished clearing the room. Bookshelves, drawers, and the wardrobe were all emptied and dusted down, the pictures stacked in a pile.

'What about the wardrobe?' asked Laura, staring at the great mahogany monstrosity that occupied one wall. 'Is Jago taking that too?'

'I think so. Yes. Mum loved it so much, didn't she?'

'It's hard to see why. God knows how he's going to transport that.'

'I think it comes apart. The top separates from the bottom bit,' said Helen, going over to the wardrobe and examining the join where the two halves met. 'Look.' She pushed the top part with her shoulder and edged it forward to demonstrate. As she moved it forward from the wall, something dropped down the back from the top of the wardrobe.

'What was that?' asked Laura.

'I'm not sure.'

'Shall we try to push it forward and see?'

They both put their shoulders to the wardrobe and, with some effort, nudged it a few inches from the wall.

'It's just an old hat, look,' said Helen, picking up a grey felt hat, thick with dust and cobwebs. But as she did so, she noticed something protruding from the wall behind the wardrobe. She looked more closely: it appeared to be some wooden beading, perhaps a door frame.

'What's this?'

Laura came over and peered behind the wardrobe.

'I've no idea. Why don't we move the wardrobe aside a bit more?'

Again, they put their shoulders to the wardrobe and, with a lot of scraping and creaking, managed to move it a couple of feet further.

It was a cupboard, built into the wall. It had a white painted door and an old-fashioned metal fastener shaped like a cross. Helen was staring at the cupboard, wondering what was inside.

'Go on. Open it then,' said Laura.

Helen turned the metal cross and pulled the door. It was stiff, but after a few tugs it opened. She peered inside. The space contained several built-in wooden shelves. Only one of these had anything on it: an old canvas bag with scuffed leather straps. Helen lifted it out carefully. She lifted the flap and looked inside. There were two dusty envelopes nestling in the folds.

Helen looked at Laura, stunned. 'There are some old letters in here.'

'Well, take them out then. What are you waiting for?'

'They're probably Mum's. She might not want us to see them.'

'Oh, come on, Helen. I'm sure Mum won't mind. We've got to pack up the house, after all. She knows we're putting it on the market.'

'If you're sure…' Helen said. Laura nodded impatiently. 'Of course. Let's see what they say.'

Helen drew the letters out of the bag with some reverence. There was a feeling of discomfort in her stomach. If she'd been alone, she would probably have left the letters in the bag and shut the cupboard again. But Laura was hovering over her, eyes expectant, her body taut with impatience.

'Well, what are they? Open one up.'

The first letter on the pile had a London postmark, was dated July 1940 and bore a Plymouth address she didn't recognise.

Miss Daisy Banks,
10, St James Road,
Plympton,
Plymouth,
Devon.

'Who is Daisy Banks?' Laura asked the question that was hovering on Helen's own lips. She shook her head, mystified.

'I've no idea. Mum's maiden name was Dawson. She showed me her passport once.' She remembered her mother proudly showing her a battered passport dated sometime in 1945, a picture of a young Daisy looking out from its pages.

'And Plymouth? Did Mum ever live in Plymouth?'

Helen thought for a moment, then shook her head. 'I don't think so. I don't remember her mentioning having spent time in Devon during the war.'

'No. She's never really talked about the war to me. I just got the impression that she stayed at home in London throughout,' Laura said.

'Do you remember when she used to talk about India?' Helen asked, recalling the stories herself. 'How she went out there once her parents had died, how she met Dad out there after the war. Perhaps it's a different Daisy?'

'I hardly think so, Helen. Are both the letters addressed to Daisy Banks?'

Helen looked at the envelopes. Underneath them were some old photographs.

The first was of two girls, standing side by side outside a terraced house. One looked to be in her early teens, the other a few years younger. The older one bore more than a passing resemblance to their mother.

'Who's the other girl?' asked Helen. Laura shrugged, examining the next photograph. 'A friend perhaps? Look at this one!'

It was of a family group, a man and a woman and the two girls from the first photograph. They were sitting on a wall at the seaside, their hair blown by the wind. The younger girl was sitting on the woman's lap. The older one was seated next to the man, holding his hand. On the back was written: *Margate, summer 1937*.

The third photograph was of a different girl altogether. She looked older. Seventeen or eighteen perhaps. She was very plump and her pudgy face was serious, unsmiling, her eyes dull. She was holding a tiny baby, swaddled in a shawl.

'Who do you think that is?' Helen asked Laura, showing her the photo.

'I've no idea,' said Laura.

There was also a picture postcard from the seaside. A sandy beach with people in bathing costumes sunning themselves in deckchairs or playing ball games. Written on the other side was:

To my darling Daisy. Be good. I'll be thinking of you all the time. Until we meet again, Love Mother.

The last photograph was of a fresh-faced young man Helen didn't recognise. He was dressed in naval uniform, with three stripes on his sailor's collar; his face was slim and fine-boned and from under his peaked cap protruded a mop of dark hair. He was staring out at the camera with a look of defiance. Helen peered closely; on the cap were the letters 'HMS' and some further letters, which she presumed were the name of his ship, but they were too dark to read. Under the photograph were printed the words, *Ordinary Seaman J. Smith. 1942.* She stared at them, puzzled. She'd never heard her mother speak of a J. Smith. She glanced at Laura, who shrugged.

'Why don't you open one of the letters?'

Helen eased a letter out of the envelope and unfolded it slowly. The paper was brittle and yellow with age and the words were written in faded blue ink in spidery handwriting. She began to read out loud.

'My Dearest Daisy and Peggy,' it began.

'Peggy?' Helen stopped reading and stared at Laura. 'Whoever's Peggy?'

Laura shrugged. 'Absolutely no idea. Go on. Carry on reading.'

'I'm so sorry your train journey got off to such a bad start, but I hope you have settled in now and that life isn't too bad with Mr and Mrs Brown. I expect you've started school by now and that might feel strange, so far from home and different from what you're used to. Please don't worry about me. They're taking good care of me, here in hospital. I broke my leg in the fall, and got knocked out, as you know, but I'm getting a bit better every day. I'll be thinking of you and hoping you will be on your best behaviour and keeping your chins up. Daisy, I know I can trust you to look after your sister. It is such a comfort to me that you've been able to go together—'

Helen stopped reading.

'Laura, this must be a different Daisy. Mum was an only child. This letter can't have been written to her, can it?'

Laura was staring at the letter, her face pale with shock.

Chapter Two

Daisy

Plymouth, July 1940

I'll never forget that night when everything changed. It was a few weeks after we'd been evacuated to Plympton, to stay with Mr and Mrs Brown. The weather was very close that night and the little bedroom I shared with Peggy was stifling. I was finding it hard to get off to sleep, as I had for weeks now. Other things were keeping me awake apart from the heat; I felt so lost in this city where I didn't belong, sleeping in a house with complete strangers. I slid out of bed to open the window wider. As I lifted the sash, I saw the first glimmerings of daylight over the roofs opposite and I was sure I could hear a rumble in the distance. Was it thunder? Perhaps a summer storm? And then a chill went through me. I stuck my head out of the window to listen. The noise was growing louder and closer. We were used to air raids by then and I recognised the tone of German engines. But something felt different this time. They were closer than I'd ever heard them before.

In a panic, I flew over to Peggy to wake her up, thinking how odd it was that the air raid sirens weren't already whining in the street. The roar of the engines got closer and closer, until it was at a deafening pitch. As I was shaking Peggy awake, the planes were directly above us and in the next instant there was a thunderous blast, followed by the sound of falling masonry from buildings in the street, and, to my horror, even closer, splintering wood; and most chilling of all, the muffled screams of people being buried by falling buildings.

I had thought that if this happened I would act quickly, knowing it was my responsibility to keep Peggy safe, but my nerves were shattered and I couldn't think of what to do as she and I sat on her bed and we clung together. The glass in the window shattered, the room shook around us, and plaster showered down from the ceiling. We stayed like that, shaking and sobbing, until the sound of falling buildings had finally subsided and all fell silent.

Slowly and carefully in the pitch-black of the room, I crept towards the door. The frame must have buckled because it took me three or four tugs to prise it open. Gingerly, I stepped outside the room and onto the landing, then stepped straight back again, stunned at what I had seen through the cloud of dust and smoke that enveloped me. Somehow, the floor of the landing and the stairs had remained intact, but the wall to Mr and Mrs Brown's bedroom was gone and the whole of that side of the house, and the next-door house too, had collapsed in a great mound of bricks and rubble. I stared, open-mouthed, not quite believing what was in front of my eyes. Beyond that, in what was left of the street, people were stumbling about in the dust, dazed, some of them covered in blood. Little fires had lit spontaneously and were burning everywhere. And at that moment, the siren started to sound. It was the familiar air raid signal, only this time it was too late.

'Peggy, we've got to get out of here quickly,' I said. I stared down at my little sister. She was four years younger than me. I'd always protected her from harm on the streets at home in London, and I'd looked after her since we'd arrived in Plymouth. She didn't really understand about the war; about how precarious our situation was. In a way, I was glad of that.

'Shall we take our things?'

'What?' I asked, dazed. 'There's no time for that.'

But Peggy was already throwing clothes from the drawer into her gas mask bag, shoving in her books and medicine.

'Mother said we mustn't lose anything.' She was moving fast. 'I'm ready now,' she said, pulling her coat over her nightdress.

I quickly pulled a sweater and trousers on over my own nightie. On an impulse I grabbed Mother's letters and some photos from home from the drawer and threw them in Peggy's bag. Tears filled my eyes at the thought of darling Mother, and that the letters were all we now had to remember her by, but I brushed them away quickly. There was no time for that now.

'Come on,' I said, taking Peggy's hand.

Coughing and spluttering, we edged our way through the rubble on the landing and began to step carefully down the stairs, which seemed to be on a dangerous tilt. Each time we took a step down, the stairs moved and gave an ominous creak as if the whole structure was about to collapse. The front door of the house had been blown off, so when we finally reached the bottom of the fragile staircase, we stepped straight out onto the street. We stood in front of the house hand in hand, covered in grime, dazed and disoriented from the blast, wondering what to do and where to go. Dust filled our eyes and nostrils, and as we stood there, it was still falling from the sky, like some sort of snow.

Not knowing what to do, stunned and reeling from the shock of the blast, I took a few steps forward, holding Peggy's hand tightly in mine. The dust swirled around us, people stumbled about, as dazed and confused as we were. I felt sick and dizzy. My mouth was full of dust. I couldn't focus my thoughts. I had no idea where to go or what to do. After a few steps forward, I stumbled over a pile of bricks and fell over, pulling Peggy down with me. We sat there for a few minutes, gathering our strength, before we got up and blundered on through the rubble and dust, directionless and disoriented.

'Where shall we go?' Peggy asked.

'We could try to get to the station,' I said, not thinking straight. 'We might be able to get on a train back to London.'

'But we haven't got any money, Daisy.'

'I know…'

We picked our way through the mountains of rubble and debris from the broken buildings towards the end of the road. There were policemen already on the street, and a group of men were approaching our house with shovels, but none of them paid any attention to us. At the sight of them there, about to start digging for people crushed under the buildings, I had an overwhelming need to get out of the street. I just wanted to get away from all this chaos and confusion.

'Come on.' I tugged Peggy's hand and we stumbled to the end of the road, through the clouds of dust.

As we turned into the next street I noticed a man striding purposefully towards us. My first instinct was to turn and run in the opposite direction, but I wasn't quick enough and, in a few seconds, he was approaching us. He was tall and forbidding and seemed to fill the pavement with his brooding presence. We stopped in front of him, afraid to walk round him or go any further. He wore a dark coat, which billowed in the dust. A chill went through me, but I wasn't sure why.

I stood in front of him, feeling intimidated, gripping Peggy's hand tightly and wondering what to do for the best. Then I noticed his white band with the words 'Billeting Officer' on his right arm. I remembered Mother's smiling face as she handed us onto the train in Paddington, happy to entrust us to a billeting officer. I felt a little reassured. Surely that was a sign that we could trust this man? We looked up at him. He was frowning at first, but put on a smile when he noticed us there.

'Hello now. Where are you two girls off to?' His tone seemed friendly, so I relaxed a little.

'Our street's just been bombed,' I said, turning to point in the direction of the Browns' house. 'We're evacuees.'

'Let me see your ID,' he said, holding out his hand and flicking his fingers impatiently. Peggy felt in her gas mask bag and held out our two brown ID cards, complete with their coat of arms on the front.

'Hmm… From London, I see,' he pondered, and paused, his brow furrowed in thought.

'We thought we'd try to get home,' I said, thinking that maybe he'd be able to help us.

'Sorry, my dear, but I'm afraid that's impossible,' he said. 'You're the responsibility of the authorities while you're here. We'll take care of you. Don't you worry.'

Then he produced a bar of chocolate from his pocket, unwrapped the foil, broke it in half and handed the halves to us. I took mine with shaking hands, and bit into it gratefully, the shock of the blast having drained me of energy and left my legs weak and shaky. The last time we'd tasted chocolate was weeks ago on the train; Mother had given us a small ration for the journey.

'No need to think about home, now,' he said in a wheedling tone. 'All school-aged children left in Plymouth are being evacuated to the countryside. How would you two girls like a stay on a lovely farm on the edge of Dartmoor? Lots of animals. There are other children there too.'

'We'd really prefer to go home,' I said firmly, glancing at Peggy, whose face had brightened at the mention of animals.

'Well, I'm sorry to say this, but I'm not sure you have that choice. I'm afraid it's a government order,' he said. He produced from his pocket a paper that had an official Ministry of Defence stamp on it, headed 'Evacuation of Plymouth'. He waved it in front of us. 'Now you just follow me. You're in luck that you bumped into me. You won't have to bother with the bus. I'll take you there myself. I know the farmer personally. Mr Reeves. He's a very generous man.'

I frowned and hesitated. Something didn't feel quite right, but the man had such an air of authority, and we had nothing to call our own and no one in the world to turn to.

I thought about Mother and felt her loss so very strongly, and of Father, thousands of miles away, fighting in Africa. So far away it felt as though he might never return. I felt so alone, as if there was no one in the world who would care, or even know what had happened to us today, no one to inform where we were going, or to look out for us, should anything go wrong. And then, grasping at straws, I remembered our neighbour, Mother's friend, Mrs Hutchings.

'Can we let a neighbour back home know where we're going?' I asked.

'If you tell me the address, I will write myself to let them know where you are and reassure them you're safe. Come along then. My truck is parked just round the corner.'

He sounded so plausible, so reassuring, and I was ready to be convinced; ready to let someone else take control of the situation. So, I said nothing and we followed him into the next street, to where a battered old station wagon was parked. At the sight of it, I hesitated again. It looked like a farm truck, not an official vehicle, but the man was so insistent, and so I swallowed my fears. He opened the passenger door and waved us inside the truck. We slid into the front seat, Peggy in the middle.

The man started the engine. He drove us through the outskirts of the town and out into the countryside, through emerald green fields and dark evergreen forests, climbing steadily upwards until we were out on the open moor. The sun was high in the sky and it was a sparkling morning.

'This is Dartmoor,' he said. 'Don't suppose you Londoners have seen anything like this before, have you?'

I stared out at the rolling moorland, dotted with grazing sheep and ponies, with swathes of gorse and heather on the higher ground. In places it rose to jagged summits of craggy rocks. I stared out at the bleak, forlorn landscape that for some reason sent shivers through me, and remained silent.

I was thinking back over the past few months. Thinking about how our lives had changed so dramatically. It seemed a lifetime ago that we'd been in London with Mother and Father, living safe and protected before the war had come along and robbed us of everything we knew and loved.

Chapter Three

Daisy

Father worked as a clerk in the City of London, leaving the house early each morning to take the Underground to work. Mother's job was to look after the family and the house. We knew all our neighbours and went to the local schools a few streets away, and each summer we would take a trip to a seaside town and stay in a boarding house for a week so we could paddle in the water and run and laugh together.

Everything changed when war broke out. I will never forget sitting round Father's wireless set in the living room that airless Sunday morning, as the prime minister announced that Britain was at war with Germany. I could see the shock and fear in my parents' eyes as they listened to his speech, but I didn't understand then what it might mean.

The first change took place that very evening, with Mother taking great care to cover every chink in the windows with heavy curtains. She and Father would speak in hushed tones more often, and I'd strain to hear what they discussed.

'Lots of children are being evacuated from London. Do you think we should send Peggy and Daisy away too, Eileen?' asked Father.

'No! Of course not. We're safe out here in the suburbs, aren't we? It's only those in the East End near the docks that need to go.'

'Well, there *is* the airbase nearby…'

'Oh, Ted, please. Can't we just wait a few weeks and see what happens?'

So, we stayed where we were for the time being, but food began to get scarce immediately, and after a few months we were sent ration books. Mother had to spend long hours queuing at the local shops to get the most basic supplies.

Things at home began to get tense. I'd never known Mother and Father argue before, but now it was a regular occurrence. I would lie awake and hear raised voices from their bedroom. Piecing together the scraps that I heard, I gathered that Father wanted to sign up to fight in the army, but Mother was dead against it.

'What about the girls?' I heard her say again and again. 'Don't forget you have a family, Ted. What would we do if anything happened to you?'

Mother was a worrier and I could see that the thought of him going to war made her anxious. But he got his way, and within a few months had signed up.

After he'd gone, Mother tried her best to keep it together for us, but I started to notice her becoming more and more withdrawn. She wouldn't say much in the evenings, and she lay in bed for longer each day, sometimes even forgetting to go out and line up for food. On several occasions we ate bread and lard for supper. Mrs Hutchings, Mother's friend, looked in on her and tried to help out. Sometimes, she invited us in for tea. She wasn't like Mother; she was much more relaxed and easy-going, her eyes full of laughter. She had a daughter, Suzanne, a couple of years older than me, who wore make-up and curled her beautiful red hair in the latest style. I started spending more time out on the streets with Suzanne and the local teenagers. We would hang about, playing ball games and hopscotch. Occasionally someone would pinch a cigarette from their mother and we would all share it, sitting behind a shed in the local playing field, enjoying the heady rush we'd get from inhaling the smoke.

Sometimes we would wander up towards the airbase, a couple of miles away, and stare at the stationary aircraft through the fence.

But that became more difficult as the fields surrounding the base were gradually cordoned off with coiled barbed wire and became parking areas for military vehicles.

A few weeks after Father left was the first time I woke in the night to the terrifying sound of air raid sirens wailing in the street and the rumbling of aircraft overhead. I sat up in bed, shock waves washing through me. The planes were flying low; it seemed as if they were only just above the roofs of our street. Everything in the room was vibrating to their sound. They didn't sound like any of the normal aircraft that regularly took off and landed at the airbase. And why were they flying in the middle of the night anyway? I switched on the bedside lamp and saw that Peggy was sitting up in bed too, her eyes wide with fear.

There followed a couple of mighty rumbling blasts, and a few seconds later, Mother appeared at the door in her nightie.

'Downstairs, quickly,' she said.

We followed her downstairs and huddled under the dining room table, which we knew from news reports was the safest place to be. It seemed to go on for ever. Wave after wave of aircraft passed above us, followed by the sickening sound of bombs exploding not far away. Eventually, when the sound of the planes had subsided, the 'all-clear' went up from the sirens. We crawled out from our hiding place and returned to our beds, but sleep wouldn't come again that night and I lay awake, watching the grey dawn steal through the tiny cracks round the edge of the curtains.

The gates of my school were padlocked when I arrived the next morning, and a notice was pinned to them proclaiming: *School closed until further notice on the orders of the Ministry of Defence.* My heart soared as I wandered home, envisaging days of leisure, hanging around with my friends or lazing at home.

Peggy and Mother were sitting at the kitchen table when I delivered the news that school was closed. Mother hardly looked up. She was busy writing, filling in some official-looking forms.

'What are you doing?' I asked.

'Peggy's school has been shut too, because of the air raids. I was talking to some of the other mothers at the gate and we all agreed that it's far too dangerous for children here. I'm going to send you away to the countryside, where you'll be safe.'

She looked up and there were tears in her eyes.

'I'm so sorry, Daisy, but it's the only way. It would be selfish of me to keep you here after last night. Your father was right and I should have listened to him.'

So that was that. We were sent details of the train we must get and the next few days were spent in frantic preparation. Mother was issued with a long list of clothes and equipment to send with us: a warm coat, several changes of clothes, underclothes, slippers and, most importantly, a gas mask each. And a few days later we found ourselves elbowing our way through the crowds as we climbed the steps from the Underground and onto the concourse at Paddington station.

I'd never seen so many children and young people gathered together in one place before. I had my gas mask bag over one shoulder and held my little leather suitcase in one hand and Mother's hand with the other. I hadn't done that for years – in any other circumstances I'd have been mortified to be seen holding Mother's hand, but today I'd abandoned all pride. I might be fifteen years old, but it was possible that I might not see Mother again for months, perhaps years.

My stomach was churning with nerves and I'd already experienced the first glimmerings of homesickness as we'd travelled from Harrow on the packed tube train that morning. We'd got up before dawn and eaten our last breakfast in the tiny kitchen at home. I'd hardly slept the night before, worrying about what was facing us in the days and weeks ahead, about how I would feel about being separated from Mother, and so far away from home.

I'd looked around the familiar room, taking in every little thing about it so I wouldn't forget. The red and white flowered curtains at the window above the old-fashioned butler sink, the row of pot plants on the windowsill, the yellow Formica table where we ate all our family meals, the old, chipped gas cooker and the kitchen cabinet with its drop-down shelf that had once been Mother's pride and joy. All these things, normally so commonplace and so familiar, suddenly became precious to me. And there was Buster, our tabby cat, rubbing himself against Mother's leg and mewing for his breakfast as she watched the toast under the grill.

I had such a big lump in my throat that I could hardly swallow the toast and jam that Mother put in front of me. She'd been saving her rations for this last breakfast, and I knew I couldn't break down and cry. After all, Peggy was only ten. I needed to be brave for her sake as well as for Mother's.

'Are we all ready then?' Mother said when we'd finished. She spoke in a bright, cheery voice, but I could tell from her rigid smile that she was finding this as difficult as I was. We took one last look in the living room to check we'd not forgotten anything. My eyes lingered on the photo of Father in his army uniform, taken before he set off for North Africa only a month or so before. I remembered how Peggy and I had both clung to him crying, and how he'd ruffled my hair and said, 'Take care of your mum, Daisy, I know I can trust you.' And now here I was leaving her behind too, despite my promise to Father.

We'd set off in the first glimmerings of daylight. There were no street lamps because of the blackout. I kept looking back at the house over my shoulder as we walked away from it. Our little three-bedroomed 1930s semi with its bay window and diamond-shaped panes of stained glass in the front door. It was the only home I'd ever known and I'd hardly ever given it a second thought, but tears welled in my eyes at leaving it.

We made our way through the teeming crowds towards Platform 10, where the Plymouth train was waiting, puffing and hissing, steam from the engine drifting along the platform. We walked along the train towards the third carriage, where our allotted seats were. All around us, mothers and children were hugging and saying tearful goodbyes. Everyone was trying to pretend that this was only temporary, but none of us had any idea how long the war might last, or whether we'd even come home at all.

We reached the third carriage and Mother paused by the door.

'This is it,' she said, her voice faltering.

A man carrying a clipboard bustled up. He wore an armband with the label 'Billeting Officer'.

'Names?' he asked Mother in an officious voice.

'Banks. Daisy and Peggy,' said Mother, drawing herself up to address him.

He ran his pen down his board.

'Ah yes. Here you are. Billeted with a Mr and Mrs Brown, 10 St James's Road, Plympton, Plymouth.'

'It's not in the city, is it?' asked Mother nervously.

'Of course not. Outside the town itself. You don't need to worry, Mrs Banks. Plymouth has been declared a neutral area anyway. They're not expecting any bombings there. Your girls will be quite safe. Now, they need to get in and find their seats. The train will be leaving soon.'

'There's another half-hour yet, surely?' said Mother, anxiety making her argumentative.

'Plenty of time, Mrs Banks, but best to get settled.'

The carriage was already almost full and the noise levels were at fever pitch. We pushed through the crowded aisle to our seats and Mother stowed our suitcases on the rack above.

'You can sit by the window, Peg,' I said, but Peggy didn't want to sit down. She clung on to Mother, her face screwed up in an effort not to cry.

Mother handed me the cloth bag containing our sandwich lunches, then she fished in her handbag and produced a brown bottle with its familiar label: Chamberlain's Cough Cure.

'Will you make sure Peggy takes this if she gets a cough?' she asked, handing it to me. I nodded and we exchanged an anguished look, remembering the times we'd been woken in the night to hear Peggy coughing and wheezing uncontrollably.

'I'll look after her, don't worry,' I said.

'Sit down, there's a good girl,' Mother coaxed, and eventually Peggy did sit down on the edge of the seat, but she still clung to Mother's arm.

Those last few minutes were excruciating. None of us knew what to say. Then the train began to pull out of the station and Mother walked along beside the carriage, waving madly and blowing kisses. But as the train gathered speed, something dreadful happened. It was as if I was watching in slow motion. There was a dreadful crash and a sickening splintering noise and before our very eyes, the platform beside the train erupted and broke up into a million pieces, rubble and dust spraying everywhere, while showers of broken glass rained down from the roof. We stared, dumbstruck, as people on the platform were blown aside, thrown onto the ground, or blown apart by the blast. There was blood everywhere.

'Mother!' I yelled. Mother was one of those who'd been flung across the platform, ending up a crumpled heap a couple of yards from the blast. All I could see of her was her bright red headscarf as she fell. A collective gasp went up from the carriage and several children screamed. The train shuddered to a halt and for a few seconds all was still. A hush fell over the carriage. Peggy started wailing beside me.

Chapter Four

Daisy

As the truck bumped across the open moor, my thoughts returned to Mother. My heart was heavy with the memory that I'd written letters to her that I'd never managed to post. I'd wanted to send them to the hospital, but by the time I'd found out which hospital Mother was in, it was too late. The next day came news of her death. To try to hold on to something solid as the truck made its way across Dartmoor, away from the city and into the unknown, I looked back through the letters and re-read them to myself.

Dearest Mother,

I hope you are getting better in hospital. I'm so sorry that we couldn't stay with you. We've now arrived at Mr and Mrs Brown's house in Plympton and are about to go to bed, so I thought I'd tell you about the journey.

It went smoothly enough. At first, we were very shocked about the bomb at Paddington and Peggy was very upset, but I put my arm round her, and tried to comfort her, and as we left London behind, she went to sleep, her head lolling on my shoulder. The sound of the train was deafening – the clickety clack of the wheels on the rails, and the chuntering of the engine up ahead. And the noise of the children inside the carriage. A few of the boys were running up and down the aisle, throwing paper aeroplanes around. Once or twice the billeting officer stood at the end of the carriage and roared for quiet, and the boys went back to their seats. But it didn't last long and after a brief respite the yelling and general chaos would resume.

I watched the countryside roll by, fields full of ripening crops, and of sheep and lambs, and once, I saw a herd of black and white cattle plodding patiently into a farmyard for milking. The farmland was dotted with villages with brick and stone cottages, some thatched, impossibly quaint.

Peggy slept for a long time. She awoke as we passed through Exeter and we ate our lunch. The wardens came round with trays full of cups of lemonade. Thank you for the lovely ham and pickle sandwiches. You must have saved up your ration coupons specially, and the bar of Cadbury's Ration chocolate. Thank you too for the lovely seaside postcards you'd left us in the lunch box. I'll look at them every day and they will remind me of our lovely seaside holidays.

I remembered that you said to look out when the train went along the sea defences at Dawlish. It was breathtaking to see the waves crashing and breaking just beneath the track.

Sometimes Peggy looked a bit sad, but I did my best to distract her. There was so much to see: boatyards full of fishing boats, the harbour at Teignmouth, chocolate-box villages, more fields full of animals. The rest of the journey passed in the blink of an eye and we were soon rolling through the outskirts of a town that looked a lot like London. Eventually the train began to slow down and we ground and jerked to a halt in a station. I leaned out of the window and saw the Plymouth signs.

Everyone piled off the train and the platform was soon overflowing. There were more billeting officers standing at the gate and as we filed through, they checked our names and told us which number bus to take. Buses were lined up in the car park outside. The names of towns were written on temporary signs inside their windows. Tavistock, South Brent, Kingsbridge, Dartmouth...

We were told to take bus number 5 marked Ivybridge. It was only a single-decker. We boarded the bus and watched it fill up with other children and teenagers. The bus pulled out of the station forecourt and we had our first glimpse of the city of Plymouth. It didn't look very different from London. There were all the familiar shops: Marks & Spencer; F.W. Woolworth, Boots the Chemist. We were soon out of the centre and into the suburbs; row upon row of red-bricked houses with no front gardens, where local children stopped their games to gawp at us.

It must have been less than twenty minutes into the journey when the bus pulled up outside a church. The driver turned round and shouted that we were at Plympton. There was a woman standing at the bus stop who spoke to the driver and handed him a slip of paper. We got off the bus with our luggage and the bus roared away. Once the smoke had cleared, we could see her more clearly. She looked as though she'd come straight from doing her housework. She wore a brown overcoat over a flowered apron, and her hair was tied up in a cloth.

She said she was Mrs Brown and told us to follow her. She set off quickly and we struggled after her, straining to keep up with our suitcases and gas mask bags. After a hundred yards or so, she turned into a street of terraced houses where the doors opened directly onto the street. Number 10 had a brown front door, which made me want to laugh, but I kept quiet and followed her inside.

Our room is a tiny box room at the front of the house that looks out over the street, with two narrow beds and very little space. *There is a small chest of drawers and a wooden rack for our clothes. While we were unpacking, Mr Brown came home from the docks. Supper was stew and dumplings and afterwards, we helped Mrs Brown with the dishes while Mr Brown sat in the front parlour, reading the paper.*

Mrs Brown said that they go to bed early as Mr Brown has to get up at 5.30 to go to his job in the docks. So, we have been sent up to bed. I'm just about to read Peggy a chapter from The Wind in the Willows. *Goodnight, Mother, I'm hoping you're comfortable in hospital and getting better all the time. I'll write again soon.*

Your loving Daisy

The next letter was dated the day after:

Dearest Mother,

I'm writing to let you know what happened on that first night at the Browns' house. It took me a long time to drift off in the strange surroundings, but I must have eventually slept. I was awoken in the night by a familiar sound. It was the rumble of aircraft flying low overhead, the wail of the sirens and the thud and crash of bombs exploding in the distance.

Mrs Brown came in. She was holding a Tilley lamp. She said that they must be bombing the dockyard and to come with her to the Anderson shelter at the end of the road. We followed her and Mr Brown as they hurried down the road, overcoats thrown over their nightclothes.

The Anderson shelter was a single-storey brick structure that had been built on some waste ground in a gap between two houses. There must already have been twenty or thirty people inside when we squeezed in through the narrow entrance. The air was dank and smelly and there wasn't much room. There were no seats, but some people had brought blankets and were sitting on the floor. The people nearest the door moved aside to make room for us, but from the way they huffed and sighed, I could sense their resentment.

The neighbours asked Mrs Brown who we were and when she said we were evacuees, they said that we shouldn't have been sent to Plymouth because it isn't safe.

I gripped Peggy's hand tightly. She was quiet but I knew she would be feeling as wretched as I was, firstly that we were sheltering from an air raid when we'd travelled all day to be in a safe place, and secondly that the people were speaking about us as if we weren't actually there. I thought about Laburnum Drive. Peggy and I are already missing Harrow.

We huddled in the shelter for another half-hour or so, until the all-clear sound wailed out from the sirens on the street, then everyone trooped back down the road to bed.

In the morning, we heard the slam of the front door at five thirty and peeped out of our window to see Mr Brown leaving the house. We got up early too, there didn't seem much point in trying to go back to sleep. After a breakfast of toast and margarine with stewed tea, Mrs Brown said we'd better set off to school.

Peggy's junior school is in the next street along from the Browns'. It's a red-brick building surrounded by walls and a bare playground. I held Peggy's hand as we went into the playground. The teacher wouldn't let me go inside with her. So, she let go of my hand and walked inside the building reluctantly. She didn't look back and I knew she was trying her best to be brave.

The senior school was a larger and taller version of the junior one. There were no children playing in the front yard, and the headmaster was stationed at the door, wearing a formal cap and gown, ushering a queue of pupils inside.

I was put in a large class of forty or fifty pupils, all sitting on benches behind scarred wooden desks. The class seems to span twelve- to around fifteen-year-olds.

The first lesson was maths. The teacher scribbled equations on the blackboard, pointing with a cane as he explained them to the class. The lesson seemed easier than at my school and I knew the answers to a lot of the questions. At one point, the teacher asked me a question directly.

Luckily, I'd already worked out the answer.

I sensed that he was disappointed that I got the right answer, and that he was trying to gain approval from the rest of the class by picking on me.

At breaktime, I was surrounded by a crowd of jeering boys. They said they didn't like clever-clogs or Cockneys.

I tried to move away from them, but they followed me wherever I went, laughing and yelling. I was determined not to cry. I knew it would give them all the more reason to taunt me.

I kept hearing your voice in my head: 'sticks and stones will break your bones but words will never hurt you.' I carried on walking, my shoulders square, my head held high.

When the bell rang for lessons, the boys followed me back into the building, but they had stopped shouting at me.

Peggy was already back at number 10 when I returned just after four o'clock. She rushed to the door and flung her arms round me as I came through it. She was feeling a bit homesick and hadn't really enjoyed school. It was all so unfamiliar. But you're not to worry, Mother, I'm sure she'll get used to it soon.

Mr Brown told us that there was a lot of damage on the dockyard. One ship, almost finished, was completely blown apart, and a lot of others were damaged. Two nightwatchmen were dead.

I will write again tomorrow. Please don't worry about us. The Browns are looking after us well, Peggy will get used to school soon and perhaps the air raids are over now.

Your ever-loving Daisy

The next letter was dated three days later:

Dearest Mother,

I hope you are still on the mend. I was hoping that the bombing raid would be the only one, but it did happen again. That night and for the next three nights. We got quite used to trooping down to the shelter in the small hours, remembering to take blankets with us so we could sit down on the concrete floor. The neighbours began to accept our presence after a time – at least they made room for us and stopped talking about us as if we weren't there.

Our schooldays have carried on in the same way. I've got several friends among the girls now. I think they have a grudging respect for the fact that I didn't let those bullies get to me.

I turned to the letter that had arrived from Mother on the third day. My heart had soared when I'd seen the envelope on the mat. I'd torn it open and read it out to Peggy over our cup of tea in the parlour. Mother had told us not to worry about her, that she was recovering in hospital and that Mr Hutchings had been to see her several times and brought her the gossip from the street. But there had been more bombing raids at the airbase, and a bomb had dropped a few streets away. 'So I'm glad you've gone away from London, to somewhere I can be sure you'll be safe. Take care, my darlings, don't worry about me, and we'll be together again very soon.' A second letter arrived from her the next day, along similar lines.

Now I knew the address of the hospital, Mrs Brown had given me some stamps and promised to take my letters to the post office for me. But before she'd had time to post them to Mother, a policeman came to the door. Peggy and I were in the front room and as we saw him walk past the window, my heart was in my mouth. Something told me, before he even knocked, that he was bearing bad news.

He spoke to Mrs Brown while Peggy and I hovered in the hallway, hanging back. When she turned to beckon me forward, the expression of pity mixed with discomfort on her face said it all.

'I'm afraid your mother passed away today at St Mary's Hospital, Paddington,' the policeman said. I don't remember his face, just that he was a portly man and his voice was kindly.

'But why? I don't understand, she was getting better.'

'Blood clot on the brain, caused by concussion,' he said, reading from a telegram. 'I'm so very sorry, Miss.'

I couldn't reply, just turned to Peggy helplessly, to take her in my arms. She was already sobbing.

'But what's going to happen to them?' I heard Mrs Brown ask the policeman. She wasn't even trying to keep her voice down.

'We'll let you know in due course. In the meantime, they stay here as normal.'

The two of us crept up to our room and sat on the edge of my bed and cried our hearts out. But no amount of crying would rid us of that empty, crushing feeling inside. I felt it as soon as I awoke each morning and remembered, and it would creep up on me all the time, each and every day whenever it felt as though I might forget for a second. It haunted my days and nights and I quickly realised that it was what they called grief.

I stared out of the window at the bleak moor rolling past, dotted with grazing sheep and with forbidding-looking rocks on the skyline. How different this was from home. Now, thinking about Mother enhanced the feeling that Peggy and I were alone in the world. Would anyone know, or even care, where we were being taken by this stranger?

Chapter Five

Helen

There were only two envelopes, each date-stamped a few days apart in July 1940. They all bore the postmark 'St Mary's Hospital, Paddington,' and were signed, 'Your ever-loving Mother'. When they first found them in Daisy's bedroom, Helen and Laura had skimmed them quickly. Later, Laura had left to go to another meeting in Exeter and Helen closed up the house. Before she set off for home, she slipped the letters into her bag.

She read them again that evening after she had eaten. It was a revelation to Helen to read about her grandmother. Daisy had never spoken about her mother, so Helen was surprised that the letters revealed that the two of them were close and that Daisy's mother appeared to be a warm, loving person.

She unfolded the letters and read each of them through again. They were fairly short, written in ink, in careful, copperplate hand. Looking at the writing closely, Helen thought, they looked as though her grandmother had learned handwriting at school, but hadn't written letters regularly. She was obviously ill, had been in an accident, but there was little discussion of that. 'Please don't worry about me. I'm getting better all the time. There's no need to concern yourselves about it.' Instead, the letters focused on gossip from the neighbourhood, passed on by someone who'd visited her in hospital, and news of recent air raids. The words were suffused with the love of a mother for her children; she repeatedly told them how much she was missing them, and gave them plenty of advice as to what they should be doing: being polite to their hosts, washing behind their ears, getting to bed early, trying their best at school. On two or three occasions she repeated, 'Daisy, I know I've said this before, but you will make sure that Peggy takes her medicine if she gets a cough, won't you?'

In the second letter she wrote:

I had a letter from your dear father this morning. Mrs Hutchings from number 55 brought it when she came to visit. It came all the way from North Africa. He couldn't say much, I expect letters have to go through the censors, but he said he is in Cairo, had been training in the desert and that he is in good health. He sends his love to you both, of course. When he sent the letter, he couldn't have got my letter telling him that you've been evacuated as he didn't mention it. I hope you two girls are praying for Father every day, and that he will be returned safely to us very soon.

Helen read these words over again and again. She wondered which regiment Daisy's father had been in. Perhaps she'd be able to look him up? Daisy had never mentioned that her father had been in the army in North Africa. Helen nibbled her thumbnail, puzzled. It was becoming obvious that much had happened to Daisy during the war and she hadn't told Helen and Laura any of it. Helen knew that Daisy had been brought up in London, that her parents had died and that she'd left to go to India at the end of the war. But why hadn't she mentioned anything else? Did she really have a sister? And for how long had she been in Devon?

Helen thought back to the rifts in their relationship; the inexplicable secrecy of Daisy's trips to the next-door farm, the way her mother seemed to put up barriers to intimacy. It was as if she didn't want people to get close to her; as if there was some danger in closeness that she didn't want to encounter. Helen was convinced that

Daisy's past held the key to these secrets. She read the letters right through several times. It struck her that there was nothing in them that might cause the recipient to want to lie about their past. She put them back into her bag with mounting frustration. Why had Daisy been living a lie all these years? She was convinced that these letters were the tip of the iceberg and that there were more of Daisy's secrets to be uncovered. But how would they ever find out the truth?

The next morning, Helen sat facing her mother in her room in the nursing home. They were both sitting in upright armchairs and the weak winter sun slanted in through the tall windows, making pale squares on the beige carpet. Helen was sipping a cup of tea that one of the nurses had brought her, watching her mother, wondering all the time about the letters.

Helen hadn't yet got used to seeing Daisy in this state and it came as a fresh shock to her each time she entered the room. She knew it was ridiculous, but the stroke and the changed circumstances hadn't dampened her feelings of trepidation each time she travelled to see her mother. A familiar sense of anxiety ran through her, as it always did when she saw her. She'd never felt quite good enough, or that she'd achieved enough, for Daisy.

'Are you OK, Mum?' she asked tentatively.

Daisy nodded. 'Not so bad.'

Helen found these occasions awkward and distressing. Daisy had been here over a month now, and the sweet nurses who took care of her reassured Helen as best they could. But the stroke had made Daisy quiet and weak. She hardly uttered a word, and the words she did try to say often came out incoherent. She was a shadow of herself, and somehow that had made things all the more awkward for Helen the three or four times she'd visited. She never knew what to say to her. To compensate, she normally ended up being gratingly cheerful. Or at least that's how it sounded to her, as she trotted out banal stories about her neighbours, about the antiques shop and the customers, about things on the news. It was doubly difficult today; normally Helen wasn't alone with her.

It always shocked Helen to see Daisy's face disfigured as it was now, her mouth slack and drooping on one side. Helen's memories were of a vigorous, youthful woman, who would think nothing of working all day in her garden, or hiking from the house to the top of Black Tor, right into her eighties. Daisy had followed a punishing routine and expected no less of Helen. She would be up early, often before dawn, go into her surgery, which was housed in a wing at the back of the house, and prepare for her day ahead. Patients would start arriving at eight o'clock and continue coming until eleven, then in the afternoon from two until five. She would do home visits between eleven and two, and again between five and seven.

Daisy, or 'Doc Cavendish' as she was known to locals, was respected for miles around. Everyone knew her ancient green Rover and farmers would pull their tractors off the narrow lanes to let her pass. Everywhere they went she would be stopped by people who wanted to thank her, or to tell her their latest news. Often a gift would arrive from a grateful farmer: a box of vegetables, half a lamb for the freezer, always a turkey at Christmas.

Daisy had once been such a strong and domineering presence in Helen's life, and she always had high expectations. Daisy had been adamant that Helen would do well at school. She would hold up Laura's academic success as an example. Laura had got into Oxford and Daisy expected Helen to be equally successful. Helen struggled with academic subjects though. She was more artistic and creative; skills that Daisy didn't appear to value. She felt worthless as she struggled with her homework, trying to live up to her mother's expectations and always failing. It made her feel as if she'd let her mother down and as if whatever she did, she would never be good enough.

Sometimes she'd admitted to Daisy that she found the work difficult, but her mother would give her a withering look and say that she needed to try harder. But as hard as she did try, she could never seem to please.

It had hurt Helen badly to see her mother's face drop when her O-level results had arrived in the post.

There were more Grade Bs than As and even a sprinkling of Cs.

Daisy's face had said it all. She didn't need to speak; Helen had known what she was thinking: that with those grades she'd never get into Oxford and fulfil Daisy's ambition for her. In the end, she'd admitted to her mother that she didn't want to go to Oxford, so her grades weren't that important.

'Well, what do you want to do then?' replied Daisy. 'You'll need a degree, whatever it is.'

'I love drawing and painting. And I'm good at it too. I might look into getting on an arts course.'

'Oh, Helen, be practical, please,' said Daisy. 'You'd be wasting your time with that. It'll never lead anywhere. Leave it to me. I'll find you something practical to do instead.'

It was then that Helen had done something she knew was forbidden. She stormed out of the house, crossed the garden, ducked under the hedge and ran across the overgrown field towards the wood. She knew that land was out of bounds, but she had no idea why, and she wanted, in that moment, to defy her mother. To gain some control in her life. She'd entered the wood at the bottom of the field. It was choked with brambles but she'd pushed her way through all the same, thorns scratching her legs and making them bleed, nettles brushing against her and stinging her flesh. When she reached the other side, she'd emerged at the top of a hill. Some derelict buildings were nestled in the valley below. They were tumbling down, overgrown with elder and buddleia. She stood there staring, until quite suddenly, she was grabbed from behind.

'What the hell do you think you're doing in here?' She'd never heard her mother so angry. Daisy frogmarched her back through the wood to the house, rage radiating from her, her tongue silenced by her fury.

'I thought I could trust you. Don't you ever, ever go on that land again. Do you hear me?' she said as they reached the garden.

'I don't see why not,' Helen said, standing firm, returning Daisy's gaze.

'Because I say so. And that should be enough. No good will come of it. It's dangerous – dangerous and… and vile down there.'

Things between them had already been difficult, but looking back, Helen realised that their relationship had never recovered from that day. Her actions had driven a wedge between them that just grew and grew as time went on.

Daisy had done her research and had found a finance and accountancy degree at Nottingham University that she insisted would help Helen forge a useful career. Helen went along with the idea because she had no choice and was desperate to leave home, but from the start, her heart wasn't in it. She'd enjoyed the student parties, making friends, the freedom she'd experienced away from home and out of Daisy's orbit, but unsurprisingly, she had failed the first-year exams. She came home in disgrace to the worst row she'd ever had with her mother, which just reinforced the distance that had grown up between them. Thinking back on it still caused her stomach to churn at the unpleasantness of it all.

'How disappointing, Helen. I expected more of you. Especially after Laura did so well.'

Helen knew then that she was never going to live up to her mother's expectations. She'd be better off alone. So, she'd left, found a bedsit in Plymouth and subsisted on a series of menial jobs. She hadn't returned home for over a year that time and a huge gulf had opened up between them.

Looking at Daisy now, it was hard to believe that she'd ever held that much power over Helen's life. And despite the hurt that had passed between them, Helen felt only sadness now, for the relationship she'd lost, and the mother she'd never really been able to get to know.

She leaned forward, reached out and took her mother's hand and held it in hers. It felt bony and cold to the touch.

'I can't stay long today, Mum,' she said.

Daisy shrugged and closed her eyes in resignation.

'Laura and I have been sorting out the house,' she ventured. Daisy's eyes widened and she put her head on one side as if she wanted to hear more.

Helen tried to work out what to say next. It wasn't easy, holding a one-way conversation like this. And so unfamiliar too. Daisy in her day had been such an eloquent speaker – and such a poor listener too. So much so that in the past it had been easy to leave her to do all the talking and to let her words flow over you. Now Helen scrabbled around for something vaguely interesting to say.

'Jago is taking some of the furniture from the house down to the shop, Mum. He'll get the best price he can for it.'

Daisy closed both eyes and sniffed deeply. Then she shrugged her shoulders. It irked Helen that even in her reduced state, her mother had found a way to communicate her disapproval of Jago. She had never liked the friends that Helen had made away from home, the life she had built for herself. And despite her own occasional niggles with Jago – she acknowledged that he was a very fussy employer, and he sometimes took Helen's work for granted – she couldn't help feeling a surge of defensive pride for her friend and boss. She stared back at her mother, wanting to retaliate, but her natural compassion stopped her from doing that.

As she looked at Daisy now, and struggled to find something to say, she thought again about the letters. *Daisy Banks*. Why would her mother have changed her name? And where was her younger sister now? The questions were hovering right there on her lips, but she took a deep breath and stopped herself from asking them. She didn't want to distress Daisy.

*

Laura was waiting at the door when Helen arrived back at the house.

'You were a long time,' she said impatiently. 'I've been here a good half-hour. Did you say anything to Mum about finding the letters?'

'No, of course I didn't. I said I wouldn't yesterday,' said Helen, stepping inside and taking off her coat.

'I thought you might have changed your mind,' said Laura. 'We'll have to broach it with her when we go there together.'

'Oh, Laura, is it really worth it?'

'Of course. If Mum had a sister, we need to know why she hid it from us. Did you read the letters again? Was there anything else in them?'

Helen nodded and told her about Daisy's father serving in the North Africa campaign.

'We could try looking him up on the internet, couldn't we?'

'Yes, I thought the same…'

'We know his surname would have been Banks, but what about his first name?'

Helen shrugged. 'She used to say her father's name was Edward. We could always try that.'

'Who knows, now? He might not have been called that at all. I'll have a look when I get home, though. Paul's out this evening.'

'OK. Let me know if you find anything. So, what's left to do today?'

'Not much really. Just the old surgery. Then I think we're more or less done.'

The keys to Daisy's surgery were where they'd always been, hanging on a hook on the back of the kitchen door. Even though it was over twenty years since Daisy had finally retired, she had refused to move anything out of those rooms. Helen had suggested, before Daisy's stroke, that she should have the wing converted into a flat where a live-in help could stay, but Daisy wouldn't hear a word of it.

'I don't need anyone to look after me. Besides, I couldn't stand to have a stranger living here. Mrs Starr does an excellent job.'

Now, Laura unlocked the door and they walked down the chilly tiled passage into the waiting room. There was an old leather sofa and armchairs, where people would wait to see Daisy, chatting or reading magazines. She didn't have an appointments system. All her patients knew her hours and they would just turn up and wait patiently to see her.

'Shall we?' asked Laura, her hand on the surgery door. They exchanged anxious looks – this had been another forbidden place.

'Here goes.' Helen pushed the door open and they went inside. She could feel Laura behind her, her hand on Helen's back. Laura was as apprehensive as she was, Helen realised, and suddenly she felt glad that they were doing this together.

It was chilly in the surgery, and it still had a clinical atmosphere despite Daisy's absence. The walls were white, the tiles on the floor still smelled faintly of disinfectant. There was Daisy's desk and chair, the couch where she would examine patients, a trolley with some equipment on it, a bookcase full of medical textbooks and a large cupboard. On the desk, beside the blood pressure machine, was a photograph of their father, standing on the steps of their house in London, wearing a dinner jacket and smiling broadly.

'Perhaps that's when he went to collect his OBE?' said Laura.

'Yes, it must be. He looks so happy, doesn't he?' Helen smiled at the photograph. She only had fond memories of her father; patient and long-suffering, he'd weathered Daisy's storms cheerfully, always supportive and mildly indulgent and a wonderful caring father until he died when Helen was nine years old.

'Well,' she said, turning back to Laura, 'where shall we start?'

'All the furniture and equipment can go to the charity shop. Let's see if there's anything in the desk drawers, shall we?'

One of the keys on the bunch unlocked the drawers in Daisy's desk. Inside the top drawer was a pile of notebooks recording her home visits.

'Shall we bin these?'

'I suppose so.' Conquering the feeling that she was trespassing on forbidden territory, Helen flicked through some pages.

'She was so meticulous, wasn't she?' she said, looking at page after page, month after month of appointments with names and a brief description of the complaint.

'But I suppose no one would have any use for them now.'

She put the pile in a bin bag and went on to the next drawer.

Inside was a file containing some artwork that she'd done for school projects. She turned each page over and stared at them, remembering. There was a sketch of Daisy sitting in the living room, a watercolour of the house, another of the open moor dotted with sheep. She remembered taking her easel out to the far side of the garden one breezy day, and the pleasure she'd taken in capturing the scene.

'Look at this, Laura. I must have been fourteen or fifteen when I did these. I'm really surprised Mum kept them. She always disapproved of my art.'

Laura said, 'No, she didn't. She was very proud of it, Helen. She was always saying how talented you were.'

'How strange! You know, I never knew that. She certainly never showed it. And she wouldn't let me study it properly.'

Laura was kneeling in front of a cupboard, taking out the contents: plates, vases, a few Petri dishes. 'You know she was fixated on ensuring we were able to make our own way in the world. She didn't want us to be dependent on anyone. It was quite an obsession with her.'

'Well, it rather backfired with me, didn't it?'

'I'm sure she only wanted what was best for you. Mum had a funny way of showing emotion. She found it so hard. Something to do with her past, perhaps.'

'Yes… although her past seems to have been quite different from what she wanted us to believe.'

'Well, you could always do it now, couldn't you?'

'Do what?'

'An art degree. What's stopping you?'

Helen shrugged. She had recently been poring over prospectuses for fine arts courses, but she hadn't got round to making any applications so far. Perhaps it was still the thought of her mother's disapproval that had been holding her back. But then Daisy *had* kept these sketches all these years. It was puzzling.

'I'm not sure. Perhaps I will one day,' she replied.

The next two drawers were filled with old invoices and receipts. Helen relegated those to the bin bags too. The bottom drawer was stiff and when, after several tugs, Helen managed to pull it open, it appeared at first that there was nothing inside. She was about to close it again when she saw there was something lodged at the back. Getting down on her knees, she put her hand inside and grasped something. She drew out a brown paper bag containing what felt like a bottle. It flashed through her mind that Daisy might have kept a secret tipple for difficult days, but she quickly dismissed that thought.

It was made of brown glass with a rusting metal lid. There was some congealed liquid in the bottom and the label on the front read: 'Chamberlain's Cough Cure'. There was a further label on the back that had been completed by hand in ink so faded that it was barely legible. It said: 'Patient: Peggy Banks. DOB: 1st June 1930: Dose, one spoonful when needed'.

'Laura, look at this.' They both peered at the bottle and looked at each other, incredulous. Helen's mind went back to the letters.

'That's what her mother said, didn't she? "Make sure Peggy takes her cough medicine." And here it is. She kept it all these years. Look, Peggy was five years younger than Mum. I wonder why Mum would have kept the bottle?'

Laura shrugged.

'Well, I've done the desk,' Helen said, looking round for something else to clear. She noticed Daisy's framed medical degree. She reached up and took it off the wall. 'What shall we do with this?'

'Why don't we take it to her?' Laura said. 'She was so proud of it; it might help remind her of happier times. I was going to take her a couple of the photos from the mantelpiece too. Her wedding, the one of her getting her degree.'

'What a good idea,' said Helen, handing the certificate to Laura, who turned it over as she took it.

'Hey, look at this!' she said.

There was a piece of card tucked in the back of the frame, secured by one of the clips that held the frame together. Laura removed it carefully and held it out for Helen to see.

It was an old black and white photograph, of Daisy standing beside a young man. Daisy looked to be in her late teens, possibly twenty. Her hair was dyed blonde, but there was no mistaking those eyes and that look of determination. She wore a cotton summer dress and she was linking arms with her companion. He was about her age, a little older perhaps, tall and skinny, with dark hair. They were leaning against a ship's rail, squinting slightly into the sun. There was no writing on the back to indicate time and place, or the identity of the young man.

Helen peered closely. Was that the sailor whose photograph had been with the letters? It was difficult to be sure.

'This must be the ship to India,' said Laura. 'Mum with someone she met on the ship, probably.'

'She looks happy, doesn't she?' asked Helen. 'I wonder who he is…'

They both stared at the photograph for a long moment, thinking, wondering.

'It must have meant a lot to her to have had it here with her in the surgery.'

'Yes,' Helen murmured, picturing Daisy taking the photograph out and looking at it when she was working at her desk at the end of the day.

'It must have meant an awful lot to her. She wasn't sentimental at all.'

'Shall we take it to her?' asked Laura, but Helen shook her head.

'Not yet, no. We need to work out a way of breaking to her gently that we've seen the letters first.'

Helen thought about what they'd found in the surgery, the secrets Daisy had kept from them and the fact that she'd hoarded her schoolgirl art. She realised that she'd never really known her mother properly and that she'd got to get to the bottom of this herself. She needed to find out why Daisy had acted the way she had, what lay there buried in her past, at the root of her secrecy and her lies. There was no point asking Daisy herself. She could only utter a few words at a time, and reminders of the past only seemed to distress her. No, Helen needed to find the truth herself.

Chapter Six

Daisy

I gripped Peggy's hand tight as the truck bumped and rattled along the long, straight road that crossed the top of Dartmoor. Peggy looked up at me, her blue eyes round, full of questions. I tucked a lock of her pale brown hair behind her ear and she leaned in under my arm. She gripped my hand in return, but we didn't speak or even look at each other. The billeting officer had stopped talking and appeared to be concentrating on the road ahead, frowning deeply, driving as quickly as the road would permit.

I stared out across the bleak moor; it was dotted with sheep on the flatter land but rose up to steep rocky crags in the distance. I'd never seen countryside like it. It was an alien landscape to me – a far cry from the domesticated farmland of the Home Counties that I was used to. This was wild and beautiful in the sunlight of the summer morning, and startlingly colourful too, with patches of purple-pink heather and bright yellow gorse breaking up the great carpet of green. I could sense its wild beauty, but at the same time just looking at that great desolate sweep of land gave me a queer feeling in the pit of my stomach. It made me feel a long way from home and from everything I'd ever known. I wanted to believe this journey would turn out well but couldn't help wondering where this man was taking us, so far from the city. The landscape was wild, untouched by war, which felt odd. It increased the feeling that we were travelling into another world.

We passed a lake surrounded by pine trees, nestled in a hollow in the hills, shimmering bright blue in the sunlight, then, half a mile or so after that, the truck suddenly swerved off the road and headed towards a dense forest.

'Soon be there,' the man said, as the truck plunged downhill and into the trees. 'Not far now.'

The thick evergreens blocked the sunlight from the lane, and the inside of the cab took on a dim, greenish glow, almost as if we were underwater. The lane continued downwards between steep banks, overgrown with bracken and ferns that brushed against the vehicle, the lane was so narrow. I glanced at Peggy and she looked up at me with round, enquiring eyes, but still neither of us spoke.

We rattled down the hill past a huge pair of wrought-iron gates that sagged between two giant granite pillars. They looked rusty and neglected and were held together with coils of chains.

'Black Moor Hall', proclaimed a carved slate sign. I peered through the gates at an overgrown drive as we passed it, and a shudder went through me. There was something about the thought that there must be a huge, empty house nestled behind those trees, full of decaying rooms where no one had ventured for years, that sent chills down my spine.

In another half-mile or so there was another sign. This time it was hand-painted crudely on a gatepost: 'Black Moor Farm'. The man turned the truck off the road, between a pair of broken-down wooden gates and onto a muddy track that continued through the trees. We bumped along and I stared out at the forest floor, carpeted brown with fallen needles. The place had an air of neglect, with piles of rusting machinery discarded beside the track, the rotting remains of a disused tractor and trailer and, most shocking of all, two dead sheep lying in a ditch, half-eaten by foxes and buzzing with flies. Peggy spotted them before I could distract her. She gasped and I saw her eyes fill with tears.

We emerged from the trees and carried on past a great muckheap swarming with flies, half-covered by a tarpaulin and held down by old tyres, past a pile of rusting oil drums, more rusting machinery and then down into a hollow between two hills. A stone farmhouse surrounded by low outbuildings stood in front of us. I wondered at first if it was derelict. A couple of the front windows were boarded up, the roof was missing several slates and some of the guttering was hanging loose. I looked at the billeting officer, confused, my knees suddenly weak with shock at the realisation that we could be alone with him in this forsaken and neglected place. Then I spotted a washing line in the overgrown garden with some greying sheets hanging on it, and I realised that people must live here, despite the dilapidated condition of the house.

Four dogs emerged from the yard and came bounding towards the truck, barking and growling, baring their teeth. Like the house, they looked neglected. Two of them I recognised to be Alsatians. Their fur was matted and their ribs were visible beneath. The other two were sheepdogs, equally malnourished. They jumped up at our side of the truck, snapping and snarling. Peggy, whose eyes had momentarily lit up at the sight of the dogs, was now clinging to my arm, quivering with fear. The man got out of the driver's seat, slamming the door.

'Get down!' he shouted at the dogs, but they took no notice.

Another man appeared from between the buildings and shambled towards the truck. He was stocky, dressed in filthy work clothes, and walked with a limp.

'Get down, you idiots!' he yelled, and the dogs immediately stopped jumping at the door of the truck and slunk back to the buildings, whimpering, their tails between their legs.

'What've you got for me today, Charlie boy?' he said, coming up close to the truck and peering inside.

Peggy and I automatically shrank back in our seats as he thrust his face into the open window. It was bloated and red, perspiring in the heat of the morning. He was unshaven, and long grey whiskers sprouted from beneath a flat cap. The window was open and I could smell his foul breath: tobacco and stale cabbage. Brown powder was sticking to his upper lip and the hairs protruding from his nose. I knew it was snuff; the old caretaker at our school used to sniff it.

The man narrowed his piggy eyes and examined us, then he straightened up.

'Little 'un doesn't look much use,' he said, displaying black and broken teeth.

The officer – Charlie – shrugged and said, 'They're sisters. Couldn't very well leave one behind. News would've got out.'

The man grumbled under his breath, then jerked his head sideways.

'Get 'em out of there. I'll get me gal to sort them out. Come inside, Charlie, and we can settle up.'

Then he cupped his hands to his face and yelled, 'Elsie! Elsie! I need you out front.'

There was a minute's pause while Peggy and I exchanged alarmed looks, then someone else appeared from the yard. It was a young girl, a couple of years older than me. She was stout, dressed in a cheap cotton print dress and filthy work boots. Her mousy hair hung lank around her shoulders, her pudgy face was pale and featureless.

'What is it, Dad?' she said. Like her father, she spoke with a heavy Devon accent.

He nodded towards us. 'Two more. Get 'em settled in the threshing barn, then come back to the 'ouse to start on dinner.'

She peered at us through the windscreen. There was a dead look in her eyes, as if she had no interest in anyone or anything. Then she came round to our side and opened the passenger door.

'Come on,' she said.

We slid off the seat and got out of the truck. I took Peggy's bag.

'Now don't you worry,' said Charlie, seeing the look on my face, 'Farmer Reeves here will look after you good. And I'll write to your neighbour today and tell her where you are.'

His words made me feel a little better as I followed the farmer's daughter down the hill and into the yard, holding Peggy's hand and carrying her little leather case.

The farmyard was huge and square, with stables and barns enclosing a brick-paved courtyard. Like everywhere else on this farm, it was neglected and unkempt. The bricks underfoot were slimy with algae and moss and grass grew between them. There was a drinking trough filled with scummy water and a few skinny chickens pecked around on the ground.

One side of the yard was lined with stables with split doors, the top halves opened and pinned back. A couple of horses put their heads over the lower doors and peered out as we crossed the yard.

'Oh look, Daisy!' said Peggy, suddenly brightening. 'Can we go and stroke them?'

'No time for that now,' said the girl, walking to the far side of the yard. She opened a barn door, beckoning to us to follow. I told Peggy to hush as we followed the girl into the barn. 'You'll be sleeping in 'ere, with the others,' she said.

I stared around me. The barn had been converted into some sort of bunkhouse, with several sets of crudely constructed wooden bunks lining the walls. A few of them had filthy bedding and pillows on them. Next to each was a broken-down chest of drawers.

At one end of the barn was a trestle table made out of an old door, with a couple of long benches either side of it. There was a sink in one corner, a couple of cupboards and, in the other, an old stove.

'Others?' I asked. 'Are there other evacuees staying here?'

She peered at me blankly for a moment. 'Don't know about that,' she said finally, 'There's others sleep in 'ere. That's all I know.'

'Where are they?' I asked.

'Out in the fields, of course,' she said. 'Workin'. Like every day.'

'Working?' I repeated stupidly.

'That's right. Like you will be later on today. They'll all be back in for dinner soon. Then when they go back out, you two can go out with 'em.'

She rummaged in a metal corn bin and produced some grubby blankets and a couple of cushions.

'I didn't know we'd have to work,' I said.

She turned to stare at me.

'Don't know what else you'd be 'ere for. Now don't you go causing any trouble. Me dad don't like troublesome ones. He'll give you a good hiding if there's any fuss, I can tell you.'

I shuddered and felt Peggy's hand gripping mine tightly.

'You can sleep over there,' the girl said, motioning to two bunks in the far corner. 'Get yourselves settled. Do you have any trousers for working?'

I shook my head. 'We could hardly bring any clothes. Our street was bombed this morning.'

She stared at us expressionlessly. I wondered if she even understood what that meant.

'Well, I'll bring some of mine for you later on. I need to get the food on now. I'll come over again at twelve. Oh, by the way, closet and buckets for washing are out back.'

When she'd gone, I took the blankets to the two bunks and spread them out. All the time I was wondering what to do, how to get out of there. Was the best way to just make a run for it? But I realised how far this place was from civilisation and how I had no idea where it was or where to go. And I didn't want to scare Peggy by telling her that we needed to run away.

'Top or bottom?' I asked Peggy, trying to make this into an adventure, even though my mind was full of unsettling questions.

'Top,' she answered automatically, but I noticed that her bottom lip was quivering.

'Don't cry, Peggy. We won't be here long. This must be some kind of mistake. Look, why don't you get up on the top bunk and see what it's like?'

There was no ladder, so she climbed up the wooden frame.

'There's no mattress,' she said.

'No. There's an eiderdown though. Have that. It's quite soft.'

'It smells,' she said, wrinkling her nose.

'Well, never mind. Perhaps we can find something else.'

'There's someone outside,' Peggy said. We both listened and could hear voices at the door, boots being scraped and removed.

The barn door opened and four people came in. At first, I thought they were our age, just taller and skinnier, but as I looked more closely, I realised that they were probably older than both Peggy and me. There were two boys and two girls. They were all dressed in muddy clothes: shapeless trousers, held up by braces, and threadbare socks. As they came in, they glanced over at us, but none of them said anything. The taller of the two boys, who had a mop of untidy dark hair, stared at us for a few seconds longer than the others, but all of them appeared subdued and uneasy. Behind them came a man. He was younger than the farmer; tall and muscular-looking, with a crop of red hair and a heavy forehead. A cigarette drooped from the corner of his mouth.

'Now what have we here?' he said with an unpleasant leer, walking towards Peggy and me at the bunk where we sat. 'Old Joe said we were due for more help. I didn't know it'd be as soon as this.'

'What's your name then?' he asked, leaning forward and peering into my face. Close up, I could see that his face was covered in freckles beneath the grime, his eyes and eyelashes pale.

'Daisy,' I answered, flinching from the stream of smoke he blew in my face. The ash fell into my lap and he laughed, straightening up.

'And who's this up 'ere?'

'That's my sister. Peggy.'

'Well, I'm Robert, but they call me Red. My job is to make sure everyone round 'ere works hard and behaves themselves. We're all working for the war effort. Growing food to feed the country, don't you know? You don't look like you're going to be trouble, but you never know… Now come and have some food at the table. Budge up, you lot!'

I thought about what he'd said, wondering if things had got so bad that children and young people were working on the land now. But it didn't feel right. Just looking at the expressions on the faces of the others told me that we'd been brought here under false pretences. That we shouldn't be here at all.

The other four had sat down at the trestle table and were waiting in silence. Red went and sat at one end of the table and Peggy and I sat at the other end on opposite sides. The others barely looked at us. I looked around at their faces tentatively, but the only one who returned my glance was the older boy. He held my gaze for a few seconds, and I saw in his eyes a look of desperation – but alongside that, something else. Could it have been defiance? All four of them looked dead beat, their eyes dull, their skin sallow. It felt awkward, sitting there with them and not even asking their names, but something told me it wasn't the time or place to try striking up a conversation with any of them.

The barn door opened and Elsie entered, carrying a huge saucepan, which she plonked down on the table.

'Get the bowls out then,' she said impatiently. 'I'll be back with the bread in a minute.'

One of the girls produced some chipped bowls and spoons from a cupboard beside the sink and in a few minutes, Elsie returned and shoved a couple of loaves of dried-out bread on the table. Red sliced the bread and handed it round, and Elsie ladled out the soup. I stared at mine for a long minute; it looked unappetising but I realised that I was ravenously hungry. Apart from the chocolate the billeting officer had given us we hadn't eaten since supper the previous day. The soup was greasy, with lumps of fatty meat floating in it, and the bread was stale and hard, but I managed to eat it all. Opposite me, Peggy was toying with her spoon. With my eyes I tried to encourage her to eat and she tentatively tried a couple of spoonfuls, but I could tell from the way her mouth turned down at the corners that she couldn't bring herself to eat the rest.

After the meal, Elsie went back to the house and returned with two pairs of old trousers and a pair of wellington boots for each of us. I looked around for somewhere to change.

'Don't mind us,' said Red in a jeering voice. 'We've seen it all before.'

I felt the colour rising in my cheeks and he laughed. I went as far into the corner of the barn as I could, next to our bunks, and changed from my slacks into the trousers. Luckily, I still had my nightie on underneath, so I slid my top off and quickly pulled on the rough shirt that Elsie had brought for me.

''Ere,' said Elsie, who'd been watching me, hands on hips. 'Them trousers will fall down, but we ain't got no more braces. You'll need this.' She handed me a length of string, which I slid through the loops on the trousers and tied at the front.

Then it was Peggy's turn. She got up from her bunk and I stood in front of her while she wriggled into the trousers and shirt that Elsie had brought, mindful that Red could probably still see from his place at the table. These fitted better – perhaps Elsie hadn't been so fat when she was younger – but the trousers still needed to be tied at the front with twine.

Red pushed his seat back and stood up. He took a hip flask from his trouser pocket and took a long swig, throwing his head back.

'Best be getting out there again,' he said, and the others got up instantly and trooped outside to put on their boots. 'Haymaking today. It's hard work, but you'll soon get used to it.'

'I don't understand,' I said and he stared at me, any pretence at jocularity gone from his face. The others all stopped too, their eyes fearful, darting from my face to Red's and back again.

'Don't understand what?' said Red. 'It's not that 'ard. We're going out to the bottom field to cut hay. I'll get you a couple of scythes from the tool shed afore we go and I'll show you how to do it.'

'But we're not here to work,' I said. 'We're evacuees from London. The house we were in, in Plymouth, was bombed this morning.'

I knew that my voice was shaking, remembering what had happened to the Browns, thinking of them lying dead under all that rubble. I could feel a lump in my throat that nearly strangled my words, but I had to protest. None of this was right and I couldn't stop myself; I needed to know what was going on.

'So you were wandering the streets down in Plymouth and Charlie picked you up, eh?' Red asked with a chuckle.

'Yes. He said he would find somewhere for us to stay.'

'And he did, didn't 'e? He brought you 'ere to stay. And everyone 'ere has to work for their keep. Nothing wrong with that, is there?'

'But what about school?' I asked. The others were still watching intently, waiting for Red's reaction, obviously astonished that I was answering back.

'What about school?' he jeered. 'I 'aven't done a day's school since I was ten. Waste of time, if you ask me. You're 'ere to work. There ain't no men any more to work on the fields. All off to war, they are, our usual workers, so we're 'aving to make do with the likes of you.'

'But we need to go to school.'

He lost patience then and he grabbed me by both arms. He lifted me up to his face and shook me hard. I could feel his filthy fingernails digging into my skin.

'That's enough of your cheek, missy. I won't 'ear any more. You can forget about your precious school. And you'll work 'cause I say so, and don't you let me catch you slacking.'

He threw me backwards onto the ground and I landed hard on my backside. Pain shot up my spine, but I got up with as much dignity as I could muster, my eyes smarting with humiliation. As I got up, I caught sight of Peggy's face. Her eyes were saucer-like with fear. I knew I must stay quiet to protect her. Then he turned on the others.

'What you all gawping at?' he roared. 'I'll tan the lot of your hides, if you're not careful. I've done it before and I'll do it again. Now get to work.'

With that, he stormed over to another door in the yard, went inside and emerged with two lethal-looking scythes.

We trooped silently out of the farmyard and along a muddy track that led downhill and through the woods for half a mile or so. My mind was in turmoil. I couldn't help thinking it was my fault and I shouldn't have trusted the billeting officer so readily. Peggy walked beside me in silence, and each time I glanced at her, I could see that she was fighting back the tears.

As the woods thinned out, the track emerged onto open farmland that skirted the edge of the moor. A patchwork of fields was spread beneath us, separated by drystone walls, stretching as far as the eye could see. Sheep and cows grazed in some, most of the others were planted with uniform rows of vegetables and a few were empty, tall grass rippling in the gentle breeze. The fields rolled on over round-topped hills into the distance. It would have been stunning, but the air felt heavy.

'Beautiful ain't it?' Red said, coming up closely behind me. His voice had a nasty edge to it; 'Black Moor's contribution to the war effort. He's a saint, our boss, and don't you forget it!'

Then he opened a gate in the wall and all of us were directed inside a huge field of tall grass. I stared across the great expanse. About half of it had been cut, the cut grass lying in wide lines.

'Get to it then!' he yelled at the other four and they trudged away, heads down.

He motioned for us and went to the nearest patch of tall grass, showing us how to swing the scythe in a circular motion so the grass fell in a certain way, then to repeat the motion in the other direction. It looked easy when he did it, but when I tried, I swung the scythe clumsily, it was so heavy, and almost cut the back of my leg. I watched Peggy. She struggled with the weight of the scythe, which was meant for an adult, but she did it carefully and slowly, with far better results.

'Come on then. I'll give you a strip each to do.'

He beckoned us to follow him until we were parallel with the others, who were spread out across the field, working in moving lines. We were each positioned a few yards apart.

'Go on then. Get started. Try to keep in line with 'em.'

So we began. After a few strokes, my arms and ribs began to ache from repeating the circular motion over and over. Soon I was out of breath and having difficulty keeping abreast of the line. Out of the corner of my eye, I watched Peggy struggling with her scythe, her face a picture of concentration. It was even heavier for her, and I could see that she had difficulty even completing one circular motion. But she wasn't going to give up. I drew myself up. If she keep trying, so could I.

'What's your name?' I asked one of the girls, who was just within talking distance. She stared at me with huge grey eyes that protruded from pale, hollow cheeks.

'Joan,' she answered in a whisper.

'How long have you been at the farm?' I asked.

She shrugged. 'A few weeks. A month maybe.'

'Where did you come from?'

'Plymouth. We were all in a home there. An orphanage. We don't have no parents.' She said it in a matter-of-fact voice, and my heart went out to her. 'One night the orphanage burned down,' she said. 'Lots of the kids didn't get out. Us four were wandering around in the dark. A man came up and said he was from the council and he would take us somewhere safe.'

'What did he look like?' My scalp tingled in alarm.

She thought for a moment. 'Dunno really. He was just a man. Tall, I suppose. Dark hair. He had an old truck. Us girls went in the front and the boys rode on the back.'

'Was his name Charlie?' I asked, my stomach clenching in shock.

'Oh yes. Yes, that was it. Farmer Reeves called him Charlie.'

I couldn't reply. Anger and frustration suddenly threatened to overwhelm me, knowing that we'd been tricked into coming here. I realised more than ever in that moment that we needed to leave. To escape, even if it meant walking for days across the moor back to Plymouth.

Chapter Seven

Daisy

That first night we spent in the threshing barn, Peggy wouldn't settle to sleep alone on her top bunk, so I climbed up there with her and we snuggled down together on top of the eiderdown, underneath the grubby blanket. It felt odd, going to bed in the same space as so many strangers. The orphans we now knew as Sally, John, Fred and Joan settled down on their bunks shortly after we'd finished the evening meal.

It was a shock to find out that Red also slept in the barn. I saw him spreading out a pillow and blankets on a bench right next to the door. Before going to bed, he disappeared for a few minutes.

'Don't any of you lot even think about going nowhere,' he said as he left. 'You know what'll happen if you do. I'll be back in a tick.'

When he returned, one of the Alsatian dogs followed him into the barn and I realised with a chill that the dog must be there to stop us trying to leave during the night. Red sprawled out on the bench, pulling a blanket over him. The dog lay down on the floor beside him, right in front of the barn door. Red had a Tilley lamp beside him. He opened a newspaper and lit a cigarette.

The upper bunk was just below a high window in the barn wall, and there was still light in the summer sky until past ten o'clock. When Peggy got under her covers, she pulled the copy of *The Wind in the Willows* out of her gas mask bag and showed it to me. She'd managed to salvage it from the devastation of the Browns' house. When I saw the book, I had an overwhelming memory of home, of being safe in our bedroom in London and Mother sitting on the edge of the bed reading it to us.

I read Peggy a chapter of the book quietly. By the end I was straining my eyes to see the print and I had to read in a whisper. I didn't want Red to hear me and tell me to stop. But despite all my attempts to comfort Peggy, she was still sobbing when I'd finished, and afterwards cried herself to sleep, her tears making a damp patch on my shoulder. Life in Plympton had been bad enough for her, but this was many times worse, and she was mourning the loss of Mother, just as I was.

Just as Peggy was dropping off to sleep, we heard the familiar rumble of an aircraft. It sounded a long way away. Could it be in Plymouth? But soon it was coming closer. Peggy, whimpering, buried her head under the blanket as the planes passed over the barn with a deafening drone, making the whole building vibrate, they were so low. It was a reminder that even though we were buried up here in the countryside, the war was never very far away.

I lay awake for a long time after Peggy had finally dropped off, staring up at the pale moonlight that slanted in through high windows, lighting up the vaulted ceiling. I thought of poor Mother, and of Father, so far away in the desert. I wondered how Peggy would get through this, and how long we would have to bear it here before we managed to find some means of getting away.

My back, arms and legs were aching from the exertions of the afternoon, and the blisters on the palms of my hands were stinging and raw. I wondered how I would get through a whole day of it. One afternoon had been difficult enough. Neither Peggy nor I could keep up with the rest of the line. Red's face was like thunder. He kept yelling at us, but in the end, even he could see that no matter how much he shouted, we couldn't do any better than we were doing. He eventually put us at the other end of the field, where our slow progress wouldn't matter. That felt slightly better, but the blisters on my hand were already sore, weeping fluid, and each swipe of the scythe exacerbated the pain, making me wince.

At around six o'clock we were allowed to down tools and walk back to the farmyard, under Red's watchful eye. When we reached the barn, Joan and the other girl, Sally, showed us a partitioned-off area outside the back, where there were a couple of buckets of water, next to a primitive-looking privy.

We sluiced the sweat and mud off our bodies in silence, dried ourselves with a threadbare towel that we found hanging over the fence, and got dressed in the clothes we'd arrived in. I tried to speak to Sally and Joan as we dried ourselves, to ask them more about what was going on here. I wanted to know if they'd thought about how they could leave, but they both looked at me with wide, terrified eyes and went completely still. In the end Sally spoke in a whisper, her eyes darting around to ensure no one was approaching.

'Don't talk like that. Please. Red will beat you. It don't matter that you're a girl. He's done it to me. He's done it to all of us. He don't like us talking about leaving. Besides, us lot ain't got no place else to go.'

I felt sad for Sally, thinking how we'd been unhappy at the Browns' house, but that perhaps we'd taken them for granted.

'Haven't you ever thought about running away?' I persisted.

'Don't!' said Sally, with a sharp intake of breath. 'John tried that in our first week here. He tried to run off while we were out working in the fields. Farmer Reeves set the dogs after him. He'd managed to get as far as the woods and was hiding there. They sniffed him out and attacked him. He's strong and he managed to beat them off. But he's still got bite marks on his arms and legs. Then Red dragged him back 'ere and beat him with a horsewhip. Bleedin', he was, 'ad to lie down for days after that. So don't you go thinking they'll let you get away easy.'

*

As I lay on my bunk that night, trying to get to sleep, I heard a rumble in the sky that set my nerves on edge. It was that sound again: the unmistakable sound of German aircraft. Why were they coming here, over Dartmoor? It felt almost as if they were tracking me down. There were several of them. I could tell by the way the different tones overlapped and separated. As the noise got closer, I felt myself sweating and automatically I pulled the blanket over my head. But they screamed overhead and carried on their way without the crash of an explosion, and gradually my heart slowed down. It was a reminder that the air raids were carrying on over Plymouth, and I wondered how many homes had been reduced to rubble, how many lives obliterated.

How could we get out of here, I wondered. My eyes smarted as I thought of Mother. If she'd still been alive, she would have come straight away, as soon as she suspected something was wrong. How my heart ached for her in that moment.

Mother's letters to us, alongside the ones I'd written to her, were tucked into the lining of Peggy's bag, which was stowed at the end of the bunk. Thank goodness that Peggy had insisted on bringing it with her after all. Taking care not to disturb her, now that she was finally asleep, I crawled to the end of the bunk, opened the bag and eased the letters out. Holding each one up to the fading light from the high window above me, I read them from start to finish.

A lump rose in my throat as I read Mother's tender words. I thought of her in her hospital bed, lying there sick, minimising her symptoms so we wouldn't worry, when all the time she was far sicker than she knew. Her news of everyday life in Harrow was boring to me when I had first read it, but now it filled me with a desperation to be back there. How I wished the war hadn't come along and destroyed everything.

If only I could get a letter to Mrs Hutchings telling her what was happening to us, she might do something about our situation, or at least inform someone in authority. But I didn't have any paper, let alone stamps. And how would I ever get out to the postbox, even if I did? I remembered that there was a pencil tucked into the lining of Peggy's bag. I could use that, but the only paper we had between us was the pages of the book. There were a few pages at the very end that had no print on them. Perhaps I could tear them out and write on those? But then I realised with a sinking heart that I would need an envelope.

I was going over and over these difficulties when I heard Red stirring on his bunk. I watched from under my blanket as he got up, pulled on his jacket and boots and lit another cigarette. I heard him say something in a low voice to the dog, who sat up and pricked up its ears. Then he unbolted the door and went outside into the yard.

I had no idea what time it was, but I guessed it must be around midnight. Kneeling up on my bunk, I could just about see out of the high window. I rubbed the dust and moss off the glass with my fingers to get a better view. Red was standing in the middle of the yard, smoking. He was holding the Tilley lamp in his other hand. It cast dancing shadows around the stable yard as he shifted around. Then I saw the glow of another cigarette approaching from the house, and I could just make out the stout figure of Farmer Reeves as he limped into the yard. The two of them stood there talking for a few minutes.

Then came the low rumble of an engine; it sounded like something large – a lorry or a tractor perhaps. Headlights appeared at the top of the slope and came to a standstill. Farmer Reeves and Red walked up the hill to where the lorry had stopped. Someone got out of the cab and slammed the door shut. The headlights were left on, casting two beams of white light down the drive, attracting a million insects. A crazy thought occurred to me then: perhaps Peggy and I could get up to the lorry and hide in the back until it took us away from the farm. But I quickly dismissed it. I didn't fancy being attacked and mauled as John had been.

The three of them stood in front of the lorry, deep in discussion. Although I strained my ears, I couldn't make out what they were saying. Then I watched as Red and Farmer Reeves walked down to the stable yard and approached one of the stables. Red appeared first, leading four ponies tied together with a rope. They were all tiny, their coats muddy and unkempt. They looked to me like wild ponies, the sort we'd seen out on the moor as we'd been driven in the van from Plymouth. Red pulled them up the little hill and round to the back of the truck. They were struggling and pulling, trying to break free from the ropes. Then I heard the clatter of unshod hooves on wood, some whinnying and shouting, and then the back of the truck was slammed shut. Reeves walked back up the hill and the three men stood together in front of the truck conferring, before the driver jumped back in and the truck reversed back up the drive and out of my line of sight. Red and Reeves stood at the top of the slope together for a while, then Red turned and walked back to the yard.

I ducked down under the windowsill for fear of him glancing up and seeing me there. Then I slid beneath the blanket, curling myself around Peggy's warm back, calmed by her steady breathing. I lay awake for a long time after that, wondering what they were up to, taking wild ponies away from the farm in the middle of the night.

In the morning, we were woken as the first dusty rays of sunlight began to filter through the filthy windows by Red walking up and down in front of the bunks, banging two biscuit tins together repeatedly. Every bone and muscle in my body was aching from the exertions of the previous day, but I knew there was no real choice but to obey him. Peggy was stretching and yawning beside me. I felt a pang of anxiety when I caught sight of her face, pinched and pale, dark rings under her eyes. After helping her get dressed under the blanket, I climbed down into my own bunk and pulled on the baggy farm clothes from the day before.

Breakfast consisted of a few slices of stale bread with lard spread on them and a cup of stewed tea. Afterwards, Red took us all out into the yard and told the other four to get tools from the shed. Then he turned to Peggy and me.

'You two are pretty useless at mowing,' he said. 'It's a waste of time trying to teach you. You can make yourselves useful in other ways. For a start you can clean out the stables.' He watched our faces for a moment, waiting for us to object, no doubt, but we both remained silent. 'There's the barrow and some muck-forks over there. You've got to pick up the droppings and put them in the barrow, then take 'em round the back and tip 'em on the muckheap.'

Peggy's face brightened at the prospect of being close to the horses.

'Don't know what you're smiling for, Little 'un,' Red said with a sneer. 'I'll be out 'ere watching you, so don't even think about running away.'

'What about the horses?' I asked, alarmed. I didn't fancy the idea of going inside the stables with the horses loose in that confined space.

'What about 'em?' he asked, a grin spreading across his face.

'They might kick us if they're loose,' I said.

'You don't look like one to take fright,' he said in a jeering voice. 'If you're scared, though, I'll tie 'em up to the wall. But I want all the muck picked up. Even where they're standing. They won't 'urt you.'

He went inside the first stable and we could hear him talking to the horse sharply as he tied it up. When he emerged from the stable, we each took one of the long-handled forks and ventured inside. There was a pungent, sickly-sweet smell of dung and straw and horse-sweat. The horse was tied up in the far corner. It was very tall and heavily built, with a thick black coat and feathery white hooves. As it moved, its muscles rippled under its skin. I noticed that it stood with one of its rear hooves rested on the ground at an angle. Did that mean it was poised to kick? I was terrified that it would break its rope or wheel round and lash out at us. I could see that it was shod with iron shoes.

As we stood contemplating the horse, we could hear Red giving orders to the other four outside in the yard. He was telling them to get up to the hay meadow quickly and carry on scything the strips.

'I'll be up to check your work in a while.'

I wondered why he wasn't going up to the field with them this morning. Perhaps the four of them were so beaten down, so terrified of him now, that he knew there was no chance of any of them trying to run.

'Come on then, Peggy,' I whispered. 'Let's get on with it, shall we? There's no getting out of it.'

But Peggy was doing something I would never have dared to do. She was approaching the huge horse's head, talking to it all the time in a low, sing-song voice. How brave she was, I thought, but how did she know what to do? I remembered how she loved books about horses. How her bookcase at home was full of them. She must have picked it up from one of those horsey books. When she got close to the horse, she leaned forward, her hands behind her back, and blew at it gently through her nose. The horse whinnied, swung its head round towards her and nuzzled her face. She straightened up and stroked its neck.

'Isn't he beautiful? He's a Shire horse, you know, Daisy,' she said.

'What's that?'

'They're used to pull carts and things. They're really strong.'

Suddenly, Red was there, pushing the door open and striding into the stable.

'Hey! What d'you think you're up to?' he said. He lunged forward, grabbed Peggy's hair and jerked her backward.

'You ain't here to make friends with the 'orses. Get on and clear up this muck, like I said,' he said, pinching Peggy's chin between his fingers and holding his face close to hers. Then he shoved her forward so she fell face-first into the straw.

'Leave her alone,' I said fiercely. He turned round towards me, his eyes narrowed, his jaw set in an angry scowl. Then, without warning, he slapped me round the face with the back of his hand. I gasped at the sudden pain and the shock of it.

'Now get on with it. I don't want another peep out of either of you this morning. I'll be out there in the yard, watching what you get up to. So, no shirking, or there'll be more where that came from.'

I hastily picked up the muck and took it out to the barrow while Peggy held the horse by its halter, talking to it gently all the time, keeping it steady. My heart pounded when I had to go near the horse's rear hooves to clean. It shifted slightly as I got close, but Peggy kept talking to it and mercifully, it stayed still. When we came out of the stable, unscathed, Red, smoking outside, at first looked puzzled, then disappointed that we hadn't been kicked or bitten, but he didn't say anything.

The next stable was empty but full of dung. I thought of the ponies I'd seen being bundled into the truck in the middle of the night. This must be where they'd been kept. But I didn't say anything to Peggy about what I'd seen. It would only have upset her.

By the end of the morning we'd finished all the stables and were covered in muck. The other four came back in from the fields and we sat at the trestle table again in silence. Red disappeared for a few minutes before the food appeared and I noticed the atmosphere of tension lighten and the others relax. John, the older of the two boys, the one with the unruly brown hair, turned to me.

'Sally said you were talking about getting out of here,' he said. He had earnest, brown eyes and he looked straight at me, waiting for a response.

'Shut up, John,' said Sally, rolling her eyes. 'Red'll be back any minute.'

'I'm planning on making a run for it again,' he said to me, ignoring Sally. 'When the time is right,' he added. 'I tried before and they stopped me.'

'When are you going? We'll come with you,' I said immediately.

He shook his head. 'Not possible. It's too dangerous. I'll tell you what, though, I'll get word to your folks if you give me their address.'

I hung my head. 'We don't have any family to contact,' I whispered and I could feel everyone's eyes on my face. 'Mother died recently and Father's away at war.'

'I'm sorry to hear that,' John said gently. 'Is there anyone else?'

'There's a neighbour. She might help, but I'm not sure.'

'It's worth a try. Give me her address anyway.'

I quickly crossed to the bunk, clambered up to the top and tore a page out of the back of *The Wind in the Willows*, grabbed the pencil and scribbled Mrs Hutchings' name and address on it. I'd just handed it to John and was sitting down again when Red came back through the door, followed by Elsie with a cauldron of soup.

'What's all this?' Red said, frowning.

'Nothing,' I said. 'I just went to the privy, that's all.'

He looked at me for a long moment. I stared back at him, my eyes steady, determined not to let guilt show in my eyes.

We ate in silence. The same filthy, greasy soup that we'd had for both meals the day before.

'Are you cycling down to the village this afternoon, Elsie?' asked Red.

'Yep, as usual. Going to see Flory, and I need to get a few bits. Dad wants some snuff.'

'Get me some smokes, would you?' he said.

'If you give me the money,' she said.

After the meal, while Red went outside for another cigarette, I offered to help Elsie wash the dishes. Looking around to check that Red was nowhere to be seen, I said, 'Is there a post office in the village?'

Even though I'd given Mrs Hutchings's address to John, I wasn't sure that he would be able to keep his promise, or that he'd be leaving the farm at all. I had the feeling that Elsie might be willing to help. I'd noticed that she was afraid of her father, and of Red too. I hoped that I could appeal to her as another girl of about the same age as me. She stared at me for a long moment, then shrugged.

'What if there is?'

'Would you take a letter to post for me?'

She looked at me with her dull, doe-like eyes.

'Not sure about that. Don't know what Dad would say.'

'Well, you don't need to say anything to him or anyone, do you?'

'What's it worth?' she asked. My mind raced, trying to think of something I could give her. Finally, I remembered.

'You could have my watch,' I said, in desperation, showing her the silver watch I'd had for my last birthday. 'It was expensive. You'd have to buy a stamp to put on the letter though. Could you do that?'

'Maybe,' she said, greedy eyes on the watch. She dried her hands on her skirt. 'Me friend Flory, her mum runs the post office. I need to go back and give me dad 'is dinner, then I'll be back down for me bike. I'll only be ten minutes. If you give it to me, I'll do me best.'

My heart soaring with hope, I dashed up to the bunk again, ripped another page out of the end of the book and scribbled some frantic words on it:

> Dear Mrs Hutchings, Peggy and I are in desperate danger. We've been taken to a farm and made to work. We aren't allowed to leave. PLEASE come quickly. It is Black Moor Farm, on Dartmoor. Daisy.

I took one of our mother's letters out of its envelope, crossed out the Browns' address and scribbled Mrs Hutchings' beside it. Then I tucked the flap back into the envelope as best I could. It wasn't perfect, but luckily the envelope hadn't torn when we'd opened it the first time.

I watched through the upper window until I saw Elsie come back down the hill and into the stable yard. Then I got down from the bunk and rushed outside. Red was still smoking outside the barn door. How could I get the letter to Elsie without him seeing? He stubbed his cigarette out.

'I've just got to go up to the 'ouse and get some money for you, Else,' he said. 'Watch these beggars for me, won't you?'

I let out a sigh of relief and approached Elsie, who was wheeling an ancient, rusting bicycle out of one of the sheds.

'Here's the letter and my watch,' I said, handing them to her. Her eyes lit up as she looked at the watch before slipping it into her pocket.

'There's a pawnshop in the village. I'm going to try to cash the watch in when I'm down there. Won't be able to wear it 'ere, what with Dad 'n Red asking questions... Who's the letter to?' she asked after a pause.

'Just a friend. It's written on the front.'

She turned to me and smiled, a sarcastic sort of smile. 'I can't read. Never learned,' she said bluntly.

I watched her push the bike laboriously up the slope. Red came out of the house and they exchanged a few words, then Elsie got on the bike and pedalled off up the drive slowly. As I watched her broad back disappearing from view, I took a deep breath and crossed my fingers. Would she post the letter for me? Could she be trusted? I wasn't at all sure of either of those things. I thought of my watch, and my father's face as he'd given it to me, full of love and hope: 'Look after it, Daisy my love, and think of me when you tell the time.' It was his last gift to me before he'd gone off to war. Tears stung my eyes and I swallowed a lump in my throat just thinking about it. How could I have parted with his final gift to me, especially now I might never see him again? But if Elsie did post the letter, it would be well worth giving up my watch, and I was sure that Father would understand.

Chapter Eight

Helen

The weak winter sun streamed through the windows and lit up the dusty bedroom as Helen sat at her dressing table, scrutinising her face in the mirror. She couldn't help comparing herself to Laura, Helen had to admit to herself. Her sister always looked so well turned out, so stylish and well-groomed, wearing her years naturally. How different they were deep down inside too. Where Laura was outgoing and confident, Helen was hesitant and introverted. It struck her that perhaps that was why Laura had found it easier to bond with Daisy over the years. It was much easier and straightforward to bond with an extrovert; it had come more naturally to both of them.

Sighing, Helen smoothed some moisturiser onto her cheeks and round her eyes, peering again at her face with its laughter lines and weathered skin. The ageing process had not bothered her much before – she'd hardly worn make-up for years; but now she reached for her tube of foundation and began to smooth it onto her skin with her fingertips, tentatively at first, leaning forward to examine the results.

She applied a thicker layer to the dark shadows under her eyes; the result of a near-sleepless night. She'd twisted and turned all night, her thoughts circling and doubling back on themselves, swooping and soaring uncontrollably.

Her mind had gone back time and time again to the wartime letters from Daisy and her mother. Why had her Aunt Peggy's existence been kept a secret for decades? And where was Peggy now? Who was the young man in the photo, standing at the ship's rail, his arm round Daisy's shoulders? Happiness and excitement radiated from the pair of them, almost leaping out of the photograph all these years later. He must have meant a lot to Daisy. And the mysterious young sailor, Ordinary Seaman J. Smith. Was that the same young man in the photo at the docks? It was so hard to tell, but there was something in his eyes that drew Helen to him. And why on earth had Daisy kept all of this from her? Had she been living a lie for the whole of her adult life? Helen planned to start by researching online to find out as much as she could, then if she had to go to the archives to track things down, she would do that too. She would stop at nothing to resolve these mysteries.

Helen double-checked in her handbag to ensure the letters and the photographs were still there. She took a deep breath to calm herself. Just thinking about diving into Daisy's past made her nerves jangle. It would be very hard, she realised that, but at least Laura might help her.

Encouraged by the experiment with the foundation, she applied some eyeliner and lipstick and sat back to assess the results. Not so bad, she concluded, although there were far too many greys in her dark hair, which was springy and unruly just like her mother's. She brushed her hair quickly and pulled it off her face into a hairslide. Perhaps she should book an appointment with the hairdresser. Why and when exactly had she stopped caring about her appearance?

She walked over and stared in the long mirror on the wardrobe. Twisting round, she examined her figure from several angles. She was carrying too much weight on her hips and midriff as usual, and the flowing floral skirt designed to mask that fact now seemed instead to emphasise it. On an impulse she wriggled out of it and reached in the wardrobe for something smarter. She picked out a straight woollen one that flattened her curves. Then she pulled on a tight red jumper and her best leather boots.

Later that afternoon, after having spent a couple of hours talking patiently to an old lady who was looking for a particular size of coffee table, and selling a chest of drawers to a young mother with a couple of unruly children, Helen took out her laptop. She started her search by tapping in the names Daisy Banks and Peggy Banks, but she was soon forced to give up that line of enquiry. There were so many that it was impossible to filter them. Instead, she began to look into the North African campaign of the Second World War. It didn't take long to find out that there were two main regiments involved at the outset, the Royal Tank Regiment and the 11th Hussars, although she discovered that several other regiments also joined later. Checking back at the letter from Daisy's mother, she realised that her father must have joined up in the early stages of the campaign, so she focused her efforts on that period. She spent a long time scanning forums where aficionados discussed the minutiae of the battles, such as the precise locations or the particular specifications of tanks used by the Germans and Italians. At one point she came across a site that contained military records. She tapped in 'Edward Banks', holding her breath, but was thwarted as hundreds of names came up. She tried again, filtering it down to the Second World War; there were fewer, but there were still dozens.

She decided to leave that for now and instead moved on to what she'd really been itching to look into. She took the photograph of the young sailor out of her bag and stared at it. She sighed, looking at his name on the cap band: *Ordinary Seaman J. Smith*. It must be the most common, unremarkable name possible. Even less remarkable than Edward Banks. So common that it was very unlikely that she would find anything about him from records online.

She looked long and hard at his face with its chiselled cheek-bones; at his fiery dark eyes with their look of challenge, staring straight at the camera, and she felt a strange connection with him. She realised that it was a familiar look; that it was a look she had often observed in her mother. Was this young man the same as the one in the picture taken on board the ship, standing side by side with Daisy at the rail, their arms linked casually as if they were comfortable in each other's company? It could be, but it was impossible to tell for certain. In that photograph, the young man's face was slightly obscured by shadow.

'Who *are* you?' she murmured into the emptiness.

Helen had never known her mother to be in love, but she wondered if this man was someone she'd been in love with. Romance was not something they'd ever really discussed, and Helen had kept her own love life away from Daisy.

She remembered how, when she'd moved back to Totnes, she'd kept her recent past a secret from her mother, suspecting that she wouldn't approve. She'd been living in a caravan with a group of travellers in Somerset, trying to make money as an artist, touring festivals and country fairs, sketching portraits for money. Her life had revolved around Quinn, a performance poet from Glasgow with a free spirit and blond dreadlocks. She'd been bowled over by the free-living alternative lifestyle and by Quinn himself, until the police turned up one day and Quinn was suddenly nowhere to be found. He was wanted for burglary. Later, he was arrested back in Scotland, where he'd returned to his wife and four children.

So, bruised by this experience, she'd returned to live near her mother and had found a job in a riverside pub as a barmaid. But she was determined to pursue her art, so enrolled in a life-drawing evening class on her night off. She hadn't expected much from it and not wanting to get involved with anyone, had kept a low profile, getting on with her work, hardly speaking to the other students. But she'd got close to one person. He was older than most of the others, wry and intelligent, with a hearty scepticism about the world in general. Despite her reserve, he would make her laugh with his witty, often cutting observations and gradually she started to warm to him. She would even chat to him during coffee breaks, when before she'd sat alone, guarding her silence.

After a few weeks he asked her out. It wasn't a conventional first date, though. He had a small boat moored on the River Dart and they pottered down to Dartmouth drinking wine while he cooked steaks on the Calor gas grill and they chatted and told each other about their lives. It was all so different from her recent experience; a million miles away from Quinn, the travellers' camp and her itinerant lifestyle, and she grasped at it like a lifeline. But it hadn't lasted; he hadn't wanted to make a commitment and Helen needed more than he had to offer, so they drifted apart. Since then she'd been alone, happy with her own company.

Without expecting much, she spent half an hour searching on military records websites, putting the name in the search engines, which came up with thousands of results. Finally, she gave up and took up the photograph again, examining it in minute detail to see if there were any more clues to his identity to enable her to narrow down her search, but she could find none.

Now, tearing herself away from her memories, she called Laura and told her of her progress.

'I haven't had much luck yet. Can you remember Mum ever mentioning anything about her father? Did she say that he'd served in the army, or even mention which regiment he might have been in?'

'No. She was always very tight-lipped about her past. It was almost impossible to get anything out of her.'

'Yes. I remember. The thing is, it's only made me more curious to find out. You know, I've been thinking about this a lot. It just goes to show, all those years of being the strong, critical one with iron self-discipline and high standards. All that must have been a front really, to hide whatever happened in her past, to cover up her own vulnerability,' said Helen.

'You know she was so hard on me when I was growing up,' she went on. 'Always comparing me to you, reminding me of how well you'd done, how perfect you were. I felt I could never measure up.'

Laura was silent for a few seconds, then said, 'I find that very hard to believe.'

'Why do you say that?'

'Because she was very strict indeed with me and I thought you were the one who had it easy. She had such expectations of my schoolwork. It made me very anxious. Whereas you seemed to get away with murder in comparison.'

'Really? But you know that's because I stopped trying in the end, began to rebel. I was never any good at academic work, don't you remember the arguments that caused? I didn't really get away with it, but she certainly gave up trying.'

'You know I always resented the freedom you seemed to have as a teenager,' said Laura. 'I remember distinctly Mum telling me that I owed it to her not to go out with boys because that would affect my schoolwork. She said she'd made so many sacrifices for me that it would be ungrateful of me not to get straight As.'

'Well, you know I used to have to jump out of the window and run away on a Saturday if I wanted to go out in the evenings. You should have heard the recriminations the next day!'

Again, there was silence from Laura's end. She cleared her throat before saying, 'I'm sorry you had cause to resent me. It's the same as the way I felt about you. I suppose it's what made us drift apart. But it seems that we were at cross purposes all along.'

Helen smiled, realising that all her childhood resentment of her sister had evaporated over the years, much like her bitterness towards her mother had softened now. She was beginning to understand now that she didn't really know her mother at all.

'Well, let's not let it happen again, hey?' she said.

'Absolutely not!' said Laura.

After they'd said goodbye, Helen glanced outside and noticed that it was dark. The clock on the wall was at ten past six. She went to the door and flipped the sign to 'Closed', and was just about to lock up when she noticed Jago walking up the street. He came into the shop with a blast of cold air.

'How are things?' he asked, and she saw from his expression that he had some news for her. Helen had known Jago since she'd returned to Totnes more than twenty years ago. They'd met when she happened to go into his shop to browse one day and they'd hit it off straight away. He was her best friend, and she normally told him everything. It would have been good to be able to confide in him about what she'd found out about her mother, but she remembered how Laura had wanted to keep it quiet, so she held back.

'Oh, a bit slow. Sold that oak chest of drawers.'

'Oh, excellent. Good stuff. The guy made an offer for your mother's bureau, by the way. Three hundred. I said I'd let him know. I just wanted to check you're happy to sell it. It's very beautiful, I thought you might find it hard to part with.'

'I know. It is lovely. But it's got to go, and it sounds a good price. I'm sure Mum would be happy with that.'

'Yes. But I thought I'd ask you first. Are you about to go home?'

'Yes, I'll just get my coat.'

As she walked away, Jago said, 'Oh, by the way, I found something in the old bureau. You must have missed it when you cleared out. One of the little drawers at the top was wedged shut, so you must have thought it wouldn't open, but I got the screwdriver to it. Found this…'

He fumbled in his pocket and produced a large key. Helen took it from him and peered at it, curious. It was old-fashioned, but it looked as though it had hardly been used. A luggage label was tied to it. On it a number was scrawled: number 342.

She stared at Jago, puzzled. 'This doesn't look like any of the keys to the house. What do you think it might be for?'

Chapter Nine

Daisy

The days wore on in much the same way as the first day and soon we'd been at Black Moor Farm for several months. I often thought about making a run for it, but I wasn't prepared to risk Peggy's life. She wasn't as strong as I was and couldn't run very fast. My sixteenth birthday came and went; I didn't mention it to anyone, not even Peggy. When we were evacuated, we thought we'd be escaping the war, but it was a constant threat even here.

It seemed that Farmer Reeves was doing his best to profiteer from the war effort. All available land was turned over to cultivating vegetables, which Reeves himself took by horse-drawn cart to market. He also had cattle grazing up on the moor and flocks of sheep grazing as far as the eye could see. The farm was cut off from the outside world but sometimes I would wake at night to the drone of engines overhead, just as I had on the very first night, and the memory of the bombings would come back to me all too vividly. It was impossible to forget that the war was raging on, that cities were being bombed, people were losing their lives and so many men were away, fighting.

Each morning, Peggy and I were made to clean the stables, and in the afternoons, we were sent out to work in the fields. A few days after we arrived, there were some new ponies in the stables when we went out to clean them. They looked just like the ones I'd seen being taken away by truck in the dead of night, wild and unkempt, their coats long and shaggy, coated in mud. They must have arrived during the night; they hadn't been there the day before. I thought I'd heard some commotion in the yard during the night, but by the time I'd got up to look out of the window, all was quiet and still. The ponies were untamed and seemed to be terrified of me and Peggy. When we entered the stable with our pitchforks, they huddled together in one corner, staring at us with the whites of their eyes showing.

In the evenings, after work in the fields had finished for the day and before the meal, Peggy and I were given another job. That was to take a bucket of corn and scraps to the chickens that were housed in an old disused barn a couple of fields away from the main farmyard. We also had to collect the eggs they laid, which Farmer Reeves would sell in the village. The barn was a ten-minute walk down a track, nestled in a hollow between two hills. A fast-running stream ran behind the building. It was a huge, red-brick, Victorian structure and had two storeys, with doors opening to the outside on both levels, like a warehouse. On the upper floor were stored sacks of grain, and we sometimes heard rats scrabbling around up there. That sound made shivers run down my spine, but despite that, if it was possible to enjoy anything in the conditions we were living under, it would have been those evening walks with Peggy down to the big barn. Since she was tiny, Peggy had always loved stories about animals but, living in London, fictional ones were the only ones she'd known up until then. It gave me some comfort to watch her excitement and pleasure at being with the horses and chickens; her love of animals seemed to temper the discomfort and fear of our situation for her. As evening approached, she always brightened at the thought of seeing the chickens, and set off for the barn with a spring in her step.

There were a dozen or so hens, which were allowed to roam around in the lower part of the barn. Our job was to spread corn and scraps out on the floor for them, check their water trough and collect any eggs we could find. The chickens would lay their eggs in different places around the barn: on straw bales, or in odd corners where they'd attempted to make nests. The first time he took us there, Red showed us what to do, but after that, he waited outside, smoking. He would bring one of the dogs with him and he always said, in a threatening voice, as we went into the barn, 'If you try any funny business, I'll set Wolf 'ere on you. He's a vicious one. Got a nasty, sharp set of teeth, I can tell you.'

After the first few days though, Red stopped coming down the track to the barn with us altogether. He would stay in the yard and let us go alone. But before we set off, he would always grab me by my shoulders and hold me close, putting his face up to mine, so I got a blast of his foul-smelling breath, and he would warn us not to escape.

So, every evening we dutifully set off to the far barn, spent ten minutes or so feeding the chickens, collecting the eggs and putting them in a bucket, then walked back up to the farmyard. Sometimes, as time went on, we would linger inside the barn, sit down on the bales of straw, watch the birds strutting and pecking around us and talk for a while. It was the one place where we could speak freely, as if we were back at home. Red didn't say anything if we took longer than usual. He seemed quite happy to lounge around on a bench at the entrance to the yard, smoking endless roll-ups, dozing or reading his paper. It was gradually becoming clear to me that Red was as lazy as he was violent and bad-tempered.

One evening as we were making our way back from the barns, we heard the sound of an aeroplane high overhead. Peggy looked at me, terrified.

'What if it drops a bomb on us?' she said. 'Shall we run back to the barn?'

'It's too high for that,' I said, but as we stared into the darkening sky, we caught sight of the lights of a stricken plane plummeting towards the earth. One of the wings was on fire; the engines were screaming, out of control. It was different from any sound we'd

ever heard a plane make before. We clung to each other, there
on the track, and watched as the plane carried on dropping and
eventually hit the earth, far out on the moor, with an enormous
cracking explosion that reverberated for miles around. At the sound,
we could hear everyone coming out into the yard, excited voices
chattering at fever pitch. We carried on walking towards the yard
ourselves, and when we reached it, Red was there too.

'Go back inside you lot, or I'll get me rifle out on you,' he yelled.
'It ain't nothing to worry about. Just a plane shot down. It ain't on
our land and the army will deal with it.'

We went back into the threshing barn with the others, subdued.
I was thinking about the crew of the crashed aircraft. Had any of
them survived? Was it an RAF plane or a German one? The engine
had been so damaged I couldn't tell by the sound it had made.
I shivered, wondering if there was a German airman wounded,
wandering about on the moor, terrified because he was in alien
territory and would soon be taken prisoner. I looked around me, at
the pinched faces of the others, at Red and the Alsatian stationed
beside the door, at our primitive living arrangements. His plight
was not so different from our own, I thought.

Peggy and I had got to know the four orphans who worked
alongside us, but it was always difficult to speak to them when Red
was around. He would pull us apart and yell at us to stop talking if
we happened to exchange a few words. Mealtimes too were mainly
spent in silence. We were able to speak a few words to Sally and
Joan though, when we were out at the back of the barn, washing
either our bodies or our clothes. I quickly realised that Sally was
the more outgoing and quick-witted of the two. Poor Joan was
like a nervous dormouse, her grey eyes continually darting about,
constantly on the lookout for danger, and when she did speak, it
was in a terrified whisper. She must have been fourteen or fifteen,
but she looked much younger, her body spindly, her face pale and
thin and mousy hair hanging lank around her shoulders.

Sally was a little bolder and more talkative. She told us that she had no memory of any home other than the orphanage, where some of the staff had been cruel, taking pleasure in humiliating the children, or punishing them physically for any minor transgression. My heart filled with pity for her when she asked why I was reading to Peggy at night. She'd never heard of anyone being read a bedtime story, or being tucked up in bed with a goodnight kiss. I didn't think she'd admit, or that she even knew, that life at Black Moor Farm was cruel. Perhaps Reeves had chosen orphans on purpose. For Sally, cruelty was all she'd ever known.

The two boys were equally different. Fred was a timid boy, a bit like Joan. He hardly ever spoke and like Joan's, his eyes were windows of fear that he mainly kept downcast, rarely meeting anyone's gaze directly. He was thin and wiry and, like Sally, not afraid of hard work.

John was different. Ever since he'd told me about his plan to escape I'd noticed something about him. Behind his restless dark eyes lurked a defiant, rebellious spirit, as I'd suspected from the first day. He was strong and a good worker, but it was obvious that he wasn't prepared to accept this forced labour, that every waking moment he was looking for an opportunity to get away. On several occasions he answered Red back, and on each occasion, Red had yelled at him, 'Less of your cheek, boy. You're here to work, don't you ever forget that,' and fetched him a slap around the face. But John wouldn't be cowed by this treatment; he would stand firm, his eyes silently on Red's face, defiance in his expression.

There was a kind side to John as well. I never forgot the fact that deep in the pocket of his trousers, he carried Mrs Hutchings's address in London scribbled on a scrap of paper torn from the back of *The Wind in the Willows*. Sometimes, in moments of fear or dread, I would start to shiver, thinking about the consequences for us if it was ever found. We didn't speak about the address again, but it was a secret we shared between us. John would sometimes give me a knowing look as if to remind me that he still had it with him, safe and sound, and that he hadn't forgotten his promise. He was kind to Peggy too, often helping her to finish tasks that she struggled with, lifting her up onto the trailer, helping her climb over tall fences. He would carry her tools for her up to the field too, ruffling her hair as he took a rake or scythe from her, and she would look up at him with shining eyes that made my heart sing to see.

I wondered why he hadn't tried to leave again. Why he was still here, all these months later. One day I asked him, as we walked side by side to the field.

'I don't want anything to happen to any of you lot,' he said simply. 'I'm worried that they'll make you pay if I go.'

I smiled up at him, my admiration for him deepening. 'Perhaps someone will come,' I replied.

We all thought we'd be found, that someone might come for us – possibly the police or someone else in authority, perhaps even Mrs Hutchings herself. I had no idea if Elsie had sent my letter – I hadn't been able to ask her; I was scared we'd be overheard. I looked out every day. Would they come down the track beside the house, or find another way onto the premises? But as the weeks and months slipped by with no sign of anyone, I began to worry that the letter had never left the farm.

I grew more and more angry with myself. I had given up Father's beautiful watch on such a slim hope of being helped. The watch was one of the very few mementos I had from home, and every time I thought of it, I could feel tears welling in my eyes, thinking of poor dear Father and remembering what I'd done.

One day, as Elsie brought the pan of stew down to the barn for the evening meal, I decided to take the matter in hand. I needed to know what had happened to my letter. I left the table where everyone sat waiting for the meal and pretended to go out the back way to the privy. Instead I skirted round the back of the barn, then doubled back into the yard. There I stood in the corner, out of sight, and waited for her. Within a few minutes she appeared on the slope, staggering a little under the weight of the huge cauldron.

'Did you post my letter, Elsie?' I hissed as she crossed the yard towards the barn.

She paused momentarily, then stuck her nose in the air and carried on walking as if she hadn't heard me. I marched forward and stood in front of her.

'I'm talking to you! Did you post my letter?'

'Get out of me way,' she said, trying to sidestep me, some of the stew from the pan slopping over the edge and spilling onto her already-filthy skirt.

'Now look what you've gone and done!' she said, her voice full of outrage.

'What did you do with my letter?' I said, trying not to raise my voice.

'Who cares what I did with it?' she said, looking at me with narrowed eyes, her lips curled into a smile of triumph. 'What yer going to do about it?'

'If you didn't post it, I want my watch back,' I said, my voice trembling with anger. She moved towards me and tried to barge me out of the way, but both her hands were holding the pan. I shoved her back, more stew spilling out of the pan and splashing on the yard.

'Too late for that,' she said. 'It ain't your watch no more, and I ain't got it anyways.'

Anger rose in me.

'Did you pawn it and keep the money?' I yelled.

I could feel angry tears welling in my eyes now. I thought again of Father, out there with the army in the desert, putting his life in danger on the front line every day. I imagined him remembering how he'd given me the watch and smiling at the thought that whenever I glanced at it for the time, I would think of him. That watch had been an invisible thread between the two of us, connecting us across thousands of miles of land and sea, and in my rash stupidity, I'd broken that link. Fury mounted inside me at the thought of it and I lunged at Elsie and pushed her backwards. The pan clattered to the ground with her and the stew slopped out and spread everywhere, making a great greasy pool over the bricks.

In seconds, Red was out of the barn and flying towards me, shouting, his face distorted with rage.

'What the 'ell's going on round 'ere?' he yelled, grabbing me from behind by both arms and yanking me backwards.

'She pushed me over,' blubbered Elsie, getting to her feet, her dress drenched in greasy liquid, her face red and sweaty.

'What you do that for, you little bitch?' he roared, twisting my arms behind my back.

'She's stolen my watch,' I said between gritted teeth, but the moment the words were out, I knew it was the worst thing I could have said.

The others had followed Red out of the barn by now and stood watching, open-mouthed. I saw Peggy's face among them, her eyes filled with tears as she watched.

'I never did. I never stole it. She give it me,' protested Elsie.

Red loosened his grip on my arms momentarily.

'Now why on earth would anyone do a thing like that?' he asked in an evil tone. 'What you give it 'er for?'

He suddenly grabbed my arms again and drew me close to him. His face was next to mine. I could smell his sweat, and tobacco on his foul breath.

'I didn't give it to her,' I protested.

'Yes, you did, you liar,' Elsie shouted, triumph in her voice. 'You give it me to post a letter.'

At that, Red pulled me even closer, digging his filthy nails into my skin.

'A letter? Really? And who was that to?'

'It was to 'er friend in London. I've got it 'ere.'

Elsie fumbled in the pocket of her dress and drew out my letter. It was crumpled and battered, but it was unmistakably my letter. Red lunged forward and snatched it out of her hand, ripped off the envelope and held the letter close, his eyes skimming the words. He was still gripping my arm with one hand, and I struggled and wriggled, trying to get away.

As soon as he'd finished, he drew his hand back and struck me round the face with the full force of his strength. I gasped and yelled out with the pain, the sickly-sweet taste of blood in my mouth from a split lip.

At that moment I glimpsed Farmer Reeves limping down the hill to the yard.

'What's goin' on 'ere?' he demanded. Red handed the letter to Reeves, who scrutinised it carefully, breathing heavily, holding it close to his face. His eyes moved slowly from side to side as he followed the lines. Then he looked up, his eyes black with anger.

'Get the 'orsewhip out of the tack room, Red,' he said, ripping the letter into tiny shreds and scattering them on the ground.

He grabbed me by the hair and pulled me towards him. I could smell the stale sweat and filth of his body and I almost retched. Then, as Red hurried off to the tack room, Reeves dragged me across the yard and shoved me forward, forcing me to bend over a trough of stagnant water. I resisted as best I could, but he was strong. He pushed me forward again, finally ducking my head under the filthy surface repeatedly, forcing the stinking water up my nostrils into my mouth, until I was gulping and choking. I had no choice then but to yield to his strength and bend forward over the trough.

My thoughts were scattering in every direction. What was going to happen to me? How would Peggy react? It would terrify her. That worried me more than my physical well-being. I also felt foolish and exposed, bending over the trough like that. Dimly, I heard a shout from the back of the yard. It was John's voice: 'Don't you touch her!' and I was aware of him lunging forward, only to be restrained roughly by Reeves.

Then I heard footsteps behind me and I sensed that Red had returned, then the steps quickened and I felt the lash of the leather whip on the backs of my legs and a scream ripped from my lungs at the evil sting of it. It happened again and again, and each time the pain ripped through my legs, causing me to yell out. When it had finally stopped Reeves yanked me upright, then threw me on the bricks so I was left sprawling on the ground.

I heard him stump away towards the house, but he stopped at the edge of the yard, shouting at the others to return to the fields, and I thought of poor Peggy having to watch what had happened. I was supposed to be protecting her and I couldn't even protect myself.

I heard their footsteps as they tramped out of the yard and up the hill and when I finally lifted my head and rubbed the tears from my eyes, I saw that I was alone. The thought entered my mind that I could make a break for it; run out of the yard and across the field to safety before anyone noticed I'd gone. But the idea was pointless. I knew I would never leave Peggy behind there alone.

My whole body ached and the backs of my legs were stinging from the lashes, fresh blood trickling from the wounds. I was shaking all over too from the shock and the pain of the beating. Slowly and painfully, I got to my feet, but I was suddenly overcome with dizziness, black spots swimming before my eyes. I was forced to sit down again to wait for the dizzy spell to pass. I sat there taking deep breaths, trying to calm myself. As I did so, there was the rumble of far-off engines and a group of fighter planes flew overhead. They flew in formation, frighteningly low, blotting out the sun. I held my hands over my ears as they passed over, trembling from head to toe. It gave me a sharp reminder that the war raged on out there, that because of it we were forgotten. No one knew or cared that we were here.

I felt so alone, so isolated, and tears sprang to my eyes once again. Then I glanced across the yard and noticed something else that chilled me to the core: the Alsatian, Wolf, was sitting there in the entrance, his teeth bared, hackles raised, his eyes fixed on my face. My feeling of being trapped was complete and I realised then that no matter what we might think, no one was coming for us. There was no escape.

Chapter Ten

Daisy

Towards the beginning of November, we were made to bring a herd of cattle into the farm from where they'd been grazing on the edge of the moor. It meant walking a long way, up a winding cart track through the woods and out into the open. It had been a few months since I'd been beaten and not much had changed. I was more aware than ever of the violent consequences of an attempt at escape, and I could imagine Peggy being hurt as I had been. And I was fearful. Where could we go, who would help us out there in the world where we had no family left? The pain of losing Mother had finally overwhelmed me, and I'd lost all hope of Father's return. But working beside John in the fields had given me at least some strength and purpose during those dark days.

When my wounds had been healing, I would often open my eyes to see John leaning over me in bed, his dark eyes full of concern. I would smile back at him, wordlessly. And sometimes, when Red's back was turned, he would bring a damp cloth and bathe my legs gently, bringing some relief to the stinging and burning left by the beating. His gentleness brought tears to my eyes. It was such a contrast to everything else that was going on around me. I would open my eyes and search for his, yearning for him to return my gaze.

I would glance over at him as we pulled weeds up together, dug up turnips or spread muck on the fields, and simply exchanging a look would send shivers of pleasure down my spine. But it would also lift my spirits, and make me feel that there was some point in carrying on after all.

Peggy still asked when we might leave, and even with John nearby, I couldn't find the strength to tell her the truth.

Red walked ahead with both the dogs at his heels. It was a biting cold day. The wind whipped around us as we walked and as we emerged from the woods onto the exposed moor, it began to rain. At first it was fairly soft raindrops that were blown towards us sideways in sheets by the wind, but gradually the rain got heavier and more persistent. After half an hour of it, our clothes were wet through, and we could feel the icy-cold water trickling through them and onto our skin. None of us had any waterproofs, just the cotton trousers, shirts and woollen jumpers full of holes that Elsie had given us.

Once the cattle had been rounded up by the dogs, our job was to help drive them back to the farm. This involved walking behind them, clapping our hands and shouting, making sure that any stragglers were sent back to the main herd. They must have been thirty or forty lively bullocks, strong and temperamental. They terrified me when they ran towards me, or tossed their woolly heads in my direction. They seemed so strong and high-spirited, I could imagine being trampled underfoot if they decided to break free.

In contrast, Peggy seemed to have no fear of the cattle. It was clear that she was enjoying this job, in spite of the cold and wet. Her eyes were alight, just as when she worked with the horses or the chickens, and her cheeks were pink with the pleasure of being with animals. Peggy had grown since we'd been at the farm. Although she was still skinny, she was taller, and, her skin brown and sallow from being in the open air.

She ran ahead and I found myself walking beside John.

'Beef's worth its weight in gold with the war on,' he said.

'But isn't it rationed though, so they can't charge too much for it?' I remembered Mother's ration books and how she would queue for hours for meat, but that it wasn't expensive, despite the shortages.

He nodded. 'Of course. But Reeves don't go through official channels. He can get much more for it on the black market.'

I stared at him. 'Are you sure?'

'Of course. Stands to reason. A man like Reeves, he don't have a conscience. That's where this meat'll be going. That's where them ponies go too.'

'Ponies?'

'He catches them wild off the moor and sells them on for meat. 'Course, folks who buy it don't know that. They pay for top-quality beef.'

I stared at him. I didn't want to believe him, even though I couldn't stop thinking about the ponies appearing mysteriously in the stable, the night-time visits from the lorry.

It took us a full two hours to get the cattle back to the farmyard, by which time we were all exhausted, shivering with the cold and soaked to the skin. Red drove the animals into a long shed opposite the threshing barn and we were then allowed to go back inside our barn. He and Elsie had started lighting the old wood-burning stove in the corner in the evenings, with sticks we'd collected during the daytime. They let it go out during the day, but it still retained some residual warmth, so we all huddled round it, trying to warm our frozen fingers.

Christmas slid by, with virtually no acknowledgement of the day. The horses and cattle still had to be mucked out, the chickens fed. Elsie brought us our meal just like on any other day, but there was no work in the fields. Reeves was drinking up at the house, and Red slumped on his bunk, swigging from a brandy bottle. Peggy and I lay on our bunks, remembering what had been happening last Christmas. Things had still been relatively normal in our household. Father hadn't yet gone to war and although there had been rationing, Mother had saved coupons and managed to buy a big chicken in place of our usual turkey. She'd saved up for vegetables and managed to cook a Christmas pudding too. My heart ached for those days, but I tried to keep Peggy's spirits up by singing a few carols and talking of home.

On Boxing Day morning, normal work resumed. Red was still ordering Peggy and me to clean out the stables. In the colder weather, this was more difficult.

'Remember Boxing Day at home, Peggy?' I said as we slipped and skidded on the ice in the yard.

She nodded. 'Mum always made a lovely lunch and we'd go out onto the common for a walk.'

'How I miss all that,' I said wistfully.

'Me too,' said Peggy. 'I miss Mum so much, but Christmas has made it worse.'

I dropped my fork and held her close for a moment, but we soon got on with our enforced tasks, our hands freezing on the forks and on the handles of the barrow when we had to take it to the muck heap to empty. We had no gloves, or even coats to wear to protect us from the freezing conditions.

I watched Peggy carefully during that harsh first winter, expecting at any moment that she would come down with a cough. It had happened most winters throughout her life. But astonishingly, she got through it in reasonable health. I could hardly believe it, especially as she now looked as skinny as all the others, her face pinched and pale. But she showed no sign of her previous illness as winter moved into spring and the weeks dragged on. Although I never had any idea what the date was, one morning I woke up to the realisation that we must have been there on the farm virtually a whole year. My spirits were low. How could I have let this happen?

It was then, during summer, when I was least expecting it, that my worst fears were confirmed; what I'd been dreading might happen did happen. Peggy started to cough. It began as her coughs always did with a troublesome tickle, but quickly worsened to a hacking, rasping cough. One morning, it was so bad I told her to stay in bed, and over breakfast, I pleaded with Red to spare her from work that day and let her rest in the barn. Red seemed preoccupied. He just shrugged.

'She can stay in the bunk today,' he said. 'Not much use anyway is she most of the time? Little weakling. More trouble than she's worth.'

I sensed that he and Reeves had been arguing. Their violent, foul-mouthed disputes were regular occurrences and getting more frequent. It was usually something to do with the ponies. I tucked Peggy up as best I could and got her to take some medicine from the bottle Mother had pressed on us, glad that it had been tucked in the pocket of the gas mask bag.

All day, as I worked beside John and the others in the field, I couldn't stop worrying about Peggy, lying there sick and alone in the barn. But there was no choice. It was far better that she was in there than exhausting herself beside us out in the fields.

That evening, when it was time to feed the chickens, Red jerked his head sideways at John.

'You go with 'er down to the barn,' he said. 'Get them chickens fed and make sure you bring the eggs back. Make sure you don't break none.'

I went to fetch the bucket, and as we set off, Red grabbed me by the shirt and said, menace in his voice: 'Now don't you dare try anything, or your sister will suffer.'

John and I walked side by side down the track to the big barn in the dusk. The night was fresh and cool and the moon was bright and high in the sky. The air was filled with summer scents of blossom and mown grass. It was the first time we'd ever been completely alone together.

'I'm still grateful to you for helping me,' I told him quietly as we walked. 'You know, when they beat me when I first came? I haven't forgotten, you know.'

'It was nothing,' he said.

'It wasn't nothing… it was kind of you. It meant a lot.'

'We need to help each other. You were really brave. Standing up to Red like that. I haven't forgotten that day neither.'

I felt a thrill go through me at his words, and looked away from him, confused by my reaction. I realised that any praise from him meant a lot to me.

Inside the barn we fed the chickens. Then we both sat side by side on the straw bale, just as Peggy and I used to do. We did it without speaking, as if we both instinctively felt the need to linger there, and for a few moments try to feel like human beings again. It felt quite natural to sit next to him like that, reassuring to feel his warmth and strength beside me. Without thinking, I rested my head gently on his shoulder. It felt wonderful to have that contact. John didn't move and we sat like that for a long time as the chickens pecked around us. Sitting like that, feeling his warmth and his closeness, I felt a sort of peace steal over me, such as I had never felt before.

'You know that you could leave the farm right now, John,' I whispered. 'Make a run for it. Now's your chance.'

He shook his head. 'Not today. You and your sister will suffer if I do. I'll not risk that.'

'You don't have to worry about us,' I said.

'Of course I do,' he replied and I felt tears spring to my eyes at his words. At his unexpected thoughtfulness and selfless kindness. I realised in that moment that he cared for me as much as I cared for him; that a deep bond had developed between us because of the appalling situation we were in, one we were facing together.

'I'll pick my moment when the time is right,' he said.

'We'd best go back,' I told him after a few moments.

'Not just yet,' he said. 'Let's talk for a bit longer. Red won't be down yet.'

He began to speak then, quietly and gently. He told me, in stumbling words at first, about his life in the orphanage, how it was all he'd ever known. I didn't interrupt him. It was as if he wanted to unburden himself.

He'd been taken there when he was a toddler. His mother had died of flu and his father was a fisherman, lost at sea, but he had no memory of arriving at the orphanage, or of either of his parents. My heart went out to him then and, quite naturally, I reached out and touched his hand. He took my hand in his and it was so comforting to feel his warm skin on mine, to feel his hand close around mine. We sat there for a while, holding hands, completely at ease with one another, united by our suffering.

When we finally got up from the bale, left the barn and walked back up to the farmyard, we walked shoulder to shoulder, and in that moment, feeling the warmth and strength of him next to me, everything felt suddenly different. It was as if I wasn't so alone; as if the future wasn't quite as bleak as I'd been imagining for the past few months.

But that night Peggy coughed continuously. I tried to help her by getting her to sit up and take sips of water and medicine. In between those times, I lay awake, listening to her struggle for breath, my mind racked with worry. I was still awake when, in the dead of night, I heard Red getting up and going outside. Determined to find out what he was up to, I knelt to look out of the window above my bed. He was gone for a long time and before too long, my knees were numb and I was shivering, so I lay back on the bunk. When I heard sounds outside, I knelt again and peered out. There he was, leading four ponies by ropes round their necks, the sheepdogs snapping at their heels. I thought of those poor, unsuspecting creatures, one moment running free on the moor, the next captured by Red.

The next morning when I checked Peggy anxiously, her face was pale and sweaty, her breathing ragged and uneven. Red took one look at her and sighed impatiently.

'She ain't going to be no good today neither. John, you'll 'ave to help out in the stables again.'

That day, although I was desperately anxious for Peggy, that anxiety was tempered by the new and delicious feeling I got as I worked side by side with John. Every time I turned my head and exchanged a quick look with him before dropping my eyes, I felt the same thrill running through my whole body. I felt a little guilty that I was feeling this new exhilaration as Peggy lay suffering, back in the threshing barn. But it didn't stop me, so deprived was I of the warmth of human kindness, so ready was I for this new giddy feeling for John to escalate and envelop me.

John and I worked together like that for three days while Peggy lay sick and alone back on her bunk in the threshing barn. He took over all Peggy's jobs: mucking out the stables, clearing the cowshed, emptying the barrow; and he performed each task quickly and efficiently. I would often look over at him, admiring the way he worked, the strength in his muscles, his easy, fluid movements. Just watching him made me feel calmer somehow.

On the second evening, when we went down to feed the chickens, we sat side by side on the bale of straw once again.

'Why don't you tell me about you?' John said.

'What do you want to know?'

He shrugged. 'Everything. Well, I know about Peggy, how close you are, what you do to protect her. But I want to know about your home… about your mum and dad. About London.'

I was so conscious of his situation that I was reluctant to speak about my own life. I couldn't help thinking about how happy my own early life had been in contrast to the sadness of his childhood. The sadness that he'd spoken about only a few days ago.

'Are you sure?' I asked.

'Of course. Go on, tell me about it.' I glanced at him and he was waiting, expectantly, his eyes caressing my face.

'Well, it's quite boring really,' I began, dropping my eyes and feeling the colour creep up my cheeks. 'We live in a quiet street of houses. They're all just like ours.'

'What's it like?' he asked instantly.

'The house? Oh, it's the same as all the others in the street – it has three bedrooms, with a living room at the front, a dining room behind it and a small kitchen at the back. Nothing special.'

'It sounds special to me,' he said with dreamy eyes, and I remembered how he had grown up in an institution, a building like a hospital with echoing dormitories and nowhere of your own to be alone. I took his hand.

'Well, of course it was special to me too. It was home. I was born there and so was Peggy.'

'Do you have your own bedroom?' he asked.

I nodded.

'Peggy has a small box room at the front and I have a bigger room next to Mother and Father's.'

'I've always dreamed of a room of my own,' he said, smiling. There was no resentment in his voice. 'Carry on. I want to hear everything.'

So, I carried on telling him about our life in London; about Mother and Father. I told him all about our house and the school Peggy and I went to, about my friends. I even talked about Buster, our tabby cat. John listened quietly, nodding occasionally, sometimes asking a question. The minute details of our ordinary, mundane existence seemed to fascinate him. It dawned on me that it was because it was so different to his own world. I carried on, just to please him, to see the light shining in his eyes, and a smile on his lips as he was transported by my words to our ordinary suburban home. I told him everything I could think of, until I came to Mother.

'She was such a loving person,' I said. 'The best mother anyone could wish for. She cared so much for us. It tore her heart out to send us away.'

'You said she'd died. I'm so sorry. What happened?'

I hung my head and felt the tears spilling from my eyes and running down my cheeks.

Once again, I felt his hand grasping mine.

'I'm sorry,' he said. 'There's no need to tell me if it upsets you.'

'I want to tell you about her. I haven't wanted to talk about her before, I've bottled it all up. When she was seeing us off on the train, a bomb hit the station suddenly. It was chaos. She was blown across the platform and injured. I don't know, but I think several people were killed outright. She got concussion from the fall. We thought she'd recovered in hospital; she even wrote us a couple of letters, but she got a brain haemorrhage…'

'I'm so sorry. That must be so hard to bear.'

'It was. Terrible. And every time I hear the rumble of planes in the distance, even out here on the moor, it brings it all back so clearly. They remind me of that moment the bomb hit the station, seeing Mother careering backward…'

I gripped his hand and stopped speaking, trying to hold back the tears. Then he lifted his other hand and wiped them away from my cheeks. And then, there in the soft darkness of the barn, he kissed me full on the lips. I'd never been kissed before, and it was as if everything else – my grief for Mother, the farm, the harsh conditions, the back-breaking days, the brutality of Reeves and Red – were forgotten, for that tender, sweet moment, when we completely belonged to each other.

Chapter Eleven

Helen

It was raining the day that Helen went back to Black Moor Hall alone. In her handbag was the key that Jago had found hidden in Daisy's old bureau. She could barely see ahead of her as she drove up the lane from North Brent and on through the pinewood, the wipers battling furiously against the downpour. The windscreen kept steaming up, the puny heating in the car insufficient to clear it. She had to keep leaning forward and wiping the mist away with her scarf.

As she drove, her mind went over the advert she'd spotted for courses for mature students in a magazine she'd flicked through at the hairdresser's the day before. The advert had included details of a website, and she'd looked it up that morning and had been writing details down on a notepad.

She wondered what was stopping her from taking the plunge and signing up to a course. Something still niggled inside her. Was it really worth it after so long? Would she be wasting her time? Her mother's words still rang in her ears. *Why can't you do something sensible like your sister?*

She couldn't help remembering a conversation she'd had with her mother, only a few years back, when she'd mooted the idea of going back to college to study art.

'You're not serious, surely, Helen? I thought it was just a hobby.'

It had taken a lot of strength to look her mother in the eye and say, 'Well, even if it is just a hobby at the moment, I've always wanted to improve and to make something of it.'

'You don't think you're a bit old to go back to school, do you?'

'Of course not. People study at all ages nowadays.'

'You had your chance to study when you were in your twenties and you couldn't even stick at it then. Things have moved on now, Helen. You've got your job in the antiques shop to think about.'

She felt tears stinging her eyes now, remembering, but she was determined not to give in to them.

Could she really do it? she thought, drawing herself up. She knew she must disregard Daisy's harsh words and take the plunge.

Now, she put the conversation out of her mind and concentrated on navigating the narrow lane. When she reached the entrance to Black Moor Hall, she had to stop and get out of the car to open the gates, bowing her head against the rain. She pulled her hood around her tightly, but the rain still drenched her face and trickled down her neck.

She drove on through the spinney towards the empty house. It looked as forbidding today in the pelting rain as it ever had, but she tried not to let that put her off her stride. She pulled up on the empty drive and ran for the cover of the front porch. This time she was alone. Laura wasn't coming today.

Once inside the hall she took off her wet mac, shook the worst of the rain out of it and hung it in the porch. She stood in the entrance hall, shivering. The house itself was hardly any warmer than outside, but at least it was dry. Daisy had always refused to install central heating.

'It's so bad for your health to be mollycoddled,' she always said if anyone asked why there were no radiators. 'There's no earthly reason why you can't just put on extra clothes in the winter. And we have the Aga and the open fires to keep us warm.'

Helen sighed, remembering waking up on icy mornings, shuddering in front of a two-bar electric fire as she got dressed in her bedroom. It would have been so nice and convenient today to flick a switch and feel the place warming up. The Aga was out and there was no fuel to light a fire.

She took the mysterious key out of her bag and examined it again, staring at the writing on the tag, wondering what the number 342 could possibly mean. Looking at the handwriting, she decided it didn't look like Daisy's, and she didn't recognise it as belonging to anyone else.

She decided to start her search on the ground floor. She began in the hall, trying the key in all the doors that opened off it, even the coat cupboard, then went on to try every other lock she could find in the house. It slid into one or two of the locks with a bit of persuasion, but wouldn't turn in any of them. She'd already spent the previous afternoon in Jago's shop, checking to see if the key would fit the locks to any of the cupboards that had been moved there from Black Moor Hall. But as she'd feared, it didn't fit anything. Jago had said it looked like the key to a strongbox – the sort that people keep deeds or important papers in. Helen didn't hold out much hope of finding any lock that it fitted in the house either, but she was determined to try.

She went from room to room on the ground floor, trying each and every door on both sides. Then she tried the doors to the surgery, and all the built-in cupboards in there. She completed the ground floor, then went upstairs. Again, she was methodical, putting the key into each and every lock that was there. She tried every bedroom door, the bathrooms, the cupboards, but as she'd predicted, it didn't appear to fit any lock in the house.

There was no furniture left in the house any more. Jago had taken the antiques and the second-hand shop in Ashburton had cleared the rest. The place felt so different without it, as if divested of its personality, stripped of Daisy's influence. The rooms seemed cavernous and unwelcoming. It sent chills through Helen to walk from room to room and see the bare patches on the walls where pictures had hung or her mother's furniture had stood. She could barely believe that this had been where she'd spent her teenage years. It certainly didn't feel like home now.

But the house had to be sold. She and Laura had agreed that it must be done, no matter how painful it might be. Daisy's care home was very expensive and it was impossible to pay for it without the proceeds from the house. Despite that, Helen found it difficult to imagine someone else living there.

She wandered into her old bedroom. It was empty of furniture, like the rest of the rooms, just wooden boards on the floor. She stood in the middle of the room and tried to picture it as it had been while she was growing up, but it barely felt like her room any more. The only thing that remained from her occupancy were the paler patches on the walls where her posters of pop stars had once hung. Daisy had taken them down years before, but she'd never bothered to decorate the room.

Helen went over to the window, staring out as she had many times at the rough meadow beyond the garden hedge. It looked just the same as it always had: unkempt and overgrown with rampant grass and brambles. She half-expected Daisy to emerge from the trees at the far end, striding out as she used to in her prime. The purposeful way she used to walk had made her look determined and strong, but her face was always preoccupied, as if she was in another world altogether.

It had stopped raining now and the sky was brightening, the clouds clearing. Helen glanced back at the field again. Suddenly she had an impulse to go there; to walk across the field, to see what was on the other side. It was very wet outside still, but she had her boots in the car.

She'd never dared to venture into the field again. Her stomach churned with nerves even now at the thought of it, but at the same time something was drawing her to it. Perhaps it was the need to find out more about her mother's secrets? That need had started with the letters and gathered momentum in her mind. The need was so pressing now that she was prepared to contemplate venturing onto that hallowed ground that had been forbidden to her for so many years. She was disappointed that her research had yielded so little to date. Perhaps there were clues to her mother's past at the farm in the hollow?

'Come on then,' she told herself aloud and, leaving the bedroom, she went downstairs to the porch and pulled the damp waterproof back on, then crossed the drive to the car to put on her wellington boots. Then she walked quickly round to the back of the house and across the lawn behind the kitchen towards the hedge. She stood by the hedge, staring over it at the forbidden field, chills going through her body. Was this really a good idea? She faltered for a moment, tempted to turn back, but the need to delve into Daisy's secrets was strong enough to suppress those warning signs. What was on the other side of that hedge that had made Daisy return there again and again over the years, and to forbid her daughters from venturing there?

Examining the hedge close up, she wondered where her mother had squeezed through. There seemed to be no obvious opening. Helen walked the length of it in both directions. At the far end, she discovered a gap that looked as if it had grown over in recent months. It was wide enough to push through sideways. She realised that this must be where Daisy had managed to get through into the field.

Taking a deep breath, Helen took the plunge. She turned sideways and began to push her way through the gap. As she squeezed through, brambles clawing at her coat, she wondered when Daisy had last done this. Had she carried on walking in the field in recent years? If so, what was it that had drawn her here? What had kept her coming back, even though she was getting old and infirm?

The hawthorn ripped at her coat, snagging on it as she tried to move away from the hedge on the other side. She had to tug it free with both hands. Then she was through and in the field, staring across it. As she already knew from looking at it from the house, it was neglected and unkempt; the grass was knee-high and there were clumps of bramble growing everywhere. At first, she thought it would be impassable, but after she had taken a few paces away from the hedge, she noticed that there was a rough path through the brambles where the grass was worn away. Her heart missed a beat at the sight of it. This must be where her mother had walked, day after day for years, the grass worn down by her footsteps.

Stepping away from the hedge, she began to follow the path tentatively, with trepidation in her heart. Half of her was desperate to find out what had drawn her mother here; the other half was terrified of what she might find. It was slow going. The path gradually wound its way through the patches of bramble towards the far side of the field. The land began to dip away and got steeper the further she walked. The field was huge and it felt as though she would never reach the other side, but eventually she came to another hedge. This one was even more overgrown than the one bordering Black Moor Hall. It was hardly a hedge any more; huge bushes of elderflower and holly towered over the hawthorn bushes, so large that they were virtually trees.

She stood staring at it, wondering how she would get through, but following the path, she soon found a gate in the far corner of the hedge: a wooden five-barred gate that was dilapidated and rotting, covered in moss and lichen. She lifted the metal latch and pulled the gate towards her. She half-expected it to disintegrate in her hand, but it opened surprisingly easily. She stepped through the opening and found herself in an overgrown spinney, the tall, dense trees choked with brambles and ferns. It was dark here, the evergreens blocking out the light, but still the path wound on, encroached upon on either side by vegetation. Helen pushed her way through the undergrowth, thorns and brambles snagging at her clothes, wet bracken brushing up against her. At the edge of the wood she came to a stile; this too was broken and rotting away, but she clambered over it, wondering how her mother had managed to do this in recent years.

She stared ahead. She'd known the old buildings were there, but there was something so forlorn about it that it brought her up sharp.

She was looking down into a hollow between the hills, completely enclosed and hidden on all sides from the outside world. In the little valley nestled a group of derelict buildings, almost completely obscured by rampant ivy and undergrowth. She could just make out the shape of a house on one side; its roof and chimneys caved in, the gables at either end still standing. All its windows and doors were boarded up, its front garden enclosed by a stone wall, a mass of unruly bushes and tall grass.

On the other side of the hollow was what looked to have been a farmyard; a set of buildings around an open square. Like the house, all the buildings were covered in ivy, nettles and creepers, buddleia growing out of the tops of the walls. The roofs were completely collapsed into the buildings, splintered beams protruding from the undergrowth.

Around the edge of the area were various mounds of earth, again covered in growth, that looked as though they had once been muck heaps, or perhaps pieces of redundant farm machinery.

A shudder ran through Helen. The valley had such a forgotten, forlorn look about it. But it wasn't just that. There was something chilling about the place too. Inhabited, it must have been thriving, full of life and movement. Now it was silent and still, derelict and abandoned. Who had lived and farmed here, she wondered. And why had they left it to rot away and be taken over by the elements? She stood there for a long time, puzzled, amazed by what lay before her. What could there possibly be about this derelict place that had drawn her mother here every day for years on end?

The abandoned farm exuded such an air of neglect and decay that she was repelled. Part of her wanted to turn back, to retrace her steps and regain the safety and security of Black Moor Hall. But she'd come this far; she knew she needed to carry on and find out what she could.

The path worn in the grass by her mother's footsteps continued down the hill ahead of her, on towards the derelict farmyard. Taking a deep breath, she carried on, following the path down the hill. It continued across the field to another fence, which she ducked under, and then on over some rough ground until at last she was down in the valley at the level of the buildings. In front of her ran a gushing stream that bubbled over rocks and down mini-waterfalls, winding its way behind the farm buildings. She stepped over the stream where the path led across it, at a point where it narrowed to rush through a gully. This was where Daisy must have crossed it time and time again. Now she was standing on a piece of flat ground directly opposite the shell of the farmhouse. She stood and stared at it, noticing that it was built of stone, and realised that it must have been very picturesque in its day. Why hadn't it been sold off like so many farmhouses in the area, restored and renovated, the barns converted to dwellings? It must be worth a lot of money.

The path petered out where it reached what must once have been a parking area in front of the house. Not knowing where to go from here, Helen walked up to the garden wall and peered at the house. The garden was full of such dense weeds and foliage that it would have been impossible for anyone to have gone in there. And the door and windows were boarded up, so it was clear that no one would be able to go inside.

She debated with herself whether or not to venture behind the house, but the garden at the side was overgrown and impenetrable.

One by one, she looked into each of the barns. In one, she disturbed a family of wood pigeons, who flew out of a hole in the roof, squawking at the disturbance; in another, she heard the scuttle of rats as she pushed open the door. But there was nothing interesting inside any of them.

She began to walk back up the short slope towards the farmhouse, disappointed, wondering whether she would be able to fight her way through the overgrown back garden and get inside the building from the back. Before she reached the house, though, she spotted a narrow path branching off the track. Her heart beat faster;

it looked just like the path she'd followed down from Black Moor Hall. It must have been her mother's footsteps that had trodden it.

She followed the path, which wound between some overgrown bushes towards the rear of the house. The ground opened out and she found herself in a large, square area that must once have been the back garden. There were the remnants of some rose bushes along one side, and some rampant camellias along the other side. Behind it was what looked to have once been an apple orchard, but the trees were overgrown and choked with weeds. She stood in the middle of the wild garden and stared back at the house; at its blind windows, crudely boarded with planks of rotting wood, at its broken roof and guttering and walls streaked with mould. She stared at it and shook her head, still wondering what had brought her mother here.

The path wound on, into the orchard. She followed it, ducking her head to avoid a branch. And then, with a bolt of shock, she saw it. The path stopped abruptly and under one of the trees was a grassy mound, about four or five feet long, on top of it a crude wooden cross. Scattered over the mound were remnants of decaying bunches of flowers, rotting away and brown with age. Flowers her mother must have placed. Her heart beating fast, Helen peered at the cross, searching for an inscription, but nothing was written on it.

But she knew that this must be what had brought her mother here again and again over the years; she was sure of it. And she also knew why Daisy had been so angry when she herself had ventured over the field towards the farm. She must have been terrified that Helen would discover this secret grave and start asking awkward questions.

She stared at the grave, wondering still.

Was this the man her mother had lost?

Chapter Twelve

Daisy

I had never imagined that I might fall in love, or even that I would ever feel safe in the conditions I found myself in on the farm, while the war raged on all around us. But I couldn't wait for the evenings, when John and I would be alone together again, the memory of that kiss sustaining me throughout the harsh next day. As we worked side by side in the stable, if our hands happened to touch, or we brushed past each other, a series of delicious electric shocks coursed through my body. That time, when we set off to feed the chickens, we couldn't wait until we reached the barn; we allowed our hands to touch as we walked down the track, and linked our fingers together.

As soon as the barn door was shut behind us, John turned to kiss me, as I stood with my back to the barn door, and we kissed passionately and urgently this time, both of us desperate to find an escape. Time seemed to melt into nothing. We were oblivious to the chickens swarming around us, clucking for their food, to the time passing, to the fact that we could be discovered at any moment. But when one of the chickens started pecking at my leg, we broke apart laughing and started spreading the scraps and corn around the barn floor, longing to resume the kiss, our faces flushed, our eyes bright with the excitement of it.

'Come and sit down on the straw,' I whispered to John, my body yearning to feel his next to mine again, to feel again the sweet heady abandonment the kiss had given me.

'No,' he said. 'Let's go up there for a few minutes,' indicating the ladder to the upper floor.

So, I followed him up the ladder, all the time my heart hammering against my ribs, my emotions racing. It was dark up there and John switched the torch off. We lay down on the dusty straw on the bare boards and kissed again. This time slowly, savouring the moment, pressing our bodies close, holding each other as tightly as we could, wanting to comfort and warm and love each other and to dispel our anger and heartbreak.

All the time I was thinking of how long we'd been there, how Red could be walking down the hill even at this moment, my ears taut, listening out for the click of the barn door. But that didn't stop me, or hold me back. Soon John was kissing my neck, unbuttoning my shirt and moving his mouth down my breasts. I didn't know how to respond, but I didn't want him to stop either, so I unbuttoned his clothes in turn, ran my arms around his back and drew him closer and closer. I had little idea what I was doing, as we moved together and I felt his hardness pressing between my legs. My friends and I had talked about this in whispered, horrified giggles as we'd shared cigarettes up at the airbase, but this didn't feel at all funny. It was exhilarating and heartbreaking all at the same time, and as I drew him closer and we moved together, I felt a rush of pure, electrifying love for him that dispelled everything else for those few brief, fabulous moments.

As we lay together afterwards, staring up at the dust-covered beams of the barn, John said, into the darkness, 'I've got to get us out of here.'

I swallowed. I didn't want to think about that. Not at that moment.

'I don't want you to take any risks.' My voice was shaking.

He propped himself up on his elbow and leaned in to kiss me.

'There's no choice. It's going to be risky,' he said.

'Please…'

I couldn't bear the thought of losing him now, the only source of love and comfort in this godforsaken place. Why did he have to go when our love was so new?

'Look, I wasn't going to tell you this, but…' He reached for his clothes, and pulled something from his trouser pocket. He hesitated before he handed it to me, and refused to meet my gaze as I took it from him. This worried me. It was an article torn from a newspaper. I took it from him and scanned it quickly.

A service was held yesterday for all those who have tragically lost their lives in bombings in our city since war broke out. Several hundred people came to pay their respects to the dead in St Andrew's Church, among them babies and children, mothers and fathers, young and old. They are all in our prayers.

There followed a list of casualties. My eyes scanned the list quickly to see if the Browns were on it, but as I reached the Bs, my heart stood still. For on the list two names leapt out at me:

Daisy Banks, DOB 15.11.1925, Harrow, London, Peggy Banks, DOB 01.06. 1930, Harrow, London.

I stared at John, the horror of what I'd read dawning on me.

'I found that in Red's paper the other day. So you see,' he said, 'no one will be coming for you and Peggy. Not your neighbour, not anyone. They all think you're dead. I've made up my mind. We're going to get out the first chance there is. We've waited long enough. We can go straight to the police, tell them what's going on here…'

I already felt a rush of anxiety at the thought of running away, the risks that it might bring. Suddenly, I needed some reassurance, that what had just happened between us meant something to him.

'But… but what about us…?'

'Don't worry. You don't need to ask. I care about you, Daisy. I need to be with you. That's why I need to get us both out of here.'

'What about Peggy?' I said, a pang of guilt rushing through me. I'd hardly thought about her at all that day. My whole being had been subsumed in this. How could I have been so selfish?

'We can go together, the three of us. I would never leave her behind. Then, once the police get here, everyone will be free. Those bastards will get what's coming to them.' I felt his muscles tense beside me as he clenched his fists in anger.

'We'd best go back,' he said, kissing me once more.

He got to his feet and started pulling on his clothes. As we both dressed and dusted the straw off our clothes and out of our hair, alongside the warm glow that filled my mind and body was a creeping feeling of regret; not at what I'd done, but that this could be over, almost before it had begun.

The next morning, Peggy looked a little better. She'd only woken once or twice coughing in the night. Red took one look at her and said, 'No reason why she can't work today. Can't spare John from the field work no longer. We've got veg to get out to market and we're lagging behind. Get up, Little 'un.'

So that morning, Peggy replaced John by my side in the stables and cowshed. She was still weak, with little colour in her cheeks, and I was anxious not to tire her, so I shouldered the burden of the work that morning. Her eyes lit up when she saw the horses, and each of them turned their head to look at her and to nuzzle her as she approached. As we worked, my mind kept wandering to John, who had trooped off to the fields with the others. He and I had hardly had time to speak once we'd left the barn the evening before, but our eyes had lingered on each other at breakfast.

After lunch, Red told us that we would be working on the potato field in the afternoon, forking up the cut plants to clear the way for harvesting the roots. They were needed to fulfil a contract Reeves had to supply groceries for the war effort.

'It's a few days' work on them spuds. It's hard work and you know what'll 'appen if there's any shirking from you lot. Now, it's bit of a walk out to that field. No funny business, mind,' Red said, glaring at me.

Two of the Shire horses were waiting in the yard, each harnessed up to an empty trailer. To my surprise, Farmer Reeves himself was there, standing beside one of the horses. I shivered at the sight of him and looked away instinctively.

'Boss is coming with us. We'll start at opposite ends of the field.'

Red and Reeves went ahead with the two trailers, leading the horses. Wolf the Alsatian trotted along beside Red. John fell in to walk beside me. The field was a long way from the farm buildings.

'This could be our chance,' he muttered to me under his breath. 'Potato field's right on the edge of the farm, I reckon. Lane down to North Brent runs right by it. It's the best chance we're going to have. Red'll be up ahead of us, occupied with the 'orse. Let's give it a try. When I run, just follow me.'

I glanced at him, my eyes wide with sudden terror at what this might mean. What about Wolf? How would we deal with him?

'We must be careful,' I muttered, thinking that he must have figured that out. I desperately wanted to touch his hand, or to squeeze his arm, to feel his skin next to mine again, to remind him of how much I cared and to give us both courage, but all I could do was to look deep into his eyes, and from the look he gave me back, I knew he felt the same way.

'Just watch me carefully,' he said. 'As soon as I go, you must both come too. Don't hesitate.'

'Please be careful,' I muttered.

Words seemed inadequate to convey what I was feeling: terror at what might happen to us, sincere hope that we'd be successful, and heartfelt gratitude that he was still prepared to help me and Peggy.

The field was a long tramp away from the farm buildings, and the sun was high in the sky. It must have taken fifteen or twenty minutes to walk there, down a dirt track between high Devon banks. When we finally arrived, I looked out across the field spread before us. It was huge; acre upon acre of cut potato plants, lying in rows, their white flowers withering among the fallen stems, giving off a delicate, sweet fragrance. It bordered a small spinney on one side and on the opposite side, through the hedge, there was a lane. The occasional motor vehicle or horse-drawn cart passed along it.

Reeves turned and looked at us. 'You three with me,' he said, nodding to me, Peggy and John. He set off towards the opposite end of the field and we followed him, stumbling on the furrows, getting tangled in the stalks of the cut plants.

'Good, the dog's not with us,' whispered John as we walked. 'And at least we're together.'

When we got to the other side, Reeves set the horse and trailer at the start of the first row of cut plants.

'Pitchforks are in the trailer. Walk behind it and fork all this rubbish up into the trailer. I want it all clear. When the whole field is done, we'll bring the spinner round and root out the spuds.'

We took the forks from the back of the trailer and did as we had been ordered. It was back-breaking work, forking the cut potato plants onto the back of the high trailer. Worse even than forking up the hay; the stalks were far heavier and weighed down with clods of mud. My body still ached from the beating I'd had months ago, each bend and stretch causing my muscles to scream out with the pain. But I gritted my teeth and got on with it, my nerves about John distracting me from the discomfort of the constant bending and lifting. Peggy was struggling to keep up, but in her usual way was determined to do her bit, a look of fierce concentration on her face as she bent and lifted.

'Peggy,' I whispered, drawing up beside her as we worked, 'we're going to try to get away. When John runs, we're going too. Just watch him and be ready.'

Her mouth fell open in astonishment, but she didn't say anything, just nodded to let me know she'd understood.

I watched John anxiously as he worked beside me. Occasionally I noticed him eyeing the hedge on the far side of the field, the one that bordered the lane. I could see no gate in it; it was dense and overgrown and I began to wonder how he planned to get through it.

As we made our way up the field behind the slow-moving trailer towards the far hedge, my stomach started to clench with nerves. I glanced at John again. Sweat was pouring from his face now, and he kept staring into the next field as he worked. I followed his gaze and suddenly realised what he was planning. There was a five-barred gate into the next field, and at the far end of that field was another gate, which presumably led onto the public lane.

As we drew closer to the gate to the next field, I watched him prepare himself; he was watching everyone around us intently as we lumbered nearer and nearer. Reeves was walking ahead, taking pinches of snuff from a tin, muttering to the horse under his breath, barely looking round.

We drew parallel with the gate and John suddenly threw his fork down. He turned and looked at me with yearning and longing. It was a promise too.

'Come on. Straight after me,' he whispered. And then he made a break for it, running hell for leather towards the gate; then he was on it, vaulting over it in two giant steps. He was off, scarpering across the other field, making for the gate to the lane.

I grabbed Peggy's hand and we set off after him, making towards the gate. My heart was pounding fit to burst and I was sweating,

Peggy's hand slipping in mine. We'd almost reached the gate when there was a yell from behind us.

'Stop,' Reeves yelled. I glanced over my shoulder and saw him, quick as a flash, whip round and take something from a shelf on the front of the trailer. It was long and metallic, flashing in the sunlight, and it was a second before I realised what it was. Then Reeves was hurrying towards the gate, brandishing it, lolloping because of his limp, but moving surprisingly quickly.

'John!' I screamed at the top of my voice, and he turned and saw Reeves. I saw him freeze for a second before turning and carrying on, running towards the gate. But he was out there exposed in the middle of the field and there was nowhere for him to find cover.

Three shots rang out from Reeves's rifle and the smell of gunpowder filled the air. Peggy and I screamed in unison. We watched in horror as John gave a sickening jerk. His arms flew out sideways from his body and he stopped dead, staggered a few steps forward, before dropping to the ground.

Chapter Thirteen

Daisy

I left Peggy and began to run across the uneven field towards John's prone body, tripping and stumbling as I went, tears streaming down my face, my heart hammering against my ribs.

'John! John! Please… I'm coming to help you,' I panted, hoping against hope that he'd only been stunned or injured, that it wasn't what I was dreading. But as I neared the gate into the next field, where he lay slumped on the ground, shock washed through me. I could see that his body was completely still, a red stain spreading rapidly on his shirt.

Lurching over the last furrow, catching my foot in a stray root, I stumbled and nearly fell, but quickly recovered and made it to the gate. I put both hands on the top bar to climb it, my horrified eyes fixed on John's immobile form.

Suddenly, from behind me a shot rang out, the bullet pinging past my right ear. I stopped, ducked instinctively.

'Where the 'ell do you think you're going?' Reeves yelled and I turned. He was standing beside the trailer, the rifle in his hand, his evil, beady eyes fixed on me. Peggy was on her knees on the ground, tears streaming down her face.

'Come back 'ere, or you'll be next,' he shouted.

Slowly, I turned round and, my whole body trembling with shock, returned to where Peggy was kneeling. I knelt down in front of her, put my arms round her and drew her close. I could

feel her body shaking too. Her tears mingled with mine as we
sobbed together.

Soon came the sound of rapid footsteps behind. I turned to see
Red approaching across the field.

'What's goin' on 'ere, Joe?'

'Little bugger only tried to run off again. 'Ad to deal with 'im,
didn't I? Can't 'ave 'im getting away and blabbering 'is 'ead off all
round the place.'

'Right. 'E was a bad apple right enough,' said Red. 'What do
you want me to do with 'im then?'

'Frank Baines'll 'ave to help out wi' this. Unhitch this 'orse and
you can take 'im back down to the farm straight away. Don't want
no one seeing nothing from the road.'

Peggy and I looked on, trembling with grief and horror as they
busied themselves with unharnessing the horse from the trailer. My
heart was in turmoil, refusing to believe what my eyes were telling
me. How could this be happening? How could it be that the boy
I'd formed such a close bond with, who a few hours ago had felt as
though I was one with, had been cut down so cruelly? I wanted to
run to him, to hold his dear face in my hands, but Reeves had his
gun trained on me. I couldn't risk being shot myself and leaving
Peggy to fend for herself.

Red led the horse towards the gate to the next field. The horse
seemed reluctant to follow, throwing its head in the air, snorting,
trying to back away. He yelled at it, whacked its neck with his stick
to make it go through the gateway, and eventually it submitted
and followed him. With a grunt, he lifted John up with both arms,
hoisted him over the horse's back, then led the horse back past us,
across the field and towards the farm.

As they passed, I covered Peggy's eyes and held her close. I'll
never forget that glimpse of John's body as he was carried past
me, slung over the horse's back. His arms flopped free, his head
bobbed from side to side with the motion of the horse. His shirt

was soaked in blood, dripping steadily onto the ground, making a red trail behind them. I could hardly see his dear face, but it swung round for a split second and what I did see shocked me to the core. His head was upside down, his hair hanging loose, and his eyes were closed.

Reeves turned back to glare at us.

'What are you two blubbering about?' he said gruffly. 'He 'ad it coming to 'im – 'e didn't learn, the rotten little scoundrel. It'll be you next, Missy, like I said, if you go trying any funny business like that again.'

We sat there staring at him wordlessly, shaking, appalled and terrified.

'Come on then,' he said.' Let's be 'aving yer. Up on yer feet now. You can fork this lot into the trailer while the 'orse is away.'

We didn't move, immobile with shock, unable to follow what he was saying.

'Get on with you!' he said. 'No point wasting time. There's still work to be done. I need to talk to the other lot. They've stopped working too. Now don't you go trying nothing while I'm gone.'

With that, he stumped off across the field, gun in hand. I glanced across to the other side of the field to where the others were standing in a row motionless, staring towards us. I could only imagine what they were feeling at that moment. John was like a brother to them. They'd known him all their lives and as the strongest personality out of the four by far. His presence and determination had kept their spirits up throughout this dreadful ordeal. How were they going to fare without him?

As Reeves crossed the field towards them, Peggy and I had no choice but to get up, take up our pitchforks again and begin to fork the cut potato stalks up into the trailer. We worked slowly, our cheeks wet with tears, our minds reliving the events of the past half-hour; the terrible thrill of seeing John's figure breaking away, running across the field towards the gate, his shirt billowing free, his desperate vault over the gate, the few steps the other side and then the shock of the shot, watching him crumple to the ground, the life gone from his body.

It wasn't until the evening that they finally allowed us to stop work, put our pitchforks up on the trailer and follow the horses slowly back down to the farmyard. My mind was running over and over the previous evening in the barn; the touch of John's body against mine, the tragic passion with which we'd clung to each other. Nausea kept rising in my throat; the delicate smell of the potato flowers, which the day before I'd thought beautiful, now sickened me, reminding me as they did of what had happened in that field.

Once we were back in the barn, I looked at the faces of Sally, Joan and Fred. It was clear from the streaks on their grubby cheeks that they'd all been crying. None of them uttered a sound or spoke a word about what had happened though; they must have been too terrified even to mention it. They'd been on the other side of the field when John was shot, but they must have been able to see everything that happened.

When Peggy and I went out to the back to wash with Joan and Sally, I still felt like I was in shock, but when I began to talk about John the two girls looked at me with wide, terrified eyes.

'Don't talk about it,' said Sally. 'There ain't no use. It could be any of us next, we need to watch our step even more now.'

I understood how nervous Sally was, but I already missed John's brave and reassuring presence. How would I survive if nobody here had any hope at all?

And as the four of us went back into the barn, Red was waiting for me, a malevolent look on his face. He leapt at me, grabbed my arm and dragged me across the barn towards the yard door. Peggy started crying immediately, and as I was pulled past them, I had a glimpse of the terrified, white faces of the others as they stood rooted to the spot with fear.

'What's going on?' I managed to mutter as I struggled against Red's grasp.

'You know what's going on. I thought one beating was enough for you, but maybe not.'

He dragged me outside as I resisted, kicking out at him, trying to wriggle free from his stranglehold.

I managed to lift my head to glance across the yard and a chill went through me at what I saw. Reeves was standing in the middle of the yard, feet splayed apart, the long horsewhip in his hand. Like Red, he was smiling, seeming to take pleasure in any opportunity for cruelty.

Red manhandled me upright in front of him, twisting my arms behind my back so it was impossible for me to move.

'You know what you've done, Missy,' said Reeves, staring straight at me with his piggy eyes narrowed.

I shook my head.

'I haven't done anything,' I said, lifting my chin in defiance.

Did they know about what had happened between me and John? Were they going to punish me for that?

'Don't come the innocent with me. You know what you've done and you're lucky not to go the same way as the lad.'

I bit my lip, trying to hold back the tears of loss and terror, to keep my breathing steady. Was he serious? Would he kill me too? I'd seen what he was capable of only a few short hours before – slaughtering an innocent boy in cold blood and carrying on his day as if he'd shot a rabbit. He had no guilt, no morals. He was an ignorant, brutal man, he was enjoying this. I thought about Peggy. What would happen to her if I were to die? She wouldn't cope here without me and she would surely die too. I thought of Mother and Father and I could no longer hold back the tears. They streamed down my cheeks unchecked. I sobbed and soon my nose was running too.

'Look at you now, cry baby,' jeered Reeves, coming up close, holding the horsewhip to my cheek, putting his sweaty face close to mine. I flinched and tried to turn away, but he grabbed my chin and turned my face back towards him.

'I thought you'd learned your lesson before when we had to deal with you, but no. You're not to be trusted. Look at what Red found in that boy's pocket.'

Shock and dread shot through my body as he pulled the folded page from *The Wind in the Willows* out of his pocket and brandished it in my face. There was a streak of blood on the page, John's blood.

'Think we wouldn't find it? Think we're stupid, do you? Country bumpkins, born yesterday?'

'No,' I sobbed. 'I just want to go home.'

He grabbed my face again and pulled it close to his. I tried not to breathe in the foul scent of his breath, the filth of his unwashed clothes, the sweat on his body.

'You might as well forget all about leaving here. No one will be coming for you and you won't be seeing 'ome ever again, I can tell you that much.'

'What do you mean?' I asked, hating myself for asking him for anything, but I was begging now. 'Please, tell me,' I said.

He released my face and pushed me backwards against Red.

'You don't need to know,' he said, then turning to Red, he said, 'Put 'er over the water trough like last time.'

Red dragged me across the yard and pushed me, face-forward, over the water trough. As I closed my eyes and gritted my teeth and waited for the lashes to come. I knew there was no point resisting; that it would only make it worse. There were ten this time; stronger and sharper than before. I counted them. Each time the whip struck and curled itself around my thighs, I yelled out, just like before, and just like before I felt the leather pierce my skin and the blood trickle down my legs. My only comfort was that Peggy and the others weren't there to watch this time; at least they were spared that trauma.

They left me to get back to the barn as best I could. I walked across the yard slowly, painfully. Then I crawled into bed without any food. I hadn't eaten anything since our meagre breakfast of watery porridge that morning, and my stomach was taut with hunger. But I couldn't have faced eating anything, even if it had been allowed. I buried my face in the blankets, trying to cope with the searing pain from the backs of my legs and the pain in my heart, thinking of John.

I heard the others sit down to eat at the table, the sound of them spooning the stew out of the cauldron, the chink of forks on plates, but no one was speaking. I was thinking of Peggy sitting down there at the table, hoping that she was able to eat something. She'd been refusing her food lately and was getting worryingly thin.

It must have been around midnight when I heard Red get up. Sally and Joan had bathed my wounds before they'd gone to bed, but the pain was inching back. It had made me think of John, of the tenderness with which he'd bathed me after the last beating, and even with Peggy beside me, holding me closely, I hadn't managed much sleep. My mind kept reliving the events of the afternoon: the shots ringing out, John's body slumping to the ground, the blood seeping from his wound, soaking his clothes.

Red was speaking to the dog gruffly under his breath. He crept out of the barn, shutting the door gently. Then came the rumble of an engine at the top of the hill. Gritting my teeth against the pain, I hauled myself up into a sitting position, careful not to wake Peggy, then manoeuvred my aching body slowly and painfully so that I could kneel up and peer out of the top window above the bunk. Sure enough, it was the same lorry as before, parked at the top of the slope, its headlights beaming down into the yard. Reeves and Red were walking towards it, Red from the yard and Reeves from the direction of the house. I could see the glow of their cigarettes as they moved.

A man got out of the cab and all three of them conferred for a few moments, just like before. Then once again the Dartmoor ponies were led up the hill, tethered together, tossing their heads, pulling against the rope.

The ponies didn't want to go up the ramp into the lorry. They reared and stamped and strained on the ropes. It took Red and the driver several attempts to coax them up there and slam the door shut. After the ponies had been shut up in the lorry, the three men stood talking in front of the truck. The driver handed something to Reeves; I presumed it to be a package of money. I watched as Reeves started to count it. He stopped after a while and handed it to Red, then stepped forward and seemed to be speaking urgently to the other man, pushing him backwards, seizing him by the collar. The other man squared up to Reeves and fought back, pushing Reeves off, and soon they were exchanging punches, pushing each other, slamming each other against the bonnet of the truck. Then Red joined in, kicking and punching the driver, and eventually the driver held up his hands in defeat. He hastily got into the truck, started the engine and reversed it. But as it turned, I saw something painted on the side that froze the blood in my veins: *J. Anderson & Sons. Specialist Butchers and Slaughtermen.*

The engine roared as the lorry turned round and sped up the farm track and away. I turned away, shivering. So that was it; what John had said was true: they were catching wild ponies and selling them for meat. It must be illegal, for them to be doing it at night like that. I thought back to John's words as we'd brought the cattle down from the moor and how he'd told me that the Dartmoor ponies were bound for the butcher's knife, for unsuspecting customers who thought they were buying beef. How right he was, how wise. And how I missed him for that.

I got back under the blankets, thinking that Red would come back at any moment, but he stayed out for a long time. Eventually I looked out again and saw that he and Reeves were still standing at the top of the hill together. They appeared to be arguing, their faces close together, hands gesticulating in anger. I watched, wondering what they were arguing about, wondering if they would begin to fight, if they would hurt each other. But after a few minutes, Red turned away and started back down the hill towards the barn. I slid back under the covers as quickly as I could.

Chapter Fourteen

Helen

Helen drove home, her mind reeling from what she'd seen at Black Moor Farm. Who was lying in the rough grave under the neglected apple trees? It was someone close to her mother, she knew that much. If it had drawn Daisy to walk down that hill come rain, come shine, year after year, taking fresh flowers, kneeling beside the grave, bowing her head, as Helen imagined… Was it the man in the photograph? The one she'd seen with Daisy setting off to India? And was he the same young man as the sailor in the other picture?

At home, she got out her laptop and tried to find information about the farm. She looked it up on the Ordnance Survey map and did various Google searches, but discovered nothing. As she searched, she thought back to when they'd moved to the house after her father had died. She'd been very young, but she recalled that her mother had been insistent that she wanted to live on the edge of Dartmoor. The location had seemed very important to her at the time. Helen recalled how angry she'd been then that her mother wanted to take her away from her friends and everything that was familiar, just at the point when she'd lost her father. But Daisy had been insistent. If Daisy's motivation had been that she wanted to be close to someone she'd lost, it was understandable. But why ever did she hide that from those she was closest to?

She found an extract from the parish register noting that the farm had been owned by a Farmer J. Reeves between 1930 and 1945, and she wondered if perhaps her mother had known him, had visited him when she was evacuated. They were not so far from Plymouth here. She searched against the name and the address without anything further coming up. She was beginning to feel frustrated by this, in danger of giving up and resigning herself to never knowing any more about the place, when she stumbled across a notice of public auction on an auctioneer's website:

Black Moor Farm, North Brent, Dartmoor, to be sold.

Lot 1: Farmhouse. In need of refurbishment and repair.

Lot 2: Stable block, outbuildings and a further, separate Victorian Barn in need of repair.

Lot 3: 100 acres of mixed moorland, farmland and woodland for sale by public auction on July 15th 1965. Land has been left fallow and needs improving. All buildings in need of refurbishment and upgrading.

Helen stared at the advert. What it told her was that the farm had changed hands in 1965, but having been down there that day, she was sure that those buildings had never been repaired or upgraded. They looked as if they hadn't been touched since the war so whoever bought it at that auction had left it to rot and had done nothing with it. Again, she wondered why someone would leave such a valuable asset to decay and sink into ruin like that?

It occurred to her that 1965 was the year her mother had bought Black Moor Hall. The year they had moved there from London. There had been no mention that the next-door farm had also changed hands at that time; that there were new neighbours, or indeed anything about it at all.

She wondered how to trace the ownership of the place. Perhaps that would provide her with some clues. She decided to call Laura.

Perhaps she'd be able to help. She must know all about this sort of thing, with her legal background.

Laura was about to go out, accompanying Paul on a factory visit. Helen quickly told her about her walk down to the abandoned farm, about the path she'd found through the woods leading down the hill to the old buildings that must have been made by their mother, and how that path had led her inexorably towards the solitary grave.

'A grave! How very sad…' Laura said. Then there was silence at the end of the line while she digested this. 'So, you think Mum used to walk down there especially to visit this grave? Who do you think it might have been? That young sailor in the photograph?'

'I've no idea. It is hard to believe that she walked down there virtually every day. She must have been grieving, but she never told us anything about it. But the path runs straight down to the grave. It starts near where she used to get through the gap in the fence, and ends in the wild garden, right in front of that grave. She must have taken flowers down there, Laura. There's a whole pile of them. All dried up. No one can have been down there recently.'

Again, there was a pause.

'I'm speechless, Helen. Why ever didn't she tell us about this? Whoever she's been taking flowers to must have been incredibly important to her.'

'I've no idea. There's so much she didn't tell us. You know, it struck me when I was wandering about those buildings that someone must own the place. I was wondering if they might be able to shed some light on all this. Is there any way of finding out?'

'Well, if the land is registered, it's easy to do a search at the Land Registry. I can do it online later if you like, when I get back from the visit. I'll look on the map so I can put in the coordinates.'

'Don't worry, I'll do it. I'm itching to know. I'll phone you later if I find anything.'

On the Land Registry website, Helen quickly put in the name and location of the farm, then entered her details and paid a fee to upload details of the title. When she clicked through to the title and opened the document, what she saw astonished her. She stood staring at the screen, open-mouthed with amazement. The person registered as the owner of Black Moor Farm was none other than Dr Daisy Cavendish, of Black Moor Hall, North Brent, Devon. Helen printed off the document, held it in her hands and stared at it again for a long time. Her mother had been registered as the owner in 1965, at the same time as they'd bought Black Moor Hall. She'd owned it all these years without telling a soul.

Chapter Fifteen

Daisy

Another Christmas came and went, and once again I couldn't help remembering our last Christmas at home with Mother and Father. My heart was aching for them, but I owed it to Peggy to put on a brave face. This time I was grieving and yearning for John too and it was harder than ever before to stay strong.

Over those weeks, as the water butts were frozen over and the high rocks on the moor were sprinkled with snowflakes, there was something else that troubled me; in among the sadness and grief, I began to fear for my own health too. I woke up one morning and vaguely noticed that my body was changing. My stomach felt tight and uncomfortable, and despite our poor and inadequate diet, my trousers were beginning to chafe at the waist. I wondered what this could mean and, in my state of confusion and distraction, I was very slow to understand. At first I wondered if there was something very wrong with my stomach due to the lack of vitamins we were eating: was it starvation that was affecting my body?

That morning, it must have been in February or early March, on one of the coldest days of the year, I decided to wear two pairs of trousers in an attempt to keep warm. I remembered the slacks I'd arrived at the farm in, and pulled them from the gas mask bag, where they'd been since virtually the day we arrived. They wouldn't normally have been suitable for working on the farm, but I thought they could be used as an underlayer. I sat on the lower bunk and pulled them up over my skinny thighs, then I pulled the waistband together to do up the button. To my astonishment, they wouldn't do up around my stomach. I stood up and wriggled about, trying to pull them together, but it was impossible. I sat down heavily, wondering if the trousers had shrunk somehow. But that was impossible. They'd never been washed.

I put them back in the bag, puzzled. But then it occurred to me: my expanding waistline could actually be a baby growing inside me. John's baby. My heart almost stopped when that thought crossed my mind. Why hadn't I realised before? But I knew the reason for that – I'd been going through the days like a sleepwalker.

That night, there was another sharp reminder that the war was still raging around us. Peggy and I were snuggled up together on the top bunk when there came the sound of bombers approaching from the direction of Plymouth. I opened my eyes and listened to their engines. I could tell by their pitch that these were German aircraft. They screamed overhead, then a few seconds later came a terrifying crash and the sound of an explosion. Everyone got out of bed and we all ran out into the yard. From there we could see a fire burning, a few fields away.

'Go back to bed,' yelled Red. 'We'll see what it was in the morning.'

After breakfast, before starting work, he allowed us to walk over to where the fire had burned in the night. It was no longer burning, but as we got closer to the place we could see wisps of smoke rising from the field. Finally, we reached it. It was a great black crater in the middle of the field. Earth had been blasted from it and was scattered all around. We stood on the edge and peered in. Inside, the crater was blackened and smoking.

'They must have offloaded their last bomb here,' said Red. 'There was another raid in Plymouth last night.'

I thought of the raids we'd experienced at the Browns' – the devastated street, the screams of those buried in the rubble. I closed my eyes. When would this dreadful war ever end?

I wondered if I was right about what was happening inside my body, terrified of what could happen if my suspicions were true. In my desperation I thought of telling Sally and Joan, asking them what I should do, but quickly realised that I couldn't do that. They would be just as shocked and terrified as I was and wouldn't know what to do. There was no way I could tell Peggy either. My first instinct was to shield her as far as I could from the worst of what was happening to us. Telling her something that anyway would be difficult to explain would only add to her stress and fear.

But later that day, when I bent down, I felt the baby move inside me, and I knew there was no longer any doubting what was happening. I tried my best to count back through the days and months and was stunned to realise that it must be almost six months since John had died. That must mean that there was only another three months to go before the baby came. And when it did come, there would be no hiding it from anyone. I knew I had to get away from the farm before the birth.

That evening, the weather was raw and cold. Peggy and I set off to feed the chickens, our clothes still damp from working in the fields, spreading muck from the muck heap behind the stables by hand in readiness for planting. It had rained that day, and we still felt chilled from our drenching. As usual, Red stayed behind in the yard and the dog followed us down the hill and waited outside the barn. On those dark evenings, Red gave us a torch to light our way down to the barn. When we got there, we began to spread the corn and scraps on the barn floor for the chickens, calling out to them as usual. They came running from all parts of the building, clucking and squawking. But as we were feeding them, Peggy started to cough. I looked at her, alarmed, concerned that it might develop into something serious as it had once before. It wasn't too long ago that she'd been laid up for days, and the weather was colder now. She was thinner and weaker too. Mother's words rang in my ears. *Look after your sister, Daisy. Make sure she takes her medicine.*

'I think we'd better go, don't you?' I said. 'Let's not stay here today. We should go back to the barn and you should get into bed and rest. I'll find your medicine bottle again.'

'I'll be all right,' she insisted. 'It's nothing serious. Let's stay, please?'

I took her hand firmly. 'No, Peggy. We need to get back. You're not at all well. Remember the cough you had last year? And the one you had at home? It lasted for weeks. And you're not really better from last time yet. You need to get back and sit by the stove.'

The stove had been lit when we got back to the barn, so I got Peggy to sit down beside it, wrapped in a blanket. I found the medicine bottle, which was tucked into the lining of the gas mask bag, and gave her a couple of spoons. She carried on coughing from time to time and her cheeks were red, as if she was getting a fever. I watched her all evening nervously, hoping against hope that the cough wouldn't develop, remembering how ill she'd become with a chest infection at home once; and that was when we were in our warm, comfortable home, with our mother ministering hot baths and steam cures. I tried not to imagine what might happen if she became really ill here. Apart from the bottle Mother had given us, there was no medicine; there was little warmth, inadequate food and no comfort. It was a miracle Peggy had recovered before, when John was still with us. I shivered, just thinking about it.

As the days continued, Peggy's cough got better, and the weather brightened, but I could no longer ignore our need to escape. Each day as we mucked out the stables, put new straw out for the animals, whose unpredictable movements and boisterous temperaments stopped me from ever fully relaxing, I become more and more aware of my promise to protect Peggy. As I watched her concentrate on her tasks, stroke the animals and calm them as she always did, I knew that it would just be a matter of time until her cough came back. It terrified me for it brought home to me that if she did become ill again, she might not get better, and I had to do something.

And I had more than just Peggy to protect now. Bending over for hours on end made me dizzy and my back ache each day, but thinking only of my baby, I hardly felt the pain. I was acutely aware of this precious new being growing inside me, my only reminder of John, and the need to guard it with my life.

The next evening, Peggy and I set off from the yard towards the barn to feed the chickens. As we walked past the end of the track that led up to the farmhouse, two yellow beams from a pair of headlights appeared at the top of the hill and a car drew up and stopped outside the house. I knew Red would notice and start yelling at me if I stopped to stare at it. It was almost dark, so it was difficult to see properly, but out of the corner of my eye, I noticed that the car had a light on its roof. My heard began to beat faster; it was a police car.

Someone got out of the car, slammed the door and walked towards the house. My mind went over the possibilities: was Reeves being investigated for John's murder? Had someone alerted the police to our presence on the farm?

Peggy and I walked down to the barn, the dancing light of the torch casting eerie shadows in the dark lane. As usual, the dog, Wolf, trotted after us. When we neared the building, he sat down and watched us carry on towards the door, his head cocked on one side, his ears pricked.

'Did you see that car?' I said to Peggy, when we were out of earshot of the yard.

She shook her head. 'I didn't really look.'

'Well, there was a car that stopped outside the house and I think it was a police car.'

'Police car?' she said, then, 'Well, why don't we run up there and tell the policeman what's happening to us?'

I thought for a few moments. It had crossed my mind too. Would it work? In the end I shook my head.

'No. It might be a mistake, Peggy. It could easily go wrong if Red or Farmer Reeves see us. I've got a better idea.'

We went inside the barn and began to throw the corn around for the hens. When we'd finished, Peggy took the bucket and went to collect the eggs as usual.

'Don't do that today,' I said and she looked at me with a questioning look.

'Put the bucket down. We're going to find another way out.'

'There isn't another way out of here. There's only one door, and Wolf's outside.'

'Come with me,' I said, going over to the rickety ladder that led to the upper platform. 'Come on up behind me. We'll have to be quick.'

I tucked the torch into the top of my trousers and climbed the ladder. I'd forgotten that it was missing a rung near the top, so I nearly lost my footing, but I managed to reach the upper floor and scrambled to my feet on the dusty boards. As I straightened up, the last time I'd been there came back to me with sudden clarity and I hesitated for a second; a lump formed in my throat as I had a sudden, desperate yearning for John, for his warmth and the comfort of his touch. But then I heard the scrabbling and squeaking of the rats running to the cover of a pile of sacks in the corner. They hadn't been there before; they must have come inside for shelter as the weather grew colder. Shuddering, trying to ignore it, I shone the torch on the ladder for Peggy as she followed me up.

'There are three doors out of here,' I said, when she was standing beside me, 'but we'll have to jump down onto the bank outside.'

With the torch, I scanned the walls, looking for the doors that I'd seen from the outside of the barn when I'd been there with John.

One of them opened onto the front of the building. This was where the dog was sitting, so was impossible to use. The others opened onto the opposite side of the barn. I went over to the back of the barn and tried to open one of them. It looked as though it hadn't been opened in decades. I tugged at it, and with a lot of effort, I managed to pull the bolt back, but try as I might, I couldn't shift the door itself, even with my shoulder hard against it. I went to the final door. There was no bolt on this one, and the door itself, although eaten away by woodworm and the hinges were decaying, opened fairly easily. It scraped over the floorboards as I pulled it back.

I peered outside into the darkness. I could hear the stream rushing past over the rocks beyond the bank, smell the damp earth and the bracken. I flashed the torch around at the bank, trying to work out where best to aim for.

'We need to jump down onto that bank,' I said to Peggy. 'Don't make a sound, or the dog will hear us.'

She nodded. My stomach was churning with nerves and I knew from the look in her eyes that she was anxious too, but she didn't protest.

'You go first,' I said, knowing that if I was the first to go, she might find it hard to follow. 'Aim for that spot there,' I added, shining the torch on a patch of heather that might provide a soft landing.

She glanced at me before she jumped and I saw the uncertainty in her eyes. But she was brave. She wasn't going to give up now. I heard her take a deep breath, then she flung herself out of the doorway into the darkness, and hurtled down towards the patch of heather.

She landed with a thump and I looked out anxiously, praying she wasn't hurt. She looked back up at me and got to her feet. Then she moved away from the patch of heather and waved back at me.

I took a deep breath and jumped too. I was taking a risk with my unborn child, I knew that, but it was a risk I had to take for its sake as well as mine and Peggy's. I felt the rush of air past my ears as, for a split second, I was plummeting down, then landed hard in the prickly heather. I felt a sharp pain as I hit the ground awkwardly, my ankle turning, the pain searing right through me. I bit my lip hard to prevent myself from crying out. Doing my best to ignore the pain, I got up and hobbled down the grassy bank towards the stream.

'Come on,' I whispered to Peggy. 'We need to walk along in the brook. It goes behind the farmyard and comes out on the other side, opposite the house.'

I pulled off my shoes and socks and Peggy did the same, then I got down into the water, gasping at the icy cold as I did so.

'Why are we walking in here?' asked Peggy in a hoarse whisper.

'It might confuse the dog,' I said. I wasn't sure that this was the case, but I thought it might be worth trying. 'Let's go.'

I began to walk slowly upstream, slipping on the rocks as I went. My teeth were already chattering. With one hand, I held the torch and my shoes, and with the other, I gripped Peggy's hand. She was following me closely, shadowing my steps. We made slow progress, clambering over rocks and up mini-waterfalls, wading through pools where the bottom was soft and muddy. After a few minutes, though, we had skirted the farmyard and were on a level with the house, staring at it across some open ground. We climbed out of the stream and stood together on the bank, hand in hand, looking at the police car that was still parked outside the front gate.

There were lights on in one of the front rooms of the house and I could see Farmer Reeves and another man talking animatedly inside. I wondered what was going on. Was the policeman questioning Reeves? Was he about to arrest him? But there was no time to speculate about that now.

'Come on, Peggy,' I said. 'We can't stand here.'

We pulled our shoes on and crept over towards the house, keeping to the edge of the open area, skirting around behind the muckheap. The smell that rose from it almost made me gag, but that didn't matter; the car was in my sights now. We were almost there.

Within seconds we were standing beside the car. My heart in my mouth, I tried the handle to the back door. It wasn't locked, so carefully, gradually, I pulled the door open, my eyes fixed on the two figures in the front room of the house. The hinges creaked as I opened the door, so I had to do it as slowly and gently as I could manage. It seemed to take an age and all the time I was watching the window, praying that no one would glance out and see us there.

When the door was open wide enough, I clambered inside the car and motioned Peggy to follow me. We both sat wedged in the well between the front and back seats. My heart was pounding now, my mind alive with all the possible things that could go wrong. What if someone came and opened the back door? What if the dog started barking and Red ran down to the barn to discover we were no longer there? What if he got suspicious anyway at the length of time we'd been away, and went down to the barn to look for himself? But I knew we'd often taken longer, sat on a bale of straw inside the barn, watching the chickens, chatting to each other.

We didn't have to wait long. Within a few minutes, we heard the front door of the house slam and footsteps on the gravel. Then the front door of the car creaked open. For a couple of seconds, the interior light came on, flooding us with light. I stared at Peggy in horror and she stared back at me, wide-eyed. Her face looked white and unhealthy in the light, dark smudges under her eyes. We heard the policeman getting into the front seat. It shifted backwards with his weight as he sat down. He slammed the door and the light went out. The engine started, then roared, and the car moved forward slowly, bumping over the rough surface. It reversed and turned round, then suddenly came to a halt. The driver put on the brake. The engine was idling, but the inside light came on again. Once again, shock went through me. I stared at Peggy again. Tears were filling her eyes, but I shook my head and held my finger to my lips to deter her; she couldn't start crying now.

The driver was fumbling in the glove compartment. He grunted as he found what he was looking for. Then came the scrape of a match, the flare of it lighting. After a second or two, I could smell the smoke from the cigarette he'd just lit. The car light went out, he let off the brake and the car began to move forward. It was moving slowly, bumping over the rough ground in front of the house and onto the track. Gradually it began to pick up pace and we were rattling towards the gate that opened onto the lane.

My stomach still alive with nerves, I gripped Peggy's hand in the dark, feeling we had a chance for the very first time, and hoping against hope that the plan would work.

Chapter Sixteen

Daisy

Crouching on the floor in the back of the police car, I felt it swing round as it turned off the farm track and onto the lane. Then I felt the car begin to descend the hill, twisting and turning, speeding round bends, plunging on into the darkness. We were jolted and thrown about, sometimes against each other, sometimes against the doors or the seats. I clutched Peggy's hand and squeezed it to reassure her, trying to keep myself steady. We could hardly see each other, but I caught the occasional glimpse of the whites of her eyes, wide and frightened. It felt as if we were going fast; too fast for the narrow, bumpy road. My instinct was to cry out, but I bit my lip in an effort to keep silent.

It was an uncomfortable ride; the floor of the car was bare metal and the space between the back and front seats where we were wedged was cramped and confined. But the feeling of elation that crept over me from being driven away from the farm was worth the bruises. I tried to cradle my belly, trying not to let Peggy see what I was doing. I was worried that the jump from the barn might have harmed my baby and that jolting around on the floor of the car could compound the damage.

The journey down the winding lanes took about twenty minutes. Then suddenly, the road became smoother and straighter, and the inside of the car was flooded with light from street lamps, shining on Peggy's pale, terrified face. I looked through the window and saw that we were passing houses and shops. We must have entered a village or small town. I was relieved that the journey must be coming to an end, and that I'd soon be able to tell the policeman everything that had happened to us in a place that was safe.

After a few more turnings, we pulled up outside a low, square building. The man got out of the driver's seat, slamming the door behind him. There followed a couple of seconds' silence while Peggy and I stared at each other and I wondered what to do next. I thought the man had gone away, but suddenly the rear door beside Peggy was wrenched open and a face thrust inside the opening.

'What the hell?' His voice was high-pitched with shock.

We both jumped at the sound of it and looked up at him, wide-eyed, terrified of what the next moments would bring.

'What are you two doing here?'

Not waiting for an answer, he grabbed Peggy's arm and pulled her out of the car. She cried out in pain and fear.

'Don't hurt her,' I pleaded. 'It's not her fault. This was my idea.'

'Get out of the car then,' he said, and I clambered across to the other side and got out onto the pavement beside Peggy.

'What's all this about?' he said, an unpleasant edge to his voice. This was a surprise. His gruff tone reminded me of Reeves. Had I made a dreadful error, putting my trust in him? I suddenly felt uncertain of my ground.

'We've come from Black Moor Farm.'

'I gathered that,' he said. 'But what are you doing in my car?'

The words came out in a rush. I was desperate to get them out; to get him to understand quickly.

'We were tricked into going there. We've been kept prisoner there by Farmer Reeves for months,' I began, but he said immediately, holding up his hand in warning, 'Now stop right there. Come on inside the station and you'd better explain what's going on properly.' He unlocked the front door and ushered us inside the chilly building. I felt a little reassured that he was taking us inside to hear our story. Perhaps, after all, he was going to take us seriously.

He switched on the lights and took us through an empty reception area to a bare room furnished with only a table and chairs.

'Sit down over there,' he said.

We did as we were told, but as I sat down beside Peggy, I noticed that her cheeks were wet with tears. The officer took off his coat, hung it on the back of the chair and sat down opposite us. Slowly and deliberately, he took a notebook and pen out of his top pocket, opened the notebook on the table and looked straight at me, making no attempts to calm Peggy. It was almost as if he didn't see her at all. I was getting the impression that he didn't care about our plight.

He was tall, with receding dark hair and a florid complexion. I could smell alcohol and smoke on his breath, even from where I was sitting across the table. Had he been drinking with Reeves?

'Now, I'm Police Constable Frank Baines. This is my police station. First, tell me your names.' I told him and he wrote in his notebook. Then he looked up. 'Well, come on then,' he said, looking at me. 'Tell me what this is all about. Slowly, now, so I can get it all down in writing.'

'We were evacuated from London to Plymouth. To stay with Mr and Mrs Brown in Plympton.'

I waited while he wrote that down.

'But it wasn't safe there either and one night, the street was bombed. I think Mr and Mrs Brown were killed. We walked to the end of the road and met a man. He said he was a billeting officer and that he would take us somewhere safe.'

The policeman looked up.

'Wait until I've written that down. Now, you say he said he was a billeting officer. Do you mean he wasn't one?'

I nodded.

'But where's your proof for that?'

I stared at him, surprised. I hadn't expected to be questioned like that.

'Well, he took us somewhere where we've been mistreated.'

I told him about the others who we met there, and how we were made to live: the food, the work, the conditions. I tried to remember the names of everyone there, gave descriptions of what they looked like. Then I told him about the list of casualties I'd seen in the newspaper, and finally, I told him about John:

'He shot a boy who tried to run away. He shot him with his rifle. We were all watching.' I was putting that part off until last, because I could hardly trust myself to speak about it without breaking down. I was worried that I might betray the fact that I cared for John in a special way, and that I was somehow blameworthy because of that, and I wanted to make sure I'd told the rest of the story first. I had to speak slowly and he kept stopping me in order to write it all down. Saying it all out loud like that made it sound fantastical, even to my own ears.

When I'd finished, he looked up and put his pen down. He leaned forward and looked me straight in the eye. There was a long silence, and finally he drew himself up in his chair and said, 'This is all a pack of lies as you well know.'

I stared at him, wide-eyed, shock waves running through me.

'No,' I protested feebly, but my voice sounded far away.

'The man who took you up to Black Moor Farm was a legitimate billeting officer. He had your best interests at heart and Farmer Reeves has been kind enough to give both you girls shelter for these past few months.' I shook my head, a lump forming in my throat.

'It's not true. You know it's not true.'

'You know the government has sanctioned the use of children for farm work? In some places they're even setting up camps for them to stay in. You're lucky you're not living in a tent.'

I stared at him, unable to reply, wondering if this were true.

'And how do you repay him?' he went on, ignoring my protest. 'I'll tell you how. By trying to escape from the farm and by spreading malicious lies about him.'

I stared at him, completely blindsided, not knowing how to respond. He looked so authoritative, sitting there in his policeman's uniform, that I even began to doubt the truth of my own story. Perhaps everything was all official and above board after all? Perhaps we were meant to be at the farm? But after a couple of minutes of thinking myself round in circles, I thought again of John.

'But Farmer Reeves killed… he killed John. We saw him do it. He's a murderer.'

The policeman shook his head, a grave look in his eyes.

'I think you'll find that Farmer Reeves fired a shot to frighten the boy. He simply wanted to stop John leaving. In fact, the boy was just winded. He's alive and well and back in Plymouth even as we speak.'

'Really?' I asked, frowning, something in my heart wanting to believe him. Could this be true? Could my precious John be alive? How did this man know so much about all this? All the time an unpleasant tingling was creeping up the back of my neck.

'Certainly. He's joined the navy. He's with his ship right now, doing his duty.'

'He was dead. I saw the blood. I saw his body…'

Again, the policeman shook his head. 'You're quite wrong. There may have been a surface wound. There might have been some blood. But the boy made a full recovery and is fit and well again, like I said.'

I stared at him, trying to make sense of what he'd said. The image of John's dead body came back to me. I shook my head. Much as I wanted to believe him, I knew it just couldn't be true.

'But I saw him…'

'You think you saw him. It strikes me that you're a girl with a very vivid imagination. You don't seem to know fact from fiction.'

'But if it's true, if it's true that he's alive and well, why can't we leave too? We don't want to be at the farm. We want to go back home to London. There's a neighbour who can look after us.'

There was a long pause, during which the only sound in the room was Peggy's muffled sobbing. The policeman carried on watching me silently. In the end he cleared his throat and spoke.

'I wasn't going to say anything. And Farmer Reeves, in his kindness, has wanted to keep it from you all these months, but I suppose you have a right to know.'

'Right to know what?' I asked, alarm sending shivers up my scalp and the back of my neck.

He put his pen down and leaned forward.

'I'm very sorry to have to tell you this,' he said, 'but I'm afraid you won't be going home because your area in London has been devastated. There's no one left to take you in.'

I found myself shaking from head to toe. I opened my mouth to speak but no words would come. Tears smarted in my eyes. What if it were true? I thought back to Mother's letters. She'd spoken about local bombings. And I knew from reading Red's newspaper that there were still bombings in London on a nightly basis.

I gripped Peggy's hand and she looked up at me, her lip trembling, her eyes brimming with tears. I squeezed her hand to try to reassure her.

'Now when you're ready, I'm going to drive you back to the farm. Old Joe will be worried about you, but he hasn't got a telephone up there, so I can't call to tell him.'

'Please,' I said, staring at him in horror, tears streaming down my cheeks. 'Please, don't take us back.'

The policeman laughed, a short derisive laugh.

'Now I'm not listening to any more of your nonsense, my girl. I know Farmer Reeves to be a kind man. He may be a bit rough around the edges – he's a country type after all – but you won't find a fairer man anywhere. He's a very busy man too, putting in so much work on his farm to produce extra food for the war effort. Now I know you want to go home, but as I've explained, that isn't going to be possible now. The alternative would be an orphanage, and I think you'd be far better off at the farm.'

'But I'm sixteen now. I can take care of us both. We don't need to be looked after.'

'Legally, you do need to be cared for, I'm afraid. And as I explained, your home isn't there any more. Your mother has passed away. I'm very sorry, but the farm is the best place for you both for the time being.'

'Time being? How long? How long will we have to be there?'

He scratched his head; I could see the impatience in his eyes. 'I'm afraid I can't answer that question, but until the war ends, at least. And who knows when that will be?'

I was frantic, trying to think of a way to stop him taking us back to the farm and everything that it would mean. How could we bear it there any longer? How would we survive? I knew we would be punished severely for trying to run away. How could I withstand another beating? What about my baby?

'Now come along. We need to get you back to that farm. It's very late now.'

He grabbed me by the arm with one hand, and Peggy with the other.

'I'm not going,' I said, planting my feet firmly on the floor.

'Oh yes, you are. Make no mistake,' he said, pinching my arm with his fingers, dragging me forward so I lost my footing and began to slide across the room after him. I yelled out for him to stop, but he took no notice. With the other hand he was dragging Peggy, who was crying, tears streaming down her face.

'You little bitch,' he said, letting go of my arm and slapping Peggy round the face, leaving a red welt on her cheek.

'Don't do that! It's not her fault,' I shouted.

'If you come quietly I won't hurt her, but if you make a fuss, I'll give her the beating of her life, and worse,' he said between clenched teeth.

I stopped resisting. He'd got me by my weak spot and there was nothing I could do about it. He continued holding Peggy tightly by her arm, dragging her out to the car. She was sobbing and protesting.

'Don't cry, Peggy,' I said, following them. 'I won't let him hurt you.'

He opened the back door and shoved me inside the car, then pushed Peggy into the front passenger seat and got into the driver's side. He turned round and stared at me, an evil, brooding look on his face.

'Don't you dare try anything else. If you do, your little sister will suffer.'

I slumped back on the seat, defeated. The policeman started the engine, turned the car round quickly, and with a screech of tyres, started back up the lane. I watched through the windscreen as the beams from the headlights lit up the high banks either side of the lane in a ghostly, grey light. The car accelerated on through the lanes and soon it was climbing a steep hill, twisting and turning as it went. Then we were travelling through woodland; great, spectral pines rose up either side of the lane, sending shivers down my spine.

All the time I was going over and over what the man had told me. Our house had been destroyed by bombs and now our last hope, Mrs Hutchings, was dead. It had the dreadful ring of truth about it, even though it was obvious that he'd lied to us about what had happened to John. I knew without any doubt that Reeves had killed him. I'd felt it in my heart as John went down.

We'd reached the farm gate now. It stood open, and the policeman eased the car off the lane and onto the farm track. The car then bumped and rocked along the track through the spinney. I thought of the first time we'd been driven along this track, reeling from the shock of the air raid in Plympton, imagining we were being taken somewhere safe and welcoming. Although I'd been a little anxious then, there had been hope in my heart. But now there was just a sickening feeling in the pit of my stomach, and a sinking dread that we were back here again.

The car emerged from the spinney and there was the farmhouse up ahead, lights shining from the front windows, illuminating the overgrown front garden. The two Alsatians came racing up to the car, barking furiously, their eyes wild in the headlights, teeth bared, hackles raised.

The front door of the house was flung open and two figures were silhouetted in the doorway: Reeves and Red. I pressed myself back against the seat, terror coursing through me at the thought of the punishments they would devise for this, the worst of all transgressions.

I shrank back against the seat as the car stopped outside the house and Reeves approached, walking with his stick, limping along but moving quickly. The policeman wound down the front window.

'What's going on, Frank?' Reeves growled.

'I've brought your two girls back, Joe,' said the policeman. 'Hiding in the back of the car, they were.'

I noticed with surprise and creeping dismay that he addressed Reeves in a respectful tone. Not at all how I imagined a policeman would treat a criminal.

'What took you so long? We've been out looking for 'em this past hour.'

'Sorry, Joe. I had to question them.'

'Question 'em?' Reeves roared, putting his red face up to the window. 'What the 'ell for? They'd run off. No need for questions.'

'Well, as I said, I'm sorry,' the policeman said in a placatory tone. 'They're here now anyway.'

Grumbling under his breath, Reeves pulled the front door of the car open and, grabbing Peggy by the arm, wrenched her out of the seat. She screamed in terror.

'Don't hurt her,' I shouted. 'It's not her fault. It's mine.'

''ere. You take the little 'un,' Reeves muttered to Red, who grabbed Peggy from him and dragged her away down the track towards the farmyard. She was stumbling and tripping as he pulled her along. I could hear her terrified cries echoing between the buildings.

Reeves opened the back door and pulled me out of the car. It was then I noticed that he had his rifle with him, slung casually over his shoulder.

'Stand there. By the car,' he said, and I saw his hand move towards the gun. My knees were trembling and I felt weak with shock. This was it. This was the end of my life. All I could think of was Peggy. How would she cope without me? However would she manage alone? Would she ever get out of here alive?

I watched in horror as he lifted the rifle and pointed it towards my head. What would it feel like to be shot? Would I feel the pain or would death be instantaneous? If I were to die, so would my baby. It would be two lives he would take. I stood there, staring at him, waiting for the shot to ring out. But it didn't come. Instead, he jerked his head sideways, towards the farmyard.

'Get walking, you little cow,' he said. 'You've been trouble right from the start. Like that young devil of a boy. And you'll go the same way as 'im if there's any more of it.'

Reeling with shock mixed with relief that I hadn't been shot, I started to walk towards the farmyard. My legs were weak and slow, and I felt dizzy and nauseous. I realised for the first time that it was a bitterly cold night and that I was shivering in the dank air. I was dressed in trousers and a threadbare pullover. I knew that Peggy must be shivering too; her clothes were thinner than mine and she had hardly any flesh on her bones.

I walked slowly down the slope towards the farmyard, my head bowed in defeat, my cheeks wet with tears, although I hadn't noticed that I'd been crying.

'Get on with yer,' growled Reeves, prodding me in the back with the rifle. I could hear the dogs snarling as they slunk along beside him.

The yard was in darkness. No lights shone from the threshing barn. I guessed the others had been told to go to sleep. Perhaps Elsie was in there watching over them. The only sounds were of the bullocks shifting and snorting in their barn, of the horses moving about in the stables. I looked around for Peggy, but she was nowhere to be seen. Alarm prickled my scalp. Where had they taken her?

Reeves prodded me across the yard towards one of the stables. I knew there were no horses in this one at the moment, but I saw as I approached that the top half of the door was flung open. The bottom half swung open as I approached, and Red came out.

'That's where you're going to sleep for the time being,' said Reeves. 'Locked in like animals to stop you running off. There's straw to sleep on. There's water in the trough. You can stay in there until you've learned your lesson.'

He pushed me inside the dark stable and slammed the door behind me. I stood still for a few seconds, listening to the bolts being pulled across, sensing that Peggy was in the corner. Then I heard Reeves unlatching the top door and beginning to close it.

'Please... please don't shut that,' I cried, rushing towards the door, suddenly terrified of being locked up.

'You can't be trusted. It's for yer own good,' he said.

I reached the door as he slammed the top half shut.

'OK. I'll stay, but let Peggy sleep with the others,' I said, hammering on the wood. 'Please!' But they didn't reply and I could hear their footsteps retreating across the yard.

I turned back into the stable and went over to comfort Peggy. I sank down on the freezing floor beside her and put my arms round her. I could feel her bony shoulders trembling through her thin sweater. She was sobbing too.

'Don't cry, Peggy. We've got to be brave,' I said, but it made no difference. A great shuddering sob racked her body. We clung together for a long time, trying desperately to get warm, but the cold from the floor seeped into our bones and chilled us to the core. Again, I thought of my baby. However would it survive this?

After a while, I felt around for the straw Reeves had mentioned. There was a bale in one corner. I began to pull straw out of it and make a pile in the other corner of the stable. At least it would keep us off the floor. It took me some time, but after a while I'd made a bed of straw big enough for both of us to lie on.

'Come on, Peggy, let's get some sleep.'

I led her over to the straw bed and we both lay down, holding each other tight to keep warm. We didn't speak, but I could feel her whole body trembling.

Sleep wouldn't come for a long time. The straw was prickly and uncomfortable, and the cold from the floor penetrated through to my bones. I was just drifting off, though, when Peggy began to cough. It started with a tickle and built up into a hacking, wheezing cough that racked her whole body. We both sat up and I rubbed her back and tried to keep her calm. There was some water in the horses' trough and I brought it to her in my cupped hands, but it didn't help.

She carried on coughing intermittently all night. In the intervals between bouts she seemed to doze off, but I lay awake, staring into the darkness, terrified of what this would do to her.

She was still coughing in the morning, when we heard the cockerel crowing in the barn down in the hollow, and the grey light of dawn began to seep through the cracks in the stable door.

Chapter Seventeen

Helen

Helen's walk to the abandoned farm was still fresh in her mind. Chills still ran down her spine at the thought of that eerie, forgotten place, nestling in the valley, decaying and neglected, slowly being taken over by undergrowth and wildlife. Visiting the grave must have been part of Daisy's regular routine. She'd successfully hidden her grief from all those closest to her. There was something about that knowledge that saddened Helen deeply. As had happened on countless occasions as she grew up, she felt excluded from her mother's life; not trusted to be taken into her confidence.

She'd called Laura to tell her about their mother owning the farm, and her sister had been as incredulous as she was.

'We really need to get to the bottom of this,' said Helen. 'You know, I can't help thinking that the key that Jago found might be a clue to getting to the bottom of all this. I checked every door in the house, Laura, it doesn't fit anything.'

'Maybe it's a safety deposit box or something.'

'It certainly looks like it. Perhaps she's got the deeds to the farm there?'

'Perhaps. I've never seen them at home, or anywhere else for that matter.'

'You know, if she had got a safety deposit box, and if she'd kept it all those years, she would have been paying for it.'

'That's true. I've got all her bank statements here. I brought them back, with all the chequebooks, when we cleared out the house. I'll have a look and see if there's a standing order anywhere in them.'

'Good idea. And if you do find anything, give me a call. I'm on tenterhooks.'

'Of course. I'll call you straight away.'

Helen paced about while she was waiting for Laura to come back to her. Her mind was spinning with everything that she'd discovered that day: the eerily derelict farm buildings with that brooding atmosphere that sent shivers down her spine; the forlorn grave with the rotting bunches of flowers; the mind-blowing discovery that her mother owned Black Moor Farm. But despite all these revelations, she had the sense that there was far more to Daisy's story. That so far she was just scratching the surface.

When her phone buzzed, she snatched it up.

'It's me, Laura. Well, I have found something, you'll be pleased to know. There's a regular payment shown in the bank statement, which I traced back to the cheque stubs. It's amazing. She kept all her cheque stubs down the years. She was such a hoarder.'

'And?'

'She was making a regular payment to the Capital and Regional Bank. Quarterly payments. Looks about the right amount for a safety deposit box.'

'That's great. I'll go to the Totnes branch as soon as I can get there. I've got to work tomorrow so I'll go in the afternoon.'

She put the phone down, her mind buzzing with new possibilities.

Chapter Eighteen

Daisy

As the day broke and the lines of light around the edge of the stable door became gradually brighter, I was slowly becoming more and more desperate. Peggy had been sitting up coughing all night; a hard, racking cough that carried on and on without respite. Between each cough, I could hear the terrifying rasp of her lungs as she struggled for air. She sat, hunched over, her shoulders slumped forward with exhaustion. She was shivering too; the straw bed I'd made had meant that at least we weren't sitting on the cold concrete floor, but it didn't do much to stop the winter chill from seeping right through to our bones. But even as Peggy shivered, sweat poured down her face. I tried to wipe it away, first with straw and then with the sleeve of my jumper. Her body was hot too; the heat radiated through her thin clothes.

'Drink some more water, Peggy,' I kept urging, trying to keep the desperation from my voice. 'That might help you.'

I had to keep going back to the water trough to get handfuls of water to carry over to her. Most of the water spilled, either between my fingers or down Peggy's chin, but she managed to sip some of it at least. I wondered how long that water had been in the trough. After we cleaned the stables each morning, we had to fill them, bringing water in metal pails from a pump in the corner of the yard. I tried to remember when we'd last cleaned out this particular stable. It worried me that it might have even been a few weeks ago, before its occupants disappeared during one of the night-time exchanges, but I couldn't remember exactly when that would have been.

I realised that I'd lost track of time; each miserable day and week of our captivity merged imperceptibly into the next one. A wave of revulsion went through me, thinking about it. I knew that the horses in that stable must have drunk from that trough on the day they left, and since then the water had stayed there, still and stagnating, attracting dust and insects. It was probably full of germs. What if it made Peggy sicker than she already was? But there was no choice. There was nothing else available to help soothe her throat and stop her from getting dehydrated.

My mind went back to all the times at home when I used to lie in the next bed while Peggy coughed her heart out through the night. Mother used to come in and, with soothing words, rub her back or sponge her brow. I couldn't bear to hear my sister wheezing and fighting for breath. I would sometimes even put my head under the pillow to blot out the sound. But now I was the only one Peggy had to help her. I knew she was my responsibility.

I thought about the medicine bottle in the bag on the bunk. If only I could get to it, it might at least give her some respite and allow her to get some rest. Neither of us had slept properly all night.

As I sat there miserably, my mind alive with anxious thoughts, I heard some footsteps in the yard and the squeak of the wheelbarrow as it trundled across the bricks. I got up and ran over to the door, hammering on it with my fists.

'Hey – let us out! Let us out of here! Peggy is sick. I need to get her medicine.'

The footsteps stopped and I heard the chink of metal on bricks as the wheelbarrow was put down. Then the footsteps approached the door.

'Shut your rattle,' came Red's voice.

'Peggy's ill,' I shouted. 'Can't you hear her coughing? She's got a temperature too. We need to get out of here or she's going to get worse.'

'I can 'ear someone pretending to cough,' he scoffed with a cruel laugh. 'Just you shut up now. I need to get on with the stables. I'm 'aving to do your work this morning, thanks to your little drama last night.'

Panic rose in my chest and I beat hard again on the wood of the door, bruising my fingers, my knuckles cut and bleeding.

'Please! Look, I'm sorry. I'm so sorry. It won't happen again, I promise. But you've got to understand, my sister has a weak chest. She's been ill before, she nearly died of pneumonia when she was tiny.'

Red gave a hollow laugh. 'Pull the other one, it's got bells on,' he sneered.

'It's true, I promise,' I said, my voice breaking with emotion. 'Can't you hear her? She's really ill. I just need to get her medicine.'

I was near to tears now but Red didn't answer. I heard him snort and stump away, the scrape of the barrow on the stable yard, the rattle of a bolt being drawn back, the bang of a door and the horse shifting in the stable as he began to muck it out.

I sat back down beside Peggy, despair and guilt engulfing me. I berated myself for getting us into this situation. Why ever did I make the impulsive decision to risk our lives by jumping out of the barn and getting into that police car? If I'd stopped to think about it, even for a moment, I might have seen the risks. I slid my arm round Peggy's shoulders and held her to me.

'I'm so sorry, Peggy,' I murmured.

For a few precious minutes she was quiet, but then the coughing returned and her body was racked by spasm after spasm. I carried on rubbing her back and holding her tight as she coughed. I didn't want her to see me crying, but I couldn't prevent the tears from streaming down my face and the shuddering sobs from shaking my own body.

I don't know how long I'd been in that state when I was startled by the sound of the bolt on the door being drawn back. I looked up and watched the top half slowly opening and a familiar face peering into the gloom of the stable.

I jumped up. 'Elsie! Please help us. Peggy's very ill. Look at her coughing. We need to get out of here.'

I expected her to laugh cruelly as Red had done, but she just peered down at Peggy with her dull, vacant gaze.

'I've got some food for you,' she said at last. 'Red's on the other side of the yard, so don't even think about trying to make a run for it. He's got 'is gun. You need to come over 'ere and get the bowls from me.'

I approached the stable door. Behind me, Peggy was still hacking away.

'You can hear her, can't you?' I pleaded. 'Could you please speak to your father and tell him she's ill? Ask him if we can at least go back to the barn while she gets better.'

She shook her head and held two bowls of grey-looking porridge up for me to take.

'Please! He'll listen to you.'

''e doesn't care about you. What's 'e going to do about it? You're in 'ere because you ran away. 'e's not going to let you out. You're going to rot in 'ere for a long time – I 'eard 'im say so last night.'

'Don't say that, Elsie! Please, talk to him for me. She needs to be in a warmer place, or she's just going to get worse.'

'I can't do that.'

'Why? Why can't you?'

'Just can't,' she said in a flat voice, and it suddenly came to me that Elsie too was afraid of her father. That she'd probably suffered at his hands since she was born and that her life was also that of a captive in its own way. I felt a rush of pity for her, even though she'd stolen my watch, given my letter to Red and been the direct cause of my first beating.

'Well, if you can't do that,' I said, gently, 'could you get her medicine? I know you're a good person really, Elsie. No one need know about it.'

'Just take the food,' she muttered, pushing it towards me, avoiding my eyes. I took the two bowls and two tin mugs of tea and put them on the floor in front of the door. I expected her to slam the top door and march away, but she hesitated. I watched her pudgy face; she was frowning, her eyes cast downwards. Behind me, Peggy had started coughing again in earnest. Elsie just stood there, motionless. I wondered why she didn't just go.

'Where is it then?' she said at last in a grudging tone. My heart leapt and I quickly told her where to find the bottle before she changed her mind.

'I'll do what I can,' she muttered and closed the top door. I listened as her footsteps retreated across the yard.

I sat down beside Peggy and we ate our breakfast; at least I ate mine and Peggy tried to eat hers in between coughing fits. She couldn't take much in, and a couple of times the coughing was so severe that she brought the porridge back up. I had to wipe it off her chin with straw. In the end she shook her head and pushed the bowl away.

'I can't,' she said, collapsing back down on the straw. She closed her eyes for a few minutes and appeared to drift off to sleep, but within minutes the coughing started up again.

I watched the stable door and listened for Elsie's footsteps. I heard the others come out of the threshing barn to start their morning's work. I could hear Red's voice, barking instructions, then I heard them collecting their tools from the shed and trooping out of the yard. It must have been an hour or so after that when Elsie's footsteps approached again. She knocked on the door gently, then pulled it open a crack. I jumped up and saw that she was holding something up for me to take: the brown medicine bottle that I'd been so desperate for.

'Thank you so much,' I said in relief, smiling into her eyes. She didn't return the smile, just shrugged.

'I'd better shut the door now,' she muttered. 'You'd better not tell Pa, or Red.'

'I would never do that.'

I opened the medicine and gave it to Peggy. There was no spoon so she had to swig it from the bottle. I watched her anxiously. She carried on coughing for a while, but soon the cough began to subside, and after a few minutes she lay down again on the straw and closed her eyes. I stroked her hair and her forehead that was damp with sweat.

'Get some sleep now,' I said, but she was already drifting off. I lay down beside her and closed my own eyes. Within seconds I was asleep, but it was an uneasy sleep full of terrifying dreams. In one dream I was alone in an enormous, dark, empty house. I went from room to room, from floor to floor, looking for the rest of the family, but every room was empty and when I looked out of the windows it was completely dark outside; an unnatural darkness through which I couldn't even make out any shapes. I found the front door and tried to get out, but it was barred and locked. I hammered on the door until my hands hurt, but no one came.

Then I was walking down a street in London. There were houses with front gardens on either side, just like our own street. Mother was walking along in front of me, Buster by her side, his tabby tail in the air; he was walking at her heels like a dog.

'Mother!' I kept shouting, but she was walking quickly and I couldn't reach her. I kept on running too, but no matter how fast I ran, she was always one step ahead. And however loud I shouted, she didn't seem to hear my voice. She just carried on, hurrying down the street, away from me, as if I wasn't there at all. Suddenly, up ahead there was a huge, rumbling explosion and the sky went dark, filled with black smoke, then bricks and rubble and pieces of pavement were flying through the air towards me. I carried on shouting for my mother, but she'd disappeared into the smoke.

I sat up, gasping, sweat pouring down my face, to hear the sound of Peggy coughing louder than ever.

'Please,' I shouted, noticing Elsie coming towards the door again. 'You're our only hope, Elsie. You've got to help.'

'Can't do that. Take these,' she said, pushing dinner bowls towards me roughly.

Instead of taking them, I reached over the door, grabbed her by the collar of her coat with both hands and pulled her towards me.

'Look at her!' I screamed, shaking her back and forth. 'You've got to help or she's going to die. I mean it. She needs a doctor. She's only young. It's not her fault we're here. Have some pity, please!'

'Leave me alone. I've done what I can,' she said, her face red and flustered. She pushed me away and slammed the top door and drew the bolt across. I heard her walk away and I sank to my knees, sobbing.

I don't know how long I sat there before I heard the sound of the bolts being drawn back. The stable door swung open again. Farmer Reeves put his face over.

'What's goin' on 'ere?' he said. He drew back the door and came inside. I shrank away from him; the sight of him with his stick, the smell of him; tobacco and filth, alcohol on his breath.

'What's up with 'er?'

I sat up. 'She's been ill for days. She's got a fever and she can't stop coughing. She needs to see a doctor.' I forced myself to look right into his eyes, even though it revolted me to.

He shook his head. 'You can forget that. No doctor's ever coming 'ere, I don't want no trouble.'

'Please! If she doesn't see a doctor, she could die.'

He shuffled forward through the straw and bent over Peggy, frowning. He placed his filthy hand on her forehead and I flinched at the sight of him touching her. He stood there like that for a minute or so, then he straightened up, frowning, scratching his head under his flat cap, with the handle of his stick.

'Pick 'er up, you two. One take 'er arms, the other 'er feet. Bring 'er up to the 'ouse.'

Elsie stared at him. 'You sure, Dad?'

He wheeled round and stared at her, menacingly. ''Course I'm sure,' he growled. 'Now get on with it.'

So we did as we were told. Elsie took Peggy's shoulders and I lifted her legs. We carried her out into the yard, where the bitterly cold morning air hit me with a fresh force. But I didn't mind that; I was glad to be out of that stinking stable, even though the daylight made me screw my eyes up and the air sliced through my ragged clothes, making me shiver harder than before. I took a gulp of fresh air and concentrated on holding onto Peggy's legs as we crossed the yard, slippery with the morning frost. We made slow progress across the yard and up the slope that led to the farmhouse. I watched Peggy's face anxiously, but her head was lolling forward and she seemed to be unconscious.

Reeves followed us slowly up the hill, and I could hear the tap of his stick on the road as he walked, one of the dogs following at his heels.

I'd never been inside the house before; in fact, I'd not been inside any house since the Browns', all that time ago. There was nothing welcoming or homely about this place. Reeves went ahead to open the front door and as we edged inside the narrow entrance hall, I got a sense of the filthy conditions he and Elsie lived in. The place reeked of a combination of greasy cooking and stagnant drains. The walls were painted brown, scuffed and torn. There was a coat stand on which hung stained jackets and macs. A couple of guns leaned against it. It had a broken mirror, and although it was virtually obscured by dust, I caught a glimpse of my face as we passed. For a split second I wondered who was looking back at me, so changed was my appearance since I'd last looked in a mirror. My face was deathly pale and sharp-featured now, my eyes sunken in my cheeks.

'Take 'er in the kitchen,' barked Reeves, and Elsie manoeuvred herself backwards along the narrow passageway that ran beside the staircase into the back of the house.

The kitchen was filthy and smelled of greasy cooking and drains. Pots and pans were stacked up and overflowing from a stained butler sink and there was a large table in the middle of the room, covered in dirty crockery, empty whisky bottles and overflowing ashtrays. But at least the room was warm. On one wall was an old-fashioned cast-iron stove in a chimneypiece. In front of it was a wooden crate in which two piglets slept, curled up together. On the opposite wall, under the window, was a sagging brown couch, rusting springs protruding from its cushions. A terrier dog and a black cat lay curled up on it. Reeves shooed them away with a swipe of his stick.

'Put 'er down on there,' he said.

We lifted Peggy onto the couch. Her breathing was rasping now, her cheeks red with the fever, and her eyes half-open but not seeing anything.

'I'll sponge 'er down,' said Elsie, going over to the sink and running the tap. She filled a bowl and knelt down beside Peggy, and began wiping her face with a grubby cloth.

'I'll do that,' I said, moving towards them.

'You'll do no such thing!' roared Reeves, turning on me. 'Don't think I've forgotten your little trick. You don't deserve to be up 'ere in the warm. You can get back to that stable and stew in your own juice until I say you can leave.'

'I need to be with her,' I said. 'You can see how ill she is.'

He lunged at me then and grabbed me by the collar.

'And whose fault is that then? If you 'adn't tried to get away, you wouldn't be in that stable, would you?'

'It's your fault,' I screamed at him then. 'You're the one who's tricked us into being here. You've kept us here like prisoners. Like slaves. Living worse than animals. It's your fault she's like this! You're cruel and evil. One day you'll be punished.'

He punched me then, the full force of his strength on my cheekbone. I cried out, but he pulled me close.

'Don't you ever talk that way to me. You're here legally. You ain't got nowhere else to go. I've given you shelter and food all these months and you've repaid me with this. Now get back down that stable afore I set the dogs on you.'

He pushed me backwards, out of the kitchen and into the hallway. I tried to resist, but he was stronger than me. The front door was ahead of me. But for Peggy I could have made a run for it, but I wasn't going to leave her. I turned to see him grabbing his rifle from the coat stand. He held it up.

'Now get down to that stable,' he said, narrowing his eyes, a look of triumph on his face.

I walked ahead of him, my head down.

'You can send me back there, but you need to get a doctor straight away,' I said.

'Like I said,' he said, prodding me in the back with the gun, 'I ain't going to do that. Elsie can look after 'er.'

When we reached the stable, he shoved me inside and slammed both halves of the door behind me. I sank to the floor on my knees, too angry and frightened to cry.

I stayed there in the same place, in the same position, for hours, the chill from the floor seeping into my knees and through the bones of my whole body until I was shivering violently. The light around the edge of the doors gradually dimmed and I heard the footsteps and voices of the others coming back from the fields.

When I could bear the cold no longer, I crawled onto the straw bed and curled up, hugging my knees to my chest. All the time my mind and my heart were full of terror for Peggy and I yearned to be with her, comforting her. Did she know I'd left her? I knew she'd be frightened without me there. Would her fever turn, now she was in a warm place? I hoped and prayed that it would.

That night, I heard the chilling sound of fighter planes echoing over the moor; a group of them flew over the farm, quite low, judging by the rumble of their engines. I lay awake, petrified, waiting for the rumble of an explosion, but none came. It was a stark reminder, though, of how small and insignificant and forgotten we were here, when the war was being played out only a few miles away.

I must have drifted off because I awoke to the sound of the bolts being drawn back and the door being opened. I sat up on my elbows, rubbing my eyes, the memory of what was happening flooding back in an instant.

Elsie stood framed in the doorway in the pale light of dawn, her shoulders drooping. I stared at her and when I saw her downcast eyes and the tears on her pudgy cheeks I knew immediately why she'd come.

'She's gone,' was all she said.

Chapter Nineteen

Helen

'I'm afraid the bank manager is with a customer,' the girl on the desk said. 'It would be best to make an appointment and come back another day.'

'I'd prefer to wait until the manager is free,' said Helen, 'But perhaps you could help me?' She put the key on the desk. 'This belongs to my mother. She's in a care home now.'

The girl looked blank.

'I think it might be for a deposit box or something like that,' Helen went on. 'You do have safety deposit boxes here, don't you?'

'I don't think so… But I'm new here, I'm afraid. Like I said, you could either wait for Mr Jenkins to help you, or make an appointment to come back and see him another time.'

'I'll wait. This is important.'

Helen sat in the reception area and waited impatiently. The time seemed to crawl by. She watched people coming in, making deposits, taking out money, chatting to the assistant. All the time her mind was running over and over everything that had unravelled over the past few days. The letters in the canvas bag in the cupboard behind the wardrobe, filled with the touching words of a mother missing her children and worrying about their welfare from afar; the key that Jago had found and that she now held in her hands. What secrets might it unlock? And the shock of stumbling upon the lonely grave in the wild garden, finding her mother's grief.

Helen shook her head when she thought about it, still unable to comprehend this news.

She took out the photograph of the young sailor and held it up to the light, tilted it to get a better look. The lights in the bank were bright, and the photograph was easier to see here than it had been at home, and she could now, just about, make out the first three letters on the cap band after the 'HMS'. 'HMS Berk…' What could the rest be?

'Miss Cavendish? I'm Adam Jenkins. So sorry to keep you waiting.'

A young man stood in front of her, dressed in a slim-fitting blue suit, his hair gelled, designer stubble on his chin. Helen stood up and shook his hand, trying to keep the look of surprise from her face. He was surely far too young to be a bank manager? She put the photograph back in the bag and followed him into a modern, windowless office.

'How can I help you today?'

Helen handed him the key.

'My mother is a customer here. My sister and I have power of attorney over her affairs. I have a copy in my bag. Here… She's recently gone into a care home, following a stroke. We found this key among her possessions. I'm wondering if it might be the key to a deposit box here?'

The man took the key and examined it, frowning.

'All our deposit boxes are stored in the Plymouth branch now. They have a purpose-built vault down there. We don't have any on these premises. And this key doesn't look like one of ours, I'm afraid. Capital and Regional have a key-card system now, and have done for the past ten years or so. Even before that our keys looked very different from this one. This old key looks very out of date.'

Helen's heart sank. She hadn't foreseen a hurdle like this.

'Do you think you'd be able to find out if it ever was one of yours?' she said. 'Please? It's very important.'

The man rubbed his chin, his eyes flicking nervously away from hers.

'Um, well…'

Why was he hesitating? Then it dawned upon Helen. He was probably thinking that she was trying to get at her mother's valuables while the old lady was incapacitated and in a care home.

'I just want to find out what's in it,' she explained. 'I don't think it's money. Something of sentimental value, perhaps. It must be something important for her to have kept it in a safe.'

He took the key from Helen and got to his feet. 'I can't promise anything, I'm afraid, but I'll call the branch and make some enquiries. If you'd like to wait in reception, please.'

Again, she waited. It was near to closing time, getting dark outside. The street lamps were on now, shops closing up, people walking home, hunched against the cold. She thought again about the abandoned farm, and it occurred to her that Daisy might not have welcomed her walking down there, prying into her secrets. She felt a twinge of guilt at what she'd done.

'Miss Cavendish?' The manager approached her again. 'I've made a few enquiries, but I'm afraid that this number is unknown at the Plymouth branch. I even read out the serial number to the security manager there – it's on the key itself, if you look closely. He has a computerised record of all serial numbers dating back to when the branch opened in 1920. I'm very sorry, but it must be for something else, I'm afraid.'

Helen left the bank feeling deflated. She'd been so sure about it being the right place to look.

In the morning, Helen got up early and logged on to her computer. She put the photograph of the young sailor on the table beside her and started to google the names of naval vessels operating during the Second World War.

There were three possible candidates: HMS *Berkshire*, HMS *Berkeley* and HMS *Berkeley Castle*. She read as much as she could about all three ships, wondering which one it was. She discovered that HMS *Berkeley Castle* was launched in 1943 and served as a convoy escort throughout the war; HMS *Berkshire* was a commandeered trawler, used during the war as an escort vehicle, while HMS *Berkeley* was a 'hunt class' destroyer that was selected for 'Operation Jubilee' in France and was hit and went down during the raid on Dieppe in 1942.

For some time Helen tried unsuccessfully to find a list of crewmembers for each ship. Then, on a specialist site for military records, she stumbled on a list of crew for HMS *Berkeley*. Her eyes quickly scanned the list and there it was: Ordinary Seaman J. Smith, and the date he signed up in 1941. This must be the same man, she thought. But what had happened to him? She turned back to the descriptions of the Dieppe raid and how the ship had been holed and finally scuppered. There were thirteen losses from the crew, she read. She tried, without success, to find a list of names. She glanced back at the photograph and the eyes of the young man seemed to be looking straight at her.

'Whatever happened to you, Ordinary Seaman Smith?' she wondered aloud. Then her phone buzzed. It was Laura. She'd only called her sister the previous evening to let her know she'd drawn a blank with the bank manager. She wondered what had happened for her to ring this early. She snatched up the phone.

'What do you want? Has something happened?' she asked anxiously. 'It's only just after seven.'

'I'm sorry, I woke really early. I've got something to tell you,' Laura replied.

'Don't worry. What is it?'

'After we'd spoken last night, I had another look through the stubs. I checked all the ones to the Capital and Regional Bank. On the first few she hadn't put anything else, but on some of the early ones, she'd written the branch. It wasn't Totnes, Helen. It was the Harrow branch. That's why the key didn't throw up any matches with Plymouth.'

'Harrow?' Helen paused, digesting the news. 'Of course! That's where she lived when she was younger, according to her mother's letters.'

They were both silent, contemplating this latest revelation.

The next day, Helen and Laura made the journey by train and tube together from Exeter to Harrow in north London. They'd decided not to drive, thinking it would be quicker and much more relaxing on the train. It would give them a chance to chat – to try to catch up on all those lost years when they'd hardly seen one another.

They spoke about their mother, how each of them had found her difficult in different ways; trying to get to know each other and understand one another better after so many years of misunderstandings. Helen remembered how she'd felt excluded and ignored when Laura had brought friends home from university and they'd gone out for outings and walks without including her.

'I'm so sorry, Helen. I had no idea. I was so thoughtless when I was young.'

And Laura had related how she'd felt a little jealous and excluded herself at the seemingly close bond that had grown up between Helen and Daisy while she was away studying.

'It didn't feel as if we were close,' said Helen. 'We were always arguing, but because we were alone together so much, I suppose we had to rub along. I'd no idea you felt that way. I'm hoping we can make up for all those difficult times now.'

Laura had spoken to the manager of the Harrow and Wealdstone branch of the Capital and Regional Bank on the phone. He'd confirmed that there was a deposit box held at the bank with the number 342.

'We don't use those old keys any more, though,' he'd told her. 'We've been gradually replacing them with more modern ones. If she still has the old one, it will probably mean she hasn't been here to open the box for a very long time.'

As the train pulled into Harrow and Wealdstone station, they both gazed out at the neat suburban houses, some semi-detached, some terraced, some clearly dating from before the war, others far more modern.

'It's amazing to think that this is the place where she grew up, isn't it?' said Helen. 'She was always so vague about her childhood and about the war. Don't you remember? If she was ever asked, she'd just quickly move the conversation on. Did you ever manage to pin her down?'

Laura shook her head, 'I gave up trying in the end. She had that way of making sure you kept your distance. Everyone knew that. I've been thinking a lot about what you said earlier, and I do think that Mum was just as fierce with other people as she was with you. She'd built a wall round herself, repelling anyone who tried to come close.'

At the bank, the manager checked Daisy's signature on the form against his records.

'This box hasn't been opened since 1956,' he remarked, looking at his screen. 'But the rental has been paid regularly. Four times a year. Every year since then.'

Helen exchanged looks with Laura.

He took them downstairs into a chilly vault: 'Three-four-two is in the older block, under the next-door building.'

They followed him along a narrow passage that smelled musty and damp. He unlocked a heavy metal door and flicked the switch for the lights.

'Number 342 is near the top on the far wall,' he said, pointing. 'I'll leave you to it then. Please take as long as you need.'

They stood in the centre of the room and stared around them. All four walls were lined from floor to ceiling with small metal box doors.

'You do it – you're taller,' said Helen, handing the key to her sister.

'If you're sure?' Laura said, touching Helen's arm and then walking forward.

Helen held her breath as she watched Laura reach up and put the key in the lock. It felt good to her that they were on this quest together now, that finally, after a lifetime of misunderstandings, they were sharing experiences and discoveries. The lock was stiff and it took her a while to turn it. Finally, with a metallic scraping sound, the door opened.

'What's inside?' said Helen, her heart beating fast. She was hardly able to bear the wait.

'I'm not sure,' said Laura, peering inside. 'Wait a minute…'

She put her hands inside and brought out a large, hard-backed book, some letters and what looked like more photographs.

'This book looks like a ledger,' she said, putting the things down on the table in the centre of the room.

Helen approached, peering at them. Nothing was written on the cover.

'Shall I?' she asked, moving to open the book.

'Yes, go on,' said Laura.

Helen picked the book up and opened the cover. It was stiff with age, but there was no dust on its surface. She expected to see columns of numbers, some sort of accounts, but instead the first page contained two or three lines of her mother's sprawling writing:

15th July 1945.

Tomorrow, we're setting off to India with hope in our hearts. We take the boat train for Southampton first thing. I'm leaving behind my old life and the girl I was before the war. What happened then changed everything and blew my life apart. I want to put it behind me and start afresh.

Have a new life in a new country with a new name. But I don't want to do that without recording what happened. So if I need proof in the future, it's all written down. I've written this record of what happened there since Peggy and I first arrived at Black Moor Farm, July 1940. Maybe one day, I'll be ready to tell the world about what happened.

Chapter Twenty

Daisy

The following months passed in a dull, grey blur. I went through the motions of the daily routines that had been forced on me, but nothing was the same without Peggy. I knew instantly that it was my fault that she'd died and from that moment I was overwhelmed with guilt. My sister was gone from my world and it was all my fault. Mother had put her in my care and I couldn't bear the grief I felt.

I begged Elsie to let me see her that dreadful morning, the day she died, and I waited desperately. The icy chill from the floor was seeping in through my bones, my teeth were clamped together with the cold, my whole frame shivering, but I didn't make any attempt to relieve the pain. I didn't even want to. I was punishing myself. I knew I didn't deserve any respite from the suffering. Not even the comfort of the straw bed I'd made, where Peggy and I had huddled together, warming and consoling each other during those long, terrifying nights.

All that day I lay there on the stable floor, staring up at the ceiling. I was in a state of paralysis, my thoughts scrambled with grief.

I listened to the sounds in the yard. I was listening so hard and feeling so desperate and confused that I even thought at one point I heard Peggy's laughter in the air, her footsteps running towards me across the yard, her voice telling me it had all been a mistake and that she was better and coming back to me. But all I could really hear was the sound of the cows lowing, the horses snorting and moving about in their stables and the crows cawing as they circled above the wood. The footsteps of others as they went out to work in the fields, the animals shifting in the stalls. Later, I heard Sally, Fred and Joan coming back from the fields for the midday meal, the sound of their subdued conversations. Then came Red's voice as he yelled at them to hurry, and I knew what they were going off to do.

The chop, chop, chop of shovels in earth stung me. It stilled the blood in my veins and I covered my ears with my hands. They were digging Peggy's grave, in the garden behind the house. And when Elsie let me out of the stable later, and I followed her across the yard, I felt cold. We walked behind the end of the buildings and through a ramshackle gate into an overgrown garden.

As I stood looking at what had become Peggy's grave, my mind scanned back through everything that had happened over the past months. I was desperately searching through my memory for a time when things had been normal, when the dark clouds of war hadn't threatened everything I knew and loved.

I realised that everything had changed for ever the day we'd listened to the broadcast on the wireless. Before that evening, our lives had been settled. After it nothing was ever the same again. I went back over all the mistakes I'd made that had led me and Peggy to Black Moor Farm; of my promises to Mother and Father, of how my stupid, headstrong actions had led to us coming to this place, of how John had represented love and hope that had been ripped from me before it had even begun. I clenched my fists so tightly that I could feel my nails cutting into the palms of my hands, blood seeping from the wounds.

As I worked in the stables each day, I could feel Peggy's presence everywhere I went, sense when she would have laughed and smiled; what she would have said at any given moment. Often, forgetting, I would turn to speak to her and it would take me a second to remember that she wasn't there. My heart was full and ached with loss. Loss of Peggy, of John, of Mother. It was too much to bear.

The others hardly remarked that Peggy had gone. They accepted it with grim resignation, just as they'd accepted John's death. Perhaps to them it didn't seem that unusual. I realised that in the world they had known, the deaths of children could well have been quite frequent.

But even if Peggy's death was unremarkable to them, I had a sense that the animals missed her presence. Those first few days after her death, they seemed to know instinctively that she'd gone. The horses would swing round with expectant eyes when I entered the stable to clean, and snort and stamp when Peggy didn't appear. Even the chickens in the big barn came running towards me, clucking and squawking, flapping their feathers when I went in with the bucket of scraps. But they quickly stopped their fussing when they saw that I was alone.

I was so focused on my grief at that time that I'd stopped thinking about the baby growing inside me. I hardly spoke to anyone, not even Sally, Fred or Joan. There was nothing to say. I retreated into my shell and pushed my body through those back-breaking days, even though in my advanced state of pregnancy the work was doubly difficult for me. I understood little of what was happening inside my body, but in the back of my mind the thought of giving birth was too terrifying to contemplate. I knew it was inevitable, but I was scared of going through something I didn't understand. Whenever I felt my baby move, or had twinges in my back from the strain of working in my condition, it was a reminder of John and of Peggy. I was comforted by it; for some reason it gave me hope.

I accepted all the tasks that were forced on me without protest, when before I'd resisted with every fibre. I even welcomed the work – it felt as if I deserved all the punishment and penance heaped on me.

I thought of Peggy constantly, of Mother, and of course of John, but there was one last hope that I tried to cling to: that Father was still alive out there, somewhere fighting this war, miraculously spared from injury or death.

I was so defeated that I'd even stopped thinking of ways of getting away from the farm. In my grief I just couldn't focus on it, and besides, I knew I needed to stay where Peggy was, to watch over her. Something kept telling me that it was what Mother and Father would have wanted. I'd even stopped thinking about my unborn baby. I suppose it was just too much for me to bear to contemplate what would happen when the baby came. I kept putting off the dreadful day when I knew I'd have to conquer my fears and try to get away from Black Moor Farm. But my refusal to face up to the reality of the situation went on too long. I left it too late and one chilly morning, I found that I couldn't ignore it any longer.

I was clearing out one of the stables alongside Joan. She'd been helping me since Peggy's death, on Red's orders. I stooped to fork up some horse muck and felt a searing pain in my lower abdomen. I paused for a few seconds and the pain retreated, but within a few minutes, it returned. It came and went and at first, I tried to put it aside and carry on forking up the muck, taking it out to the barrow as usual. But the pains soon got so strong that I couldn't ignore them any longer. When a particularly fierce one overtook me, I was forced to stop working. I leaned on the pitchfork, panting with the intensity until it was over and I could breathe normally again.

'What's wrong with you?' Joan asked, looking up from her work. 'Have you got a bad stomach?'

I shook my head, but couldn't speak; another spasm of pain had gripped me fiercely. It grew and grew until I cried out and sank to my knees.

Joan came closer, a concerned frown on her face.

'It looks bad. Maybe it's appendicitis. One of the kids got that, back in the orphanage… I remember how she yelled out with the pain all night. Had to go to 'ospital.'

I shook my head again, concentrating on getting through the next contraction – I knew now that was what these pains were – waiting for the vice-like grip it had over my body to subside.

'Shall I get Red?' Joan asked. 'He's out in the yard, having a smoke.'

'No!' I said fiercely. 'Don't… please don't.'

But as I sank down again, panting and heaving with the next contraction, she took no notice of my pleas. She ran out into the yard.

I looked up to see Red standing in the doorway, staring at me. At that point I was doubled up, fighting yet another contraction. I don't know if he guessed who the father was and it was on the tip of my tongue to plead with him for help, but even gripped with pain I was clear-thinking enough to stop myself. My pride resurfaced as I thought of his cruelty, his brutality. I knew I'd rather die than ask him for help.

'I can 'elp you,' he said. 'Ain't no different to lambing or calving.'

I looked up at him. 'No!' I said. 'Get away from me. Don't you dare come near me.'

Anger flashed across his face. 'Ave it yer own way,' he said, stepping back. 'I'm going up to the 'ouse to talk to the boss about this.'

Once he'd gone, Joan crept to my side and I felt her taking my hand in hers. She stroked my sweating brow.

'I've seen babies born…' she whispered, '… in the orphanage. Sometimes girls would come in. Girls in trouble…' I turned to her in surprise but felt relief at her words. I never would have thought she knew anything about childbirth. 'It will be all right, you'll see,' she went on. 'You'll need to grip my hand when the pain comes and breathe steady. The baby will soon be here, I can tell. Here, I'll get some more straw to make you more comfortable. I'll be back in a moment.'

She moved away from me and, as another contraction gripped my body, I immediately missed her presence. I needed her there beside me. But she was soon back with some more straw to put under my knees, and she held my hand again through the shuddering pain, whispering soothing words, stroking my back, giving me strength.

The pains were reaching a crescendo a while later when Elsie appeared in the doorway, carrying a blanket, some rags and a bucket of water.

'Dad sent me,' she said simply. I was too absorbed coping with the pain to wonder why he'd sent her down to the stable, instead of leaving me there to give birth with only Joan by my side.

Elsie knelt down on the floor beside me, spread the sheet over the straw and helped me onto it. The pains were so strong and so frequent now that I knew instinctively that the baby would be coming soon. And when it did finally come, a pressing, bursting feeling between my legs, I held Joan's hands so fiercely that she cried out in pain herself.

Instinctively, I pushed down, yelling like an animal. The pain was immense and seemed endless, but at last, after one huge, shuddering push, it was over. Elsie picked up the slippery, wriggling creature streaked with blood. She held it up to inspect it, patting its back until it started yelling.

'It's a boy,' she announced.

I sat back, exhausted, weeping with relief and exhaustion, and held out my hands to receive my son. And lying there, I felt an overwhelming rush of emotion, seeing that tiny creature that John and I had created from our love. I instantly felt a connection to him and through him, directly to John. I held him close to me and stared into his beady eyes. I decided to call him Edward, after Father.

I'd never witnessed any of Reeves's and Red's fierce, volatile arguments directly, but we'd heard plenty of them from the barn. I remembered how I'd seen the two of them punching each other after the exchange of horses once in the dead of night. For reasons I didn't yet understand, Reeves insisted on me and Edward staying in the house, and, over the coming weeks, the arguing intensified.

I was relieved that Reeves's attention wasn't on me and my son. I struggled to get my strength back and being inside helped me greatly, and I knew it was a safer place for my baby than the barn, but I had no idea why he was taking pity on me now. All the same it felt wonderful to be there in the shelter and relative comfort of the kitchen, snuggled up with my newborn. I'd had no idea how I'd react to motherhood, but it just came naturally to me, those overwhelming feelings of warmth and love for my baby.

The first night I was there, I heard Reeves sitting down at the table and pouring himself a large whisky.

'To our newborn,' he'd said.

I tried not to react to his words, but I was feeling more and more uneasy around him, feeling as though his behaviour was becoming odder. Was this how he always acted in the house? Why was he comfortable having me there, relishing the birth of my child? I'd have preferred to have gone to the threshing barn with the others, even if it was cold and uncomfortable, than to be here under Reeves's roof, where he ate and slept, under his direct control.

Elsie cooked me three meals a day and made me a regular supply of tea. She helped me bathe and change the baby. On the day after the birth, she gave me some baby clothes: a knitted blue baby suit and woollen jacket and booties. I looked at them in surprise.

'These are lovely, Elsie. Where did they come from?'

'Dad give 'em me,' she said, in her flat voice. 'They belonged to me little brothers.'

My scalp prickled in alarm. 'Little brothers?' I asked weakly.

She nodded.

'None of 'em lived beyond a couple of days. Mum 'ad four little boys altogether. Two older 'n me and two younger.'

'What happened to your mum?' I asked, already suspecting the answer.

'She died. Giving birth.'

'Another little boy?'

Elsie nodded. 'He died too,' she said in a matter-of fact voice. 'That was when I was four year old. I 'ardly remember me mum.'

'I'd prefer to go back to the barn,' I told her, suddenly fearful.

'He won't let you do that,' she said immediately.

My scalp prickled in alarm.

'Why ever not?'

''E thinks the baby needs to be up here in the warm.'

'Why does he care?'

Elsie fell silent and dropped her gaze to the floor.

And then Reeves came for Edward. 'You can start work again today, girl,' he said to me. 'Can't spare you no more. You should be ready for work again now.'

I stared at him. 'But what about the baby?' I asked.

'No need to trouble yerself about 'im. Elsie can look after 'im now. She'll take good care of 'im.'

'But… but what about his milk?' I stuttered, dread descending on me as I realised what this meant.

'We've got bottles and teats, 'e can take cow's milk from now on.'

'But… but… I'm his mother…'

Reeves got angry then; his face quickly became a violent red. ''E was born on my farm and it's up to me what 'appens to him now,' he said.

So, I went back to work that morning, taking up all the jobs I'd been doing before I was forced to leave Edward in the house. First, I worked in the stables, then the cowsheds, then out to the fields to weed between the lines of cabbage plants in the soaking rain, all the while thinking of him.

It tore my heart out to think that my baby was there, less than a hundred yards away from me, crying his heart out for his mother's touch. And I worried that one day he would eventually stop crying and forget all about me. I lay on my bunk at night, pining for him, wondering if he was comfortable; whether Elsie was gentle with him, showing him kindness, feeding him properly. I knew that there was no such thing as love in that violent, crazy household, and sometimes in the dead of night when my mind was going into overdrive, I even feared for his life. I approached the house many times, trying to reach him. I tried to reason with Elsie, with Red or Reeves, but no one would listen.

The months wore on, and gradually the months melded into years. I went through the days of my dreary, backbreaking routine hardly noticing the passing of time. My constant focus was the house. I wondered how my baby might be faring up there, looking out for any opportunity to go to him, but those opportunities never came. Every morning I saw Elsie walk out with the pram, up the drive and out onto the lane. How I wished that it was me pushing my baby, smiling into his eyes, singing him nursery rhymes. In my sadness, I neglected myself, growing thinner and thinner all the time, retreating further and further into my shell. Red ignored me now. He'd got what he wanted; he'd beaten me down into a defeated, submissive shadow of my former self. I no longer presented any threat to him or to anyone.

It felt strange as I walked down that dark track alone one night towards the big barn, into the mist, trying to decide what to do. I carried the bucket for the chickens. I felt unsteady and a little afraid as I took each step. I kept looking back, checking to see anyone was following me. And as they focused more and more on protecting the house, using the dogs to guard it, I realised that while in the past it would have been possible to escape, into the fields that surrounded the farm, I could never do that now. I looked back at the farmhouse, shabby and neglected, knowing that my little boy was inside. Despite everything, I knew I was bound to that desolate place.

I let myself into the barn and glanced at the bale of straw that Peggy and I used to sit on as we watched the hens, talking about home. Just the sight of it brought tears to my eyes.

And then I heard a sound that made me freeze.

The hair stood up on the back of my neck. It sounded as though there was someone else in the barn. Was my mind playing tricks on me again, imagining Peggy was here when I knew very well she wasn't? I stood stock-still for a few seconds, straining my ears, and there it was again.

'Hey!' A whisper was coming from upstairs in the hayloft. I turned and listened.

'Don't be scared. I'm not going to hurt you.'

I turned round and walked slowly to the base of the ladder, my heart pounding. When I reached the bottom, I shone the torch upwards into the void.

'I'm up here.'

Hesitantly, I walked up the first two rungs of the ladder and stopped, shining the torch upwards, peering into the gloom.

Then I saw him. Caught in the spotlight, a boy's face. He was not much older than me. His face was pinched and thin, streaked with dirt and framed with a mop of filthy dark hair. I frowned and peered, unable to believe what my eyes were telling me. The face had changed, but I would never forget those dark eyes. He was kneeling at the top of the ladder, looking down intensely into my eyes. He held his a finger up to his lips.

Chapter Twenty-One

Helen

Helen had read some of Daisy's letters to her mother, and the first part of Daisy's journal. She'd read part of it on the train home from Harrow, and part of it when she got home that night. She was intrigued and appalled at what she was discovering about Black Moor Farm and what had happened to her mother and her sister there.

Although she'd tried before, she did some more internet searching for Black Moor Farm. There was very little about it at first, but then she put the name into an ancestry-tracing website. To her surprise, it came up with an entry in the Register of Births.

County of Devon, Register of Births and Deaths; District of North Brent.

Name: Joe Edward Reeves; Place of Birth: Black Moor Farm; Date: June 11th 1942; Father Robert Jones, Farm Labourer, Mother Elsie Freda Reeves, spinster.

She stared at the entry and chills coursed through her. Did Elsie and Red have a baby together, or did they register Daisy's baby as their own? Why did they call him Joe, if so? Would Farmer Reeves have insisted on that? If that was the case, and she thought that was probably what had happened, she was looking at the registration of her own older brother on the screen. It looked strange, seeing it there in an official register in black and white. This gave credence to what she'd been reading in Daisy's diary and letters, which at times had felt almost unreal and hard to believe. But here was evidence of what had gone on, as plain as day.

Inspired by that, she tried more searches of Black Moor Farm, but drew a blank. She decided to expand the search to cover North Brent. She found a local history site covering Dartmoor and its villages. She scrolled through the entries for the war years. There were a few columns describing bombs being dropped on parts of the moor and another that described how a German plane had crashed after a bombing raid on Plymouth.

> *The pilot was still alive in the cockpit, although badly burned. He was rescued by local firefighters and taken to hospital in Plymouth to recover. On discharge, he will be detained as a Prisoner of War.*

Helen thought of the air crash that Daisy had described in her journal, how her mother and the others on the farm had watched the fire from afar and how it had brought it home to her that the war was raging on, despite the fact that she was a prisoner on that remote farm. Helen wondered if it was the same incident as the one described here and, again, reading about it here made Daisy's journal entries all the more real and believable.

She carried on scrolling down the news items, and stumbled upon one that made her breathe a sharp intake of breath:

> *7th September 1944: North Brent Constabulary. Today was sad to report that Constable Frank Baines was found dead in the station in North Brent this morning. It is believed that Constable Baines took his own life and that there was no other party involved. Constable Baines is a sad loss to the force*

and the community. He had been a policeman for twenty-five
years, the last five of which he served at North Brent.

Constable Baines. That was the policeman Daisy had written about, who had refused to help her and Peggy and instead had taken them back to the farm and to Reeves. He was clearly corrupt, and facilitating Reeves's criminal activities, but what had led him to take his life like that, not so many months after the incident Daisy had described? Perhaps he'd realised, after the fire, that his activities would have been exposed.

Shaking her head, she carried on through the archives of the North Brent local history society, trying to find anything else relevant to her mother's story, but drew a blank.

Looking back at the early pages of her mother's journal, thinking about how Reeves was using children and teenagers as slaves on his farm to boost his contribution to the war effort and thereby his profits, Helen began to wonder if this was an isolated incident, or if it had happened elsewhere during the war.

She fetched herself a coffee and settled down in front of the computer to do some further research. After a few false starts, she learned that the experience of evacuee children during the Second World War was not always happy; some suffered at the hands of 'cruel or indifferent hosts'. Although many children enjoyed their experiences in the countryside immensely, others were homesick and longed for their families. There was even mention of some being exploited by their hosts; either they were made to work on the land, or had their ration books taken from them and the food that should have been theirs went to the host family.

She did some reading up on agriculture during the war, hoping that it would give her more of an insight into Reeves's operation. In the process she stumbled upon an article describing how the war effort, and the blockade of the Atlantic, meant that British farmers had to plough up what had formerly been grassland to produce vegetables and livestock in an attempt to make Britain self-sufficient in food.

As well as this push to produce more food, more and more young, fit farm workers signed up to join the military. Farmers became reliant on volunteers and the Women's Land Army, although in the early years of the war membership wasn't huge and didn't extend to all parts of the country. Child evacuees were often relied on to help with the harvest; the Ministry of Agriculture even resorted to setting up Agriculture Harvest Camps for both children and adults to ensure sufficient workforce was available. Children were relied upon throughout the war, it seemed, as a source of cheap labour.

It had been common for local schools to supply schoolchildren to help with the harvest even before the war, so it wasn't considered unusual at all at that time for children to work on the land. Helen's heart broke to think of this. It wasn't unknown for children to go on strike during the harvest in protest at not being given any breaks during the day, and she imagined just how easy it would be for someone terrible to exploit these children. Legislation was even passed to enable children to be absent from school during term-time to labour on farms.

Helen thought about Reeves. He was an unscrupulous, selfish man, who had no compunction about exploiting others for his own ends. It wasn't surprising, she thought, if children were commonly used as cheap farm labour, for Reeves to go one step further and secure his own source of free labour. He'd got away with it because of the remoteness of his farm and because he'd managed to get the police and probably other officials in his pocket.

Helen turned back to the journal to read the final pages. What she'd discovered in her research had helped her to understand how Daisy and Peggy had come to be exploited alongside the other orphans, but she was still puzzled about the birth certificate. She opened the next page of the journal and read on.

Chapter Twenty-Two

Daisy

My mouth dropped open. I was frozen to the spot.

'Daisy,' he whispered. 'It's me.'

I looked up at him, speechless, my heart bursting with emotion as I took in his appearance. He was dressed in a uniform: dark blue, worn and shabby; the knees on the trousers were shiny and thin, his boots scuffed and without laces.

'I came back for you,' he said.

I tried to swallow but my throat was dry. I couldn't answer. No words would come. It was the shock of seeing him there, when I'd seen him die, had been mourning his death for such a long time.

'Is it really you?' I finally managed to say.

'Of course. Of course it's me.'

As I stood there, our eyes locked together and it felt as though time had stopped. The moment seemed to expand until it seemed as if I'd been standing on the top of that ladder shining the torch up into John's face for an age. I was drinking in his expression. The openness and honesty in his gaze that kept me hovering there. I recalled how it spoke directly to my heart.

There was something about his voice that had taken me by surprise too. I'd grown so used to aggression and brutality that it was strange to be spoken to gently again. I peered into his eyes and hesitated, unsure how to react.

'Come up here,' he said, breaking the silence.

Slowly, hesitantly, I climbed up beside him and he took me in his arms. We held each other for a long time, clinging to each other, sobbing wordlessly. I couldn't believe that this was for real, that I wasn't dreaming.

Finally, we broke apart.

'I thought you were dead,' I said, looking into his eyes, tracing his face with my fingertip. 'What happened? We all thought you were dead… I saw your body going past on the horse.'

I shook my head dumbly, and as if from nowhere, tears suddenly filled my eyes.

'Hey, please don't cry,' he said. 'I'm back now.'

'I thought you were dead,' I repeated, shaking my head in wonder. 'I can't believe it. I've been so…'

He put his fingers on my lips to hush me, and held me close again.

'What on earth happened that day? And where have you been?'

'In the navy,' he said. 'At war. That's why I couldn't come back.'

I stared at him, remembering what PC Baines had said to me about John… '*He's alive and well, and back in Plymouth…*'

So, it was true; but how could I have distinguished that truth from all the lies I'd been told that night?

'John,' I began, my voice breaking, 'there's something I need to…' I spoke with trepidation, wondering how he would react when I told him that I'd borne his baby, but that I'd allowed Reeves to take him from me. How could I find the words to tell him that devastating news? 'What happened that day when Reeves shot you?' I asked instead. 'I was sure you were dead. I thought they were taking you away to… to hide your body. I was convinced of it. We all thought you were dead.'

'I nearly did die,' he said. 'I must have been unconscious for days. When I woke up, at first, I couldn't understand where I was. It turned out I was in a cell at the police station. The policeman had been looking after me, giving me food and water, making sure I stayed alive. The bullet grazed past me. Even so, I was wounded and there was a lot of blood. He'd bandaged me up, and even though I'd lost a lot of blood and was weak, I managed to pull through.

'I don't know how long I was there, weeks maybe, but he kept me locked in that cell. When I got stronger, he said that he'd arranged for me to sign up for the navy. He said he had close links to some regiment in Plymouth. It was wrong; I was only seventeen and too young to sign up. He knew that. I tried to tell him about Joseph Reeves and what was happening at the farm, but he just shook his head and laughed at me. He said Farmer Reeves was an honest man, doing his best for his farm and workers and doing great things to help feed the nation during the war. I asked him if that was the case, if Reeves was such a great man, how come he had tried to kill me, but he said he was just trying to stop me leaving, for my own good. None of it made any sense. I knew the man was a criminal, just like Reeves.

'He said he would keep me locked up until I agreed to sign up for the navy, and that I wasn't to breathe a word about Reeves and the farm to a soul, or he'd see to it that I never made it home, and he'd make sure all you others on the farm suffered too.

'So, a few days later, he took me down to Plymouth in his police car and the next thing I knew, I was in the naval base in some office, signing my life away. I was given a medical and put in a bunkhouse in some barracks with a load of other lads in the naval dockyard, and the next day we started training to go to war. Oh, and they took this picture of me.' He reached into his pocket and fished out a small portrait of him in full sailor's uniform. His face looked thin and pinched, and he stared straight at the camera with a defiant gaze. The inscription underneath read, '*Ordinary Seaman J. Smith*'.

He handed it to me. 'You can keep it, if you like,' he said.

I took it and hid it deep in my pocket.

'I'll treasure it,' I said.

'I was desperate with worry about you and the others. I tried to tell a couple of the lads about the farm, but I don't think they really believed me, or maybe they just didn't want to know. Their minds were on the war, going to sea and fighting, and what we were about to face. I didn't dare say anything to the officers.'

He fell silent suddenly and dropped his gaze. There was a long pause and I thought about Red. I'd been so absorbed, I'd almost forgotten where I was, and that I was risking everything by being here too long.

'Go on,' I said.

'Well, before I knew it we were out at sea on naval exercises, accompanying ships in the Atlantic, bringing supplies from America. I was a gunner, so I was trained for action, but we were lucky those months, didn't see much fighting. A few close shaves with German U-boats. We saw a couple of other ships in our convoys being sunk. It was all from a distance, but it could have been us. That brought it home to me. All I could think about those months was getting back to you and the farm, Daisy. But then, in the summer, our ship was called back into port. It was obvious there was something big being planned. And before we knew it, we were sailing for France in another convoy. Only this time it was for real. We were going to invade France at Dieppe—' Again, he stopped and looked away. 'It was hell on earth, Daisy.'

'Dieppe?'

'Our ship was meant to be giving cover to Canadian troops landing on the beaches at Dieppe. But when we reached the harbour, word was going round the crew that the raid was a disaster. And then, all of a sudden, the ship was being bombed by German aircraft. They came out of nowhere, strafing the deck with machine-gun fire. We were out on deck, ready for a fight and sitting targets. All the lads I'd made friends with during training were slaughtered around me. Every single one. I was the only one to survive.'

I gasped, appalled.

'Then the ship went down and it was chaos,' he went on. 'There were no lifeboats anywhere to be seen so I just swam for it, but all around me the water was on fire. The oil tanks had been hit and the oil was burning on the surface. I dived under the water, to avoid the flames, but I came up in the middle of it. My lungs were bursting and I had to take a breath. I must have breathed in some of the burning fuel because then my lungs were on fire and I could hardly breathe at all. But I had to keep going. I kept on swimming for hours, even though every breath was agony and my body wanted to give up at every stroke. It was freezing cold too. Eventually a fishing boat came up beside me and hauled me on board and took me back to Portsmouth. I can hardly remember the next few months. I was taken to hospital and almost died – I was there a long time. Only thoughts of you kept me from giving up.'

I reached out and took his hand. He grasped mine tight, like a lifeline. I felt the power of his pain in that grip.

'I was sent back into training, but after a while it was clear I couldn't keep up. I was signed off sick and discharged from the base. The medical officer told me to rest up and report back each month but when I left the base, I knew what I had to do. I knew I needed to get back here to you. Back to the farm to help you get away.'

I stared into his eyes, trying to imagine what he must have gone through. Suddenly the desperate look in his eyes was beginning to make sense. My heart went out to him and I put my arms round him and held him close.

He sat back on his heels and his face was suddenly serious, his eyes full of pain.

'I'm… I'm a failure and a coward. I know that.'

His distress was so sudden and so intense that it frightened me. But at the same time, I felt the same powerful connection with him I'd felt before.

'Of course you're not. How can you say that?' I whispered. 'You're incredibly brave. Look what you've been through. And you survived.'

He looked at me then, frowning, his eyes boring into mine. 'I don't expect you to understand. Look at me. Here I am, safe and sound, when so many are dead. They died in the line of duty, and I can't even get back out there and fight for what they died for.'

I held his hand tightly and looked deep into his eyes; those eyes that I loved, that I'd longed to see again in all those desperate months.

'It's not your fault,' I said. 'It's not your fault that you survived and the others didn't. And it's not your fault you were injured either.'

He shook his head helplessly.

'How long ago were you signed off?'

'Not long. Ten days, maybe a fortnight. I've lost track. I had hardly any money, or anywhere to go, so I had to walk across the moor. I've been hiding out in barns and outhouses, trying to get back here without being noticed.'

'So, have you been hiding up here in the barn for two days?'

He shook his head. 'Not up here, no. There's an empty house through the wood on top of the hill. Huge place it is, all boarded up. Black Moor Hall. I saw the name on the gate. It's deserted, so I figured it was safer to camp out up there than right under Reeves's nose. I came down here and hid up here on the off-chance that you and Peggy would still be feeding the chickens every evening.'

'Peggy died, John,' I said. 'She fell ill. It was my fault…'

'I'm so sorry,' he said. This time it was his turn to comfort me. He put his hand out and touched my cheek, brushing away the tears. He didn't tell me not to cry, or ask for an explanation. He just stood there, his eyes on my face, waiting patiently for my crying to stop.

'How can you think it was your fault?' he said at last. 'It was Reeves. He's the one to blame.'

I shook my head, 'No, it was my fault. If I hadn't tried to escape…'

'Why don't you sit down and tell me about it,' he said as my tears subsided.

Then the words came pouring from me. I told him about how we'd jumped from the barn and hidden in the back of Baines's car, how he'd questioned us and brought us back to the farm, and how Reeves had imprisoned us in the cold stable as a punishment. I cried as I told him, and he held me close as my body shuddered with sobs.

'It's not your fault,' he kept saying. 'Let's get out of here now then, shall we? We can make a run for it before they notice. Hide out at Black Moor Hall. I don't know how you got away tonight, why they haven't come to find you yet, but this is our chance, we might not have another.'

I took a deep breath. 'There's something else,' I said and, my head bowed, not daring to look him in the eye, I told him about our baby, about how Reeves had taken him from me. I took out a photograph I'd found among Elsie's things in the barn of Elsie holding him. When I'd found it, I couldn't resist keeping it. It was the one reminder I had of my precious Edward. With trembling hands, I held it out to John. He took it, staring at it, his eyes wide with amazement.

'He's beautiful,' he breathed.

'I'm so, so sorry, John,' I said, looking up anxiously into his eyes. Searching them for his reaction.

'Don't be sorry. Nothing's your fault… I don't know what to say,' he said at last. 'If only I'd known…'

'What difference would it have made?' I took the photograph back and hid it deep down in my pocket again.

'I don't know… I could have tried to come back sooner… Reeves…' He clenched his fists. 'He won't get away with this.'

'I'll have to go back now,' I said, suddenly remembering how long I'd been away.

'Don't go yet. Let's think about this for a minute… Look, is there any way you could get Edward out of there?'

I shook my head. 'I'm not even allowed to see him.'

'Do they ever take him outside?'

'Elsie takes him for walks in the push chair. She must go out on the lane. She might even take him to North Brent to see her friend. I've seen her pushing him up the track. But if I followed her out there, I'd be spotted.'

'So that's when I'll get him, then? If you come with me now, we can come back and get him together once you're free.'

I was suddenly besieged by nerves, of fear of what we were planning. It all felt so quick, so rushed; how would we manage it, after all the failed attempts, the beatings, everything that had happened before?

'But what about the others?' I said, remembering Sally, Joan and Fred. 'We can't just leave them here.'

'When we get you out, we can go to the police and report what's going on here.'

'But that's not going to work. You've already said, the police are in on it too.'

'They can't all be, can they? Not everywhere. We can go somewhere else. To London, maybe?'

'We could try, but why would they believe us? London's too far away.'

'Look, Daisy, we can't get the others to come with us now. We'd never all make it. Getting you out and going to the police later is our best shot.'

Reluctantly, I agreed that he was probably right.

'Come on then,' he said, taking my hand.

'No! Not yet. I need to go back and get Peggy's bag. There are letters in there from Mother. Photographs. I can't leave them behind. They're all I've got left of them.'

He stared at me for a long moment. I realised then that he had nothing left of his family, and that he might not understand, but finally he said: 'So, let's do it tomorrow evening. Come down here to feed the chickens as usual. Is there any way of distracting Red to make sure he's busy for a while?'

I fell silent, trying to think of something.

'I might be able to, but what about Wolf?'

'I'll catch a rabbit and skin it so we have some meat for the dog to distract him if he follows you. Then we can slip away and hide in Black Moor Hall until tomorrow. It'll take them a while to notice you've gone and they won't want to search until the morning. Then tomorrow morning, when Elsie takes the baby out, we can be waiting in the woods. I'll get her talking – she won't recognise me at first – and you can grab the baby.'

'It sounds so simple when you say it,' I said, nerves churning my stomach again. 'But you know them, John. They're just not going to let the baby go that easily.'

'Daisy, we must do this. We need to be together as a family now. It's amazing what you've done all by yourself. You brought our baby into the world. I'm desperate to meet him. That's why we've got to try.'

'It won't be easy though,' I persisted.

He grabbed me by my shoulders and put his face up close to mine. 'You've got to stop thinking like this or you'll never get out of here,' he said, his eyes fierce. 'We've got to try it, Daisy. It's our only hope.'

Chapter Twenty-Three

Daisy

That night, I barely slept. I lay awake staring at the cobwebs above my bunk, worrying about what I'd agreed to and what that day would bring. The plan had been so hastily hatched, I knew it could easily fail and that within twenty-four hours I could either have been severely beaten again, locked up in the freezing stable, or perhaps even shot dead. I sweated all over at the thought of it.

In the morning, I went through my usual chores, unable to keep my mind on the tasks. As Joan and I worked side by side in the cowshed, I tried to speak to her, to let her know what I was planning. I wanted to tell her that if I got away, I would be doing my best to get her and the others out of there, but when I started to speak, she looked at me with fear in her eyes, held a finger to her lips and said, 'Don't talk like that, Daisy. Please. I don't want no trouble.'

'But don't you want to get out of this place?'

She shrugged and turned to me with a look of shame in her eyes.

'Not sure what I'd do out there,' she admitted. 'And I don't want to get shot, neither. Look at what happened to John.'

'But John's alive,' I said in a hoarse whisper, looking around to make sure no one else could hear. Joan frowned and looked at me with disbelief.

'It's him who's helping me,' I said. 'He came back to help us get away from here.'

"'E can't be. We saw 'im with our own eyes. 'E was dead.'

I tried to convince her, but she just didn't believe me. It was almost as if she didn't want to believe it, or even to be helped at all. In the end I stopped trying.

'Please, just tell Sally and Fred that if I get out of here alive, we'll make sure you all get out too,' I said.

After the day's work in the fields, the time arrived for me to go down to feed the chickens. I looked around the gloomy barn that had been my prison for so long, at the others sitting silently round the table waiting for their food, just like they would any other evening. As I glanced up at the bunk that I'd shared with Peggy, I felt an inexplicable pang of regret at leaving it behind. There was her gas mask case on top of the bunk. It contained Mother's letters, Peggy's medicine bottle and our only book. I knew it was crazy to even think of taking the case with me, but it was only small, I thought, and it represented my only remaining connection with Peggy. I couldn't help myself; I just couldn't leave without those mementos of my family. I quickly grabbed it from the top bunk, stuffed a spare pair of trousers and a sweater into it, then slipped it in the gap behind Red's bunk beside the door of the threshing barn.

I went out into the yard, trembling in the knowledge of what I was about to do. I'd managed to devise a way of making sure Red and Reeves would be distracted for some time, but the thought of executing it made me go hot and cold with fear of what might happen if it went wrong. I went to fetch the bucket of scraps for the chickens, then I returned to the yard and, looking around to make sure no one was watching, went to the stable, where the latest group of ponies was being kept. They'd arrived the previous night, a day after the lorry had taken the previous batch away. I'd heard a commotion in the middle of the night and peered out of the window to see Red bringing them in from the moor, ropes round their necks, the sheepdogs snapping at their heels.

Slowly, so as not to make a sound, I pulled back the bolt on the stable door. Then I made clicking sounds with my tongue to attract the ponies' attention. One of them looked up, startled, and started moving over towards the open door. I hurried back to the threshing barn. I could already hear their unshod hooves trotting across the stable yard as I grabbed the gas mask bag. Then, chicken bucket in one hand and gas mask bag over one shoulder, I set off down the track to the big barn, my heart pounding fit to burst.

I had almost reached it when I heard shouting from the stable yard; Reeves's voice cursing and swearing, yelling at Red, the dogs barking too. I couldn't make out Reeves's words, but I smiled to myself, knowing that soon the two of them would be fighting, as they had so many times before over the ponies. I knew that Reeves would be blaming Red for them escaping. He'd be unleashing the full force of his ugly temper on him.

I lifted the latch of the chicken barn and went inside. The chickens surrounded me as usual. I emptied the bucket of scraps hastily onto the floor, then ran to the bottom of the steps.

'John?'

'I'm here,' came his voice immediately. 'Did the dog follow you?'

'I don't think so. They're all up in the farmyard.'

'Come on then. Let's go. Climb up here and we can jump out of one of the doors on this floor.'

I paused, my heart sinking. 'No. We can't do that. We'll have to go out of the front. They sealed the doors up when Peggy and I jumped out up there.'

'It's all right. I noticed that. I've already taken the nails out and opened it up. Come on up. Hurry!'

I clambered up the ladder.

'What have you got there?' he asked, frowning.

'It's Peggy's bag. I had to bring it.'

He didn't argue, just kissed me quickly on the lips and took it from me. I noticed a cloth bag slung over his back, blood oozing from it onto his jacket.

'That's the rabbit. In case the dog comes. If 'e doesn't, we can eat it ourselves later on.'

He'd already opened one of the doors. It was the one Peggy and I had jumped from, and I paused; but there was no time to waste looking back to that day, so I put it out of my mind and focused on what I had to do.

'You go first,' said John. 'Then I'll chuck the bag out.'

I only hesitated for a second before I leapt out, landing as before on the bank of the stream, sprawling on the short grass. I turned to look up, just as the bag came hurtling towards me. Then John landed with a thump on the bank next to me.

'Come on,' he said getting up, 'we've got to move quickly.'

I gave him the torch and followed him downstream, away from the barn, away from the farmyard. As I stumbled along behind him, I kept thinking I could hear snatches of angry shouting from the direction of the stable yard, but I tried to put Red and Reeves out of my mind, sure it was each other they were focusing on. They wouldn't be thinking about me – surely we were safe?

I followed John downhill along the length of a dry-stone wall that bordered several fields. It was heavy going, the ground rough and rocky. I kept slipping on the wet grass, tripping on rocks. I was soon out of breath, but that didn't matter. I pushed myself on, determined to keep up with John.

But we hadn't gone far before he stopped, leaned against the wall and doubled over, gasping for breath. I ran to him and put my arms round his shoulders. I could feel his body shake as he struggled to take in air, his lungs rasping. Instinctively, I held him close, trying to calm him, stroking his back, speaking gently to him. Gradually, his gasps eased and he started to take normal breaths. After a few moments he turned to me.

'I'm sorry,' he said. 'That happens sometimes.'

'Let's go more slowly,' I said.

'We're going in the wrong direction for Black Moor Hall,' he said. 'But once we reach the wood we can double back and start climbing up to the big house.'

'Is it far?' I asked.

'Not too far,' he said. 'Come on, we should get going again.'

We set off again, more slowly this time, walking side by side. I slipped my arm through his and helped him along.

As we neared the point where the fields met the pinewood, we heard a series of sudden bangs from the direction of the farmhouse.

We stopped and exchanged alarmed looks.

'What the hell was that?' asked John, but we both knew what it was. It was the sound of shots being fired from a rifle. I shuddered, wondering what or who had been shot. Perhaps one of the ponies had injured itself as Red and Reeves tried to catch it? I felt a pang of guilt at the thought that an innocent animal might be suffering because of my actions. I hoped against hope that it wasn't a pony who'd been shot, and that instead it was either of the two men.

We climbed over the wall and started uphill through the pinewood. It had rained that day, and there was no path to walk on. We had to push our way through the undergrowth, the dripping ferns and bracken, the brambles and nettles. Soon, I was wet through and shivering. But I hardly noticed that, I was so focused on keeping up with John in the meagre light of the torch, and on the fear that Reeves or Red might notice I'd gone and already be coming after us with the dogs.

It took us half an hour or so to climb the hill through the wood. There was a fence on the other side, which we ducked under. Then we were walking through a boggy field of high grass, our shoes sticking in the mud, the wet grass soaking our thighs through to the skin.

At last we came to a gate in a hedge. John stopped and leaned on the gate, his breath making clouds in the torchlight.

'There it is,' he said, shining the torch at a building up ahead, brooding and enormous. It was difficult to see it properly in the dim torchlight, but I could just make out black stone walls, three floors of boarded windows and a gabled roof.

I exchanged glances with him. It didn't look at all welcoming.

'Who does it belong to?' I asked.

He shrugged. 'What does it matter? They can't care about it or it wouldn't be like that. Come on. Let's go inside.'

We climbed the gate and crossed the overgrown lawn to the house. John had broken one of the locks on a back door and I followed him into a dark passage.

'Come on through,' he said and I followed him along the echoing passage, across a galleried hallway and into a vast room with huge bay windows.

'This is where I've been kipping,' John said, casting the torch around the room. I saw some faded red curtains laid out in front of the fireplace. 'I took those down from the windows,' he explained. 'I'll make a fire. I collected some logs from the wood. They're a bit wet, but once they get going, it gets quite warm in here. And we can cook the rabbit if it gets hot enough.'

He put the bags on the floor and started to pile sticks onto the fireplace.

'Take your wet things off and wrap yourself in one of the curtains. You'll soon warm up.'

I did as he suggested and watched as he lit the sticks and kindled the flames. A tiny glow soon grew and spread, and soon the logs were roaring in the grate. Shivering, I crept closer to the fire and warmed my hands. John put his arms round me.

'Thank you,' I whispered. 'For getting me away from there.'

He didn't reply, just hugged me tighter, and we sat there silently, feeling the warmth and closeness of each other, just staring into the flames for a long time. It wasn't over yet. Not by any means. All I could think of was Edward, our beautiful baby boy. I knew that getting him away from Elsie wouldn't be easy, and it involved going back up the lane that led past the entrance to Black Moor Farm. I was terrified of doing that, and terrified too that something would go wrong. What if I lost John for ever?

That night, after we'd cooked the rabbit over the flames of the fire and eaten some of its dense, rich flesh, we lay down together on the floor, wrapped ourselves in the red curtains and, our bodies moulded around each other for warmth, finally fell asleep in the flickering, dancing firelight, my thoughts, as always, on Edward.

In the morning I awoke with a start, wondering where I was. But when I sat up, rubbing my eyes, there was John crouching in front of me, relighting the fire. The room was dark apart from the shafts of dusty sunlight penetrating cracks in the boarded-up windows. He turned and smiled at me and I remembered what had happened the day before, and what we were about to do.

There was no need to speak much, and anyway, we were both far too nervous for conversation. We dressed quickly in our still-damp clothes, then crept back through the great house, down the echoing passageways, and stepped out of the back door into the weak morning sunlight.

We walked quickly down the overgrown drive, leaving the brooding mass of Black Moor Hall behind us. The boggy track wound through some woods and petered out at a metal gate obscured by brambles and ferns. John climbed it first and jumped down on the other side, and I followed, brambles snagging my legs, the thorns piercing my skin. We crossed a rotting wooden bridge that spanned a stream and found ourselves on the metalled lane that ran between high Devon banks, shaded by evergreens. I hesitated for a second, remembering how we'd been driven down this lane by Charlie, the false billeting officer, and again by Frank Baines the night Peggy and I had escaped.

'What if someone comes?' I asked, suddenly nervous.

'We'll be able to hear an engine from miles away. We'll have time to hide in the trees.'

'What if it's a bike, or someone on foot—'

John stopped walking, turned to me and took my face in his hands. He looked deep into my eyes.

'There are risks, Daisy. We know there are. But we've got to do this, haven't we? If we see someone on a bike or walking, we can get into the trees too. Or we could just say hello. Tough it out.'

'You're right,' I said. 'Sorry… I'm just worried, that's all.'

He took my hand in his and we walked side by side up the lane. It was the first time I'd been free for more than four years, but I didn't feel any different inside. I was still that terrified, beaten girl who'd lost her spirit, and, as long as my baby was still a prisoner in that house with Reeves, I knew I wouldn't experience any joy. All I could feel as we walked was fear of what might happen when Elsie appeared with the pram.

It was a mile or so before we caught sight of the dilapidated farm gate up ahead. We finally reached it and drew level with it. My nerves were taut as we walked past, the thought of the farm and everything that had happened there striking such terror and panic into me. I gripped John's hand fiercely as we walked a little further up the hill. We stopped fifty yards or so from the gate and he said, 'Let's get up into the woods here and wait for her to come.'

So, we clambered up the bank and into the trees, and found a mossy log to sit on.

It was a long wait and we hardly spoke as we sat there on that damp log, the wetness seeping through to my thighs and into my bones. I fixed my eyes on the gateway to Black Moor Farm until my vision was blurred and my head was aching, but I didn't want to take them away from that spot for a second in case I missed Elsie when she appeared with the pram.

'What if she doesn't come?' John asked after a while.

'She will come,' I said vehemently, wishing he hadn't given voice to the niggling doubt at the back of my own mind. 'She always takes him out for a walk. Every morning at ten o'clock, it's her routine.'

'Maybe she went early today and we missed her. We're only guessing what the time is, after all.'

'Please, don't…' I said, angry tears springing to my eyes.

I felt his arm round my shoulders. 'Don't worry, Daisy. If she doesn't come, we'll find another way.'

But, at last, she did come. First, we heard the squeak of the push-chair wheels on the track, then finally, the push-chair appeared with Elsie plodding behind it, bending her head with the weight of it, her plump face red with the effort.

We watched, holding our breath as she pushed it through the gate, over the little bridge and onto the lane. She stopped and straightened up, pausing for breath. Then she leaned forward to speak to the little boy, her voice crooning and high. I leaned forward, desperate to catch a glimpse of him.

'Are you ready?' John whispered. 'I'll go and get 'er talking, then when I grab her, you come down and push the pram away. You'll have to be quick, she's strong.'

I nodded and watched him walk quickly down through the trees and scramble down the bank. I followed him forward quietly, my heart thumping, and came to a halt behind a tree at the top of the bank.

Elsie looked up, startled, as John scrambled down the bank and stood in front of her on the lane, dusting down his clothes.

'Hello there,' I heard him say. 'Am I glad I ran into you! I'm completely lost. I don't suppose you know the way to North Brent, do you?' he asked, in a casual voice.

Elsie was immediately suspicious. 'You made me jump! What were you doing in the wood?'

'Like I say, I got lost. I've walked from the other side of Princetown—'

'Princetown? From the prison?'

''Course not. I've been working on a farm over there… Lost me job.'

I held my breath, waiting for John to grab Elsie as we'd planned so I could jump down and whisk the pram away.

'But you've got sailor's uniform on. Why aren't you out there, fighting for the country? Strong-looking lad like you?'

John took a step closer to her. *Why don't you just grab her?* I kept thinking, poised to run forward. *What if she recognises you?*

''Ere… don't I know you?' Elsie said suddenly. John lunged then and grabbed her arms. I was about to rush forward when suddenly all hell broke loose. Elsie let out a squeal and started yelling: 'Dad! Dad! Help me. Please. I'm being attacked!'

A shot rang out from the opposite direction and I took a step back and hid between the trees. Farmer Reeves stood in the farm gateway, rifle to his shoulder.

'Leave 'er alone, yer bastard!' he shouted, limping forward.

John let Elsie go.

'You'll regret this. I've come for the little boy,' John yelled back at him and Reeves stopped short and took a step back. 'You've got no right to keep him and if you don't give him up, I'll come back with the police,' John shouted.

Reeves came to life then and fired another shot at John. John started running down the lane, back in the direction of Black Moor Hall. For a split second I wondered why he hadn't come back to me in the woods, then I realised and was grateful. He didn't want to lead Reeves to me. Reeves stood in the lane, swearing and yelling abuse and firing the gun in John's direction. Shot after shot rang out. He carried on shooting until John had disappeared round the next bend. All the time Elsie screamed hysterically, then the baby started up too.

I stood there, paralysed with shock, frozen to the spot behind the tree, my mouth dry, my heart beating so fast, I felt vomit rise in my throat.

When Reeves stopped firing, he went back up to Elsie, his face purple with anger.

'What were you doing, talking to that navy lad, eh? That were that farm boy. Nothing but trouble 'e was.'

'Nothing, Dad. 'E said 'e was lost.'

'Didn't I tell you? Don't talk to no one. Who knows what 'e might do, lad like that, in uniform.'

'I'm sorry, Dad,' Elsie sobbed.

'We're gonna 'ave the police onto us because of you,' he said roughly. 'All these years, I've kept them off my back, and now 'e's going to bring 'em 'ere. Baines should never 'ave saved his miserable life.'

'Oh, Dad…'

'Come on now, get back to the 'ouse,' he said. 'From now on, you're not going out of the farm with the little 'un.'

'But, Dad…'

'Too risky. What with that little bitch running away, and that lad poncing about the place in uniform. Anything might 'appen. Frank's been out looking for 'er and when he catches that little whore, she's gonna be sorry. Until then, we've got to be careful.'

He put his arm round her shoulders and they turned back towards the farm, pushing the push-chair away from me. I stood there watching them go, helplessness and desperation washing over me. Would I ever see my baby again, would I ever hold him in my arms and smell his sweet skin next to mine? I broke down behind that tree, sobbing uncontrollably.

Chapter Twenty-Four

Daisy

It took me a long time to find my way back to Black Moor Hall that morning, after our failed attempt to snatch the baby. I didn't dare go down onto the lane, which was the quickest route back. Instead I climbed up the hill a little way and made my way back through the forest, away from the road, terrified that PC Frank Baines would be out looking for me. Twice I heard the sound of a vehicle on the lane and hid behind a tree, trembling. The first time it was a farm truck, its engine clanking and straining as it struggled up the hill towards Dartmoor, but the second time my heart stood still when I saw that it was a black saloon car. When I heard the sound of the engine, I was convinced it was Baines's police car, but from where I was hiding, I only caught a glimpse of its sleek paintwork as it roared past, down the hill towards North Brent. After that I was even more careful to keep out of sight among the trees. Once I drew roughly parallel with the entrance to Black Moor Hall, I had to summon every ounce of my courage to scramble down the bank and dash across the lane to the entrance.

When I'd pushed my way through the brambles and climbed over the wrought-iron gate into the grounds of the big house, I caught sight of John waiting for me in the spinney. He came running towards me and took me in his arms.

'Thank God you're safe,' he said, holding me tight. 'I was terrified Reeves would see you.'

I found myself sobbing with relief, unable to speak as we clung to each other.

'I'm so sorry, Daisy,' he kept saying. 'I messed it up. I should have tried to grab Elsie much sooner. I was trying to get her trust, but it all went wrong.'

'There's nothing you could have done. Reeves must have decided to follow her with his gun. He'd have stopped us somehow anyway. It's lucky neither of us got shot.'

'When I mentioned the police, he looked as though I'd triggered something inside him, he looked so out of control,' John said.

We broke apart and walked back to the house in silence. Once inside, I told John what I'd overheard Reeves say. That Frank Baines was out looking for me, and that if he found me, they would probably kill me.

John took both my hands in his and looked into my eyes.

'We have to go to the police and tell them what's going on down there at the farm,' he said. I started shaking, thinking about Constable Baines, about how mistaken I had been to place my trust in him, about how he'd treated John.

'We can't go to North Brent,' I said. 'That's where Baines is.'

'I know. We'll go to Ivybridge instead. There's another police station down there. A bigger one. If we go now, we can be there by mid-afternoon.'

I hesitated, the memory of the traumatic experience in Baines's police car coming back to me.

'What if they're in on it too? Reeves's criminal activity?'

'It's probably just the people round here who're in on it,' he said.

'But you said yourself Baines had connections in the navy.'

'That's true,' he said, rubbing his chin, his eyes deep in thought. In the end he said, 'We'll have to take a chance, Daisy. Just like we did running away from the farm yesterday. Sometimes you have to do that. Let's go down there and decide once we're there. Look, I've got plans for getting us right away from here. Having a completely new start. A mate in the navy kept telling me about his brother, who works for a tea plantation in Darjeeling. I've got his address. They're always looking for young men to run them. They pay your passage and give you accommodation. Once the war is over, we could go. How about it, Daisy?'

I stared at him. It was difficult to think beyond today, getting Edward back, but the thought of the two of us stepping onto a ship with our son, leaving all this behind, was appealing all the same.

'Let's think about it once this is over,' I said.

'OK. So, come on. Let's get moving.'

'All right. I suppose there's no choice.'

I got to my feet, seized with a feeling of urgency, wanting to get it over with.

We shoved our few belongings into the gas mask bag, let ourselves out of the back door and set off across the moor. When we'd found our bearings, we followed an old cart track and headed west towards Ivybridge, a little town that John said was on the south side of Dartmoor. The walk took us many hours, sometimes on rough tracks or sheep paths, sometimes trudging across open moorland, climbing dry-stone walls, wading through bog and bracken, gorse thickets and woodland. We couldn't walk on the lanes, for fear of someone spotting us and telling Baines, and we couldn't go anywhere near North Brent for the same reason.

Despite the fear and panic with which we walked, it was wonderful to feel the wind in my hair and the cool air on my cheeks and to gaze out over the wide open countryside and the clear skies. I began to feel the first glimmerings of relief that I was away from the farm, away from Reeves and his madness, but of course that relief was tainted with the knowledge that Edward was still there and that Joan, Fred and Sally were still prisoners and slaves, at his mercy. But I strode beside John with a purpose. We were doing everything we could to get them out of there, even taking our chances that the Ivybridge police might be corrupt, just like Baines.

Midway through the afternoon, we reached the top of a craggy tor and stood there catching our breath, looking down at the patchwork of meadows beneath us and the little town of Ivybridge nestling in the valley, with its mill chimneys belching smoke and its rows of stone cottages. From where we stood, we could see the red-brick railway station clearly, and the railway track too, snaking along the valley beside a fast-flowing river.

We made our way down to the town and through the quiet streets. The police station was a single-storey stone building in the centre of the town, opposite a Victorian church. It was dark by the time we got there, but the lights were still on inside. We stood hand in hand on the pavement outside.

'What do you think?' John asked. My stomach was turning over with nerves, but something told me I had to trust the situation. We were far away from Black Moor Farm and this little town, with its feeling of bustle, its mills and railway station, felt connected to the outside world, unlike North Brent, insular and cut off as it was by miles of bleak moorland.

'Let's go in,' I said, my heart in my mouth, and arm in arm we went up the steps and entered the station.

Two hours later, we were sitting in the back of a police car behind two policemen as the car made its way through the winding lanes towards Black Moor Farm. It hadn't taken us long to persuade them to investigate the farm. If I'd been alone, I think I would have had a hard time convincing them that I was telling the truth, but they seemed ready to listen to John. I think the fact that he was in uniform had a lot to do with that.

The constable on the desk had a friendly face and an avuncular manner. He'd smiled when he noticed John's naval uniform and quickly put us at our ease. He showed us through to a bare little interview room at the back of the building.

John did most of the talking as it was obvious from the start that he had the most chance of being believed. The policeman listened to him attentively. He seemed very deferential towards him.

'We've come about a kidnapped baby and three orphans being kept on a farm on Dartmoor. They're being made to work against their will,' he began. The constable's eyebrows shot up, but he nodded and indicated for John to carry on. So, John told the whole story, from Charlie the fake billeting officer taking us all to the farm under false pretences, to the conditions we'd been forced to live and work in, the theft and trade in Dartmoor ponies, the beatings, the shooting, the death of Peggy and finally the way Reeves had stolen Edward.

The constable wrote it all down, sometimes shaking his head in wonder, sometimes asking John to repeat his words or to clarify something. I could tell by the way he kept glancing up at us as he wrote that he was finding it hard to believe everything John was saying. Especially when John told him about Constable Baines and how he'd returned me and Peggy to Black Moor Farm after we tried to run away. At that point he peered at me and asked, 'So why would a policeman have done a thing like that?'

I shrugged. 'I'm not quite sure, but I think he must be paid by Farmer Reeves to keep things quiet. John has mentioned the ponies. Reeves is obviously stealing them and selling them on for meat, passing it off as beef. Perhaps Frank Baines is taking bribes to keep that quiet. I don't know, but I do know that he's a bad man. And he's in with Farmer Reeves. For some reason he knew where Peggy and I came from and about our house in Harrow being bombed. He knew all about the orphans being kept as slaves on the farm too…'

The policeman raised his eyebrows and carried on writing. When we'd told him everything, he put down his pen and stared at me.

'How old are you, lassie?'

'Eighteen now.'

'And who was the father of your baby?'

'It was me,' John said quickly. 'Before I went away.'

I stared down at the table, my cheeks burning. I was ready to cry, tears of embarrassment and shame, but instead I took a deep breath and with a monumental effort managed to keep the tears at bay. At last it was over. We'd told him everything.

Now, as the car wound its way up through the woods towards the farm, the stout policeman turned to us and said, 'When we get there, you two stay in the back here, out of sight. We'll go into the house to speak to Farmer Reeves and see what he has to say. Don't show yourselves or things could get difficult.'

I gripped John's hand and glanced at him in the darkness, wondering what the trip to the farm would bring. Would we be leaving later on this evening with baby Edward in our arms? Would the policemen arrest Reeves, Red and Elsie and let the orphans go free? We sped on up the steep lane through the evergreen forest, beside the rushing brook.

'Here's the gate up ahead,' said John, leaning forward. The driver swung the car between the gateposts and drove on down the rutted, bumpy track towards the farm. My heart was racing now as the headlights lit up the pine trees and the piles of rusting machinery beside the track. Then we rounded the bend and there was the farmhouse in front of us in the hollow.

But as it came into view we all took a collective gasp and the car skidded to a halt. The sky in front of us was alive with fire; the house was blazing, in the midst of an inferno so huge, it was hard to make out the shape of the roof or the walls. And it wasn't just the house; the whole of the stable block and the barns were blazing too. Bright orange flames lit up the sky and debris showered from the buildings like shooting stars.

'My baby!' I yelled, grabbing the door handle, trying to get out.

I felt John's hand on my arm. 'You stay here. I'll go.'

'Stay where you are, son. I'll radio the fire brigade,' said the constable.

But John ignored him, and in seconds he was out of the car and running down the hill towards the blaze.

'John,' I yelled, and got out of the car myself. I began to run towards the burning buildings after him, but he was way ahead of me and within a few steps I felt the arms of the policeman round mine and he was pulling me back, forcing me to stop.

'My baby's in there,' I sobbed, my eyes burning, my throat full of smoke.

'The fire engine's on its way. There's nothing you can do.'

'But what about John?'

'Come back to the car, lassie. He won't get far. It's too far gone. We've radioed for help, the fire engine will be here soon.'

They forced me back to the car and I waited, on the back seat, paralysed with fear, tears streaming down my face, my eyes fixed on the burning buildings in the hollow. Now I wasn't just terrified for baby Edward and the orphans, but for John too. I understood why he'd gone down there to try to get into the house – I'd been desperate to myself – but now I was terrified that I'd lost him too. Every minute that passed without seeing him stumble back up that hill was agony for me.

It seemed an age before the fire brigade arrived. It must have taken them a long time to find their way up to the farm all the way from Ivybridge. They arrived in their red wagon with ladders on the top, the bell ringing frantically. I watched breathlessly as they charged down the hill and pulled up outside the house. They ran around trying to find a water source. In the end they found a tap in the yard, but the pressure was very low, the hoses making no impression on the rampant flames, so they scrambled down to the stream with buckets and threw water at the flames. It was a long, long time before the flames began to subside, and as they died down gradually, I could see that the house had been completely gutted by the fire, part of the roof caved in, the windows smashed in the heat and the frames burned away. Tears streamed down my face thinking that baby Edward had been in there and that John could well have perished too; but as I looked on, two figures emerged from behind the building and started to make their way up the hill towards us. My heart leapt. As they got closer, I could see that one was John. He was being helped along by one of the firemen.

I jumped out of the car and ran towards him. Close up, his face was black with soot and sweat was pouring from him. I flung my arms round him and held him as close as I could.

'I'm so sorry, Daisy,' he said, his voice cracking. 'I tried to get in there, but there was nothing I could do.'

Chapter Twenty-Five

Helen

Helen was driving to the care home. She was tired. She'd sat up long into the night, reading the journal and letters in the deposit box. After she'd shut the journal, she'd sat in silence for a long time, just staring into space. Her mind was back in 1945, imagining Daisy and John making their way to Paddington station, stepping onto a steam train bound for Southampton. She knew now that the sailor in the portrait was the same person as the young man on the ship with Daisy. And she knew, too, that he had been on board HMS *Berkeley* when it went down at Dieppe, although she also knew that he'd survived. His story had touched her heart; an orphan boy who had struggled so hard to help her mother and who'd shown such bravery in battle.

Her eyes were tired from devouring the closely written pages of her mother's scrawling handwriting. As she'd read, she'd sensed that Daisy had written the journal in a hurry, racing against time to get everything down while she had the chance.

Helen shook her head slowly in wonder, thinking back over what she'd read. Her mind was reeling with shock at the hardships her mother had suffered; the traumas, the grief and the violence. As she'd read, her eyes had filled with tears several times with pity for Daisy.

It had taken Helen two days to read the journal and letters all the way through. She and Laura had agreed that Helen would read it first, then pass it on to Laura once she'd finished. She'd started it on the train back from London to Exeter the day they'd discovered it in the bank vault in Harrow, and she'd carried on that evening and well into the night, unable to put it down.

Helen had been appalled at what had happened to Daisy and the others on the farm. She was finally beginning to understand her mother; to piece together the reasons for some of her behaviour. That she'd been shaped by her circumstances and the dreadful ordeal she'd been through. Helen was overwhelmed by a feeling of compassion for Daisy. She needed to go to see her mother straight away to tell her she understood, she was sorry for the way things had been between them and to make things right.

As she drove, she wondered if anything that had happened on Black Moor Farm had ever come to light. It was so unjust, Helen thought, that no one would have been punished for the cruelty that had taken place on the farm. Even Frank Baines had been too cowardly to face the truth and had taken his own life.

She remembered what she'd found out through the research she'd done into the treatment of evacuees during the war. That many were exploited, that their rations were used for their host family while they themselves went without. That some others were made to work on the land without pay. But in all her searching, she hadn't been able to find anything on the scale of what had happened to her mother.

She'd been desperate to finish the journal, reading long into the night the day before. When she'd reached the point where Daisy had described Peggy's death her heart had gone out to her mother, and she'd thought back to that forlorn grave under the neglected apple trees in the orchard at the abandoned farm. She felt tears in her eyes as she envisaged Daisy trekking down through those overgrown woods on foot day after day over the years since she'd bought Black Moor Hall, carrying flowers to lay on her dead sister's grave, kneeling there in the rain and in the snow, nursing her private grief. But because of her misplaced guilt she'd been unable to share that grief with anyone, not even her daughters. At least, not until now.

She'd wondered if anything that had happened on Black Moor Farm had ever come to light, although, as Reeves had perished in the fire, and Baines had hanged himself, there was no one to punish. She'd done some hasty research on the internet. She finally turned up an article in the *Western Morning News* about the fire at Black Moor Farm. Four charred bodies had been found, but it was thought that more had perished with no identifiable remains. The words still had the power to shock; the ring of a dreadful tragedy. It was so unjust, Helen thought, that no one would have been punished for the cruelty that had taken place on the farm. Frank Baines had taken his own life…

When she arrived at the care home, Helen was shown straight in to see her mother. For the first time in her life, she felt deep sympathy and a real connection with Daisy as she entered the room and caught sight of the familiar figure sitting in her usual position in the bay window, staring out across the moor. She crossed the room quickly, approached Daisy's chair and touched her mother on the shoulder. Daisy turned and looked up at her.

'Don't worry, Mum,' she said straight away. 'Laura and I went to the bank in Harrow. We found your journal in the vaults there, and some letters too.'

Daisy caught her breath, gripped Helen's hand and nodded slowly. Then she bowed her head and closed her eyes for a few seconds.

'Did you read it?' she asked, her eyes searching Helen's.

Helen paused and smiled at her mother, amazed that she'd been able to utter a full sentence. Then she pulled up a chair and sat down beside her, and leaned forward. When Daisy opened her eyes, she said, 'Yes. I understand now, Mum. I know what happened to you during the war.'

At those words, Daisy drew her brows together in an anxious frown, and Helen noticed a look of fear enter her eyes.

'I know how you were tricked into going to the farm and how you were mistreated there,' she went on. Then she paused, letting the words sink in, but Daisy's eyes still conveyed her distress at remembering, and now there were tears in them too.

'I know all about how you lost your sister; that you blamed yourself at the time and that you've been blaming yourself ever since. It's why you bought the farm and kept it like a memorial to her. I know about John too, and baby Edward. Oh, Mum, what you must have been through!'

Daisy looked up at her with tears in her eyes.

'And I can understand, too, why you were so angry with me when you caught me walking down there when I was a teenager. I couldn't understand it at the time and it grew into that great rift between us that lasted years, but now I know why. I'm so sorry, Mum.'

Daisy hung her head and felt for Helen's hand. It wasn't much, but it was a start.

'Don't worry, Mum. Please don't look like that. You don't need to be afraid of anything now. There are no secrets between us any more. I think it's amazing how you survived all that and went on to do the things you've done. Became a doctor, helped so many people. Your strength… it's unbelievable.'

The anxious frown softened, and Daisy released Helen's gaze and looked down at her hands.

'It must have been… well, words can't describe what it must have been like for you. You're so strong to have got through that experience. So unbelievably strong, Mum.'

Daisy shook her head and gave Helen another searching look, almost pleading.

'And I understand too, some of the reasons why… well, why you are the way you are. You were trying to protect yourself from getting hurt, weren't you? Putting a shield up around your heart?'

Daisy frowned and drew herself up stiffly in the chair.

'I'm sorry, Mum. What I meant was that you needed to be strong to cope with what had happened to you during the war, and that meant being tough with Laura and me too. Setting high standards; never letting up.'

Her mother inclined her head slightly again. Was that a trace of a smile on her lips?

'And I'm beginning to understand, too, why you bought Black Moor Farm, and why you needed to keep it a secret from us.'

She'd stayed with Daisy for a couple of hours, talking about what she'd read in the journal; about Daisy's life in Harrow before the war, about her mother and father. Daisy had smiled and nodded and held Helen's hand. She'd seemed genuinely relieved that the secrets of a lifetime were finally being brought to the surface. And Helen got a sense now that Daisy was beginning to understand everything, that she was fully focused for the first time since her stroke.

When Helen left the home just before Daisy's lunch was served, she felt her heart lifting, as if the misunderstandings and bitter disagreements they'd had for decades were finally being aired and put to rest.

She'd driven back to Totnes to mind the shop for Jago for the afternoon while he went to an auction. But at the end of the day, pulling the blinds down at the shop windows and preparing to lock up and walk back to the house, she thought again about what she'd read, and reminded herself that there were many more questions to be answered. What had happened to Daisy and John in India? She thought about the photograph of the two of them standing beside the rail of the ocean liner, the wind in their hair, the expressions on their young faces. They must have been on their way to Darjeeling together when that was taken. Had John and Daisy gone their separate ways once they were there?

She wandered down the hill and through the lamplit streets to the house, letting herself into the dark entrance hall. She wondered if she might find out these answers from Daisy herself, but knew that she was still very ill. Too unwell to speak too much.

Later, with questions about the journal and what happened to John burning in her mind, she sat down at her computer and logged on, wondering if she might be able to find some information about him on the kind of sites specialising in family history and research into ancestry where she had discovered her half-brother's existence.

Helen made herself a cup of tea and went straight upstairs to her computer table. She took out the art college prospectus and flicked through the pages, letting her imagination roam. Wouldn't it be wonderful to be able to devote herself to her art to the exclusion of everything else? To put her own desires first for once. Forget about the shop for a while, put her skills and potential to the test and see if her talent could blossom. She thought back to the conversations she'd had with Daisy. Now that she understood the reasons behind her mother's disapproval of frivolity, she felt sure that Daisy hadn't really meant to be so hurtful when Helen had suggested going to art college before. And the knowledge that she had kept Helen's schoolgirl art in the desk in her office for all those years had made her realise that underneath it all, Daisy was proud of her. Smiling, she made a note of the telephone number. She would give them a call in the morning and find out about places for next year.

Chapter Twenty-Six

Helen

Helen was awoken the next morning by her mobile phone buzzing.

'It's me – Laura,' came the breathless voice at the other end. 'Sorry it's so early, but I've just dropped Paul at the station. He's got a debate in Parliament today.'

'What time is it?' asked Helen.

'Oh, just after six thirty. I've been thinking about Mum. You've read everything in the deposit box, I take it? What's it all about?'

Helen sat down on the bed.

'It'll take a bit of time to tell you,' she said.

'I've got all the time in the world,' said Laura. 'Fire away.'

So, Helen told her about what she'd read in the letters and journal. About how Daisy and Peggy were abducted to the farm and forced to work; about John and how he escaped but they thought he'd been killed, about Peggy and how she'd died, and finally, about baby Edward and the fire.

'I can't quite believe it,' said Laura when she'd finished. 'The things she went through! I've been awake most of the night, wondering about it. It's been going round and round in my head.'

'Mine too. I can't stop going over it. I've been dreaming about it too.'

'She had a baby! That's the most astonishing thing of all, Helen. Edward… just think, he was our brother. How very sad that he died in the fire. Poor Mum! It explains a lot, doesn't it?'

'Yes, I've been piecing everything together too. It all fits now, Laura. The way Mum was with us, with everyone, the way she led her life… She put a shield up around herself. She disciplined herself ruthlessly, punishing herself for what had happened to Peggy and to Edward. It wasn't rational and it was completely understandable given what she'd been through. The way she treated us, held us to such high standards, wouldn't let us get close. I understand all that now. She was terrified of her own vulnerability, and she guarded it at all costs.

'I also understand why she was so angry when I went down towards the old farm that night after my O-level results. It was the closest she'd come to being found out and it must have terrified her. No wonder it drove a wedge between us that we're only just removing now everything is out in the open.'

'You're right. I wonder what happened to John though?'

'Yes. I really want to fill in the gaps too. What happened to Mum and John when they went to India? Why did they part and how did she meet Dad?'

'I'm sure we'd be able to find out some more if we tried. I could have a go this morning. And we could always see if Mum could tell us about it herself, but she's so reluctant to talk and so unwell that she can't say much anyway. One thing occurred to me while I was reading. Maybe Mum wrote to Mrs Hutchings after she left for India. They were very close, so if she wrote to anyone, it would have been to her. It might be a long shot, but perhaps we could go and look for Mrs Hutchings in Harrow?'

'Surely she must be dead by now. She was middle-aged in the war, after all. She'd have to be well over a hundred if she was still around.'

'But it might still be worth going back there, don't you think? We know from the letters that Mother's address was in Laburnum Drive, which we can find, and Mrs Hutchings lived at number 55.'

'I suppose so…' Helen said slowly.

'So why don't we go today, then? No time like the present. If you come straight up to Exeter, we could get on the nine o'clock train.'

A wave of guilt washed through Helen. That would mean letting Jago down yet again. How would she be able to tell him that she wasn't going to be working in the shop again today?

'Helen? Are you still there? You're not worrying about Jago, are you?'

'Oh, Laura. I *was*, sort of. How did you guess?'

'Because I know you. You're just too kind. Jago's perfectly capable of looking after the shop himself.'

It was early afternoon when Helen and Laura opened the garden gate of 55 Laburnum Drive in Harrow and went up the front path between the neat flowerbeds. They exchanged apprehensive glances as they approached the front door and Laura pressed the doorbell. There was silence for a long time and they were just on the point of turning away when they heard the sound of footsteps coming quickly down the hall and the bolts being drawn back. The door was opened a fraction, held taut on a chain. The face of a woman appeared in the crack. She was tall and thin, and her hair was dyed a startling shade of red, making her skin look dull and pale. She wore bright red lipstick. She looked about the same age as Helen and Laura's mother. When she saw the two of them standing there, she frowned.

'How many times have I told you people? No Jehovah's Witnesses,' she said sharply.

She moved to shut the door, but Laura put her foot inside before she could. She said quickly, 'Please. We're not Jehovah's Witnesses. We're here to do some research into family history. We're looking for someone who used to live in this house.'

The door was drawn back a fraction and the old woman's face appeared again.

'Really? And who might that be? I've lived in this house most of my life.'

'We're looking for a Mrs Hutchings. We've recently discovered that our mother lived in this street when she was growing up before the war. From her letters, we're pretty sure that this was the Hutchings' house.' Helen and Laura exchanged looks again as the old lady pushed the door for a second time, but this time she removed the chain and then opened it wide.

'Well, I'm *Miss* Hutchings,' she said, this time with a smile. 'Miss Suzanne Hutchings, that is. Mrs Hutchings was my mother. She passed away more than twenty years ago now. What did you say your mother's name was? I might remember her myself.'

'Daisy… Daisy Banks.'

The old woman frowned for a moment, her face puckered up in concentration, then her expression cleared and she smiled. Her face was transformed, her eyes sparkled with memories.

'Oh, Daisy! Yes, of course I remember Daisy. Daisy Banks and her little sister Peggy. Would you like to come inside? I'll put the kettle on.'

They followed the old woman down the narrow hall and into a small, square kitchen.

'Do sit down at the table. I take it you'd like some tea? Have you come far?'

'Tea would be lovely. Yes, we've come up from south Devon this morning.'

'Gosh! Quite a journey. So, what can I do for you two girls?' Miss Hutchings said, putting a kettle on an old-fashioned gas stove as Helen and Laura settled themselves at the kitchen table.

'We're trying to find out a few things about what happened to our mother during the war,' said Helen. 'And we'd like to find out something about our Aunt Peggy. We've only just discovered her existence.'

'Daisy and I were friends, sort of, although she was a little younger than me. I think she used to come and visit Mum towards the end of the war. Mum had a soft spot for her because she'd lost her own mother, I suppose. I was off doing my nursing training and working away from home until in Mum's final days when she needed help. Daisy and her sister were evacuated in 1940, but I expect you know that.'

'It's a long story,' said Laura, 'but we think that our mother might have visited Mrs Hutchings – your mother – before she went off to India with her friend John in 1945. We're not sure what happened to them there, and we were wondering if Mum ever wrote any letters to her that might help to explain. We'd like to find out what happened to John if we can.'

Miss Hutchings put three steaming mugs of tea on the table, then sat down between them.

'What an extraordinary story,' she said, and paused for a few minutes, her eyes far away. 'I suppose the war separated lots of people, did dreadful things to families… But what does Daisy herself say about all this? Have you tried to ask her?'

'She recently had a stroke and we only just found out about it through reading a journal she kept during the war,' said Helen. 'It's dreadfully sad, but the stroke virtually robbed her of the power of speech. She can only say a few words at the most now. It was only clearing out her house that we found some letters, which started us looking into what happened to her during the war.'

'How very sad,' said Miss Hutchings, shaking her head. 'Daisy used to hang around with us older girls and boys at the aerodrome. We all used to go up there for a smoke sometimes. Thought it was sophisticated.' Her eyes shone as she remembered. 'I got rid of most of Mum's papers and letters after she died, but I did keep a few of them. I stashed them away in a box under the spare bed if they had unusual stamps. I didn't read them, of course. I thought

I might take up stamp collecting in my old age, but do you know, I haven't got to that stage yet. Too busy by half!' She smiled.

'It would be amazing if any of them are from our mother,' said Laura.

'I'll go and look for them right now. It would be wonderful if I could help you. The sad death of your grandmother affected the whole street for years afterwards. I'll always remember it.'

'That's incredibly kind of you,' said Helen.

'You just wait there. I won't be long. They're up in the spare room.'

Helen and Laura hardly spoke to each other while they waited for Miss Hutchings. They listened to her going up the stairs, walking along the landing and opening a door at the front of the house. Then all went quiet.

'She's very sprightly for her age,' whispered Laura. 'She's that bit older than Mum... she must be well over ninety.'

'She's astonishing,' said Helen. 'I thought she was going to be a bit difficult at first, but she's got such a twinkle in her eye! Did you notice?'

Laura nodded, smiling. Then there was a sound in the passageway.

'She's coming back,' said Laura, putting her finger to her lips.

Miss Hutchings came back into the room carrying an old shoebox.

'I think I might have found something,' she said. 'There *are* some letters in here from India. There are others from Australia, and Canada. My uncles travelled for work a lot and always wrote to Mum... but here are the Indian ones. Different handwriting. I've never opened them.'

She fumbled in the shoebox and, one by one, laid four dusty, faded envelopes on the table. Helen stared at them. They were all made of airmail paper, virtually transparent, with a blue airmail sticker on the top. On each envelope were many stamps, some blue, some red, with King George VI's head in the middle and the words 'Indian Postal Service' around the edge. They were smothered in postmarks. One said 'Calcutta', but the others were indistinct. Helen looked across at Laura, who was also staring at the letters. The handwriting was unmistakably Daisy's. Helen would know it anywhere, now she'd spent so much time deciphering it while reading the journal.

'Look familiar?' asked Miss Hutchings.

'It's definitely Mum's handwriting.'

Miss Hutchings gasped and put her hands to her mouth. 'Are you sure? How marvellous if they are.'

'Yes. Quite sure,' said Helen.

'Well, in that case, would you like to take them home with you?'

'We'd love to, but they belong to you really.'

'No, my dear. They belong to you,' said Miss Hutchings, putting her hand on top of Helen's. 'If my mother were alive it might be different, but since she's dead, and since they might be of some use to you…'

'That's very kind of you indeed,' said Laura. 'We could send you the stamps back, once we've read them.'

'No need. I don't suppose I'll ever get round to stamp collecting in reality. Sounds a bit too sensible for me. But if they're helpful, it would be lovely if you could let me know what you find. I'd love to know if they've helped to solve your mystery.'

Chapter Twenty-Seven

Daisy

August 1945

My dear Mrs Hutchings,

It is many weeks since we said goodbye. Thank you for showing us so much kindness when we arrived in London. I don't know how we'd have coped without you.

Even now I can't stop thinking about my father's death, but know that I don't blame you for being the one to tell me. It was heartbreaking to find out, on top of everything else, especially as he must have died thinking that I'd been killed in the bombing in Plymouth. I wonder if he just gave up, having lost his whole family? If only he'd known I'd survived, things might have been different. But I can't think like that. I must learn to grieve him, just as I've learned to grieve everyone else.

Our ship docked in Calcutta yesterday so today's the first opportunity I've had to write. I have so much to tell you. I promised I would let you know how we got on once we'd arrived in India.

The train down to Southampton was packed with people heading for the docks, taking ships to the colonies now that the war was over. We kept to ourselves in the corner of the carriage; hardly speaking and hardly looking at our fellow passengers. We were both nervous. We knew nothing about the ship that we were taking, or what the voyage would be like. On that journey down to Southampton I began to wonder if we could trust Alfie, the pub landlord who'd helped us get tickets and passports, including a new identity for me. As you know, I wanted to leave everything about my old life behind, to start afresh. So I left Daisy Banks with you. I was so pleased with my passport and how sophisticated I looked in the photograph. I'm looking forward to being Daisy Dawson and having a fresh start.

I knew that John wouldn't have asked Alfie too many questions about the journey and about what awaited us in India, so desperate was he to get away from England and to make a new life.

When we arrived at the docks, we found the office of the P&O shipping line and showed our tickets to the man behind the counter. My heart sank when it turned out that we were to travel on a ship that was also transporting a couple of battalions of soldiers. Neither of us knew that all P&O liners to India had been commandeered and converted to transport troops at the beginning of the war. Now that the war in Europe was over, more soldiers were being sent out to India to defend the empire against the independence movement.

There were two decks reserved for passengers. Alfie and his friends obviously had contacts in high places if they'd been able to get us a ticket in those circumstances.

We boarded the ship and were directed to our cabins. They were a few doors down from each other. They were very basic, with a simple bunk, a basin and a shelf for a suitcase. Neither had a porthole and they were on the inside of the ship, so airless and claustrophobic. Since we weren't married, it would have been against the company's rules for us to share.

When we left the port, got clear of Southampton Water and were finally out to sea, John and I went out on deck and watched the green downs of the Isle of Wight slip away from view as we headed south into the English Channel. A man with a camera on a tripod offered to take our photo, so we agreed, although I felt very self-conscious being photographed like that when I was running away on a false passport. The man said he would mail the picture to our address in Darjeeling once we got to India.

The journey to Calcutta took almost a month and was uncomfortable and tense. For the first few days the sea was rough as we crossed the Bay of Biscay and I was very sick. But even when the ship moved into calmer waters, the sickness continued, and after a few days it dawned on me that I could well be expecting again. When I told John, he held me close for a long time and we both cried together; partly with joy at the knowledge of this new life we'd created and partly with grief for the loss of our firstborn child.

'When we get there, we'll get married,' he said and I agreed. We'd both known all along that we would, but now there was a reason to do it quickly.

It was wonderful to go out on deck and feel the wind in my hair and watch the endless shimmering ocean blue as far as you could see. I imagined what Peggy would think of it. There were a few young men, like John, going out to take up jobs on plantations, or in the Indian civil service, and there were some older couples too, returning to homes and jobs in India that the war had interrupted. We hardly spoke to any of them, we didn't wish to appear rude, but equally, we did not want anyone to ask us about how we'd spent the war.

We weren't allowed onto any of the troop decks, but we could hear the soldiers doing their exercise drills out on deck in the morning, the loud hum of conversation from their canteens during mealtimes, and occasionally loud, tuneless voices singing bawdy songs from the bunkhouses in the evenings.

On the last week of the voyage, John became sick with fever. I'm not sure what had brought it on – although the food in the third-class canteen was very poor – but when I went to his cabin one morning, I found him scrunched up on the bunk, his teeth chattering with the cold, goosebumps on his skin, but at the same time his body pouring with sweat. He was gasping for air and I was terrified for him – he was still broken from the war. I ran along the metal gangways, up three decks to the sanatorium and managed to convince a doctor to come to the cabin and examine him. The doctor told me to bathe him with a cold flannel and make sure he drank plenty of water. He didn't seem too perturbed, pronouncing it to be some type of flu. I did as I was told, hardly leaving John's side for four days, while he sweated and twisted in delirium. It reminded me so much of Peggy's illness that I was desperate for him to get better. I was worried too about catching whatever illness he had, terrified that it might harm my unborn child, but I knew I was the only person who could help John get through it, so I put my fears aside and nursed him as best I could.

I missed a great deal of the journey, holed away in John's cabin. But as the ship put in to Colombo, I went out on deck and watched the teeming life on the docks below. Hawkers shouting about their wares, porters carrying luggage to and fro, bullock carts and rickshaws jostling for space on the quayside. I would have loved to go ashore, attracted by the exotic sounds and smells, the balmy air *and the beautiful buildings on the seafront, but I knew I had to stay with John.*

On the fifth day he was well enough to get up. I managed to persuade him to come out on deck, so we went up and leaned on the ship's rail, enjoying the warm breeze, watching the eastern coastline of India slip past on the far horizon. But as we turned to go back inside, he was seized by one of his dreadful coughing fits and I had to support him as he walked downstairs to the cabin.

The next morning, we crossed the Bay of Bengal and entered the channel between the swampy islands at the mouth of the Hooghly River. Even though John was still coughing and wheezing, we stood together at the rail the whole morning, entranced by the scenes on the banks of the river as the ship made its way up the estuary towards Calcutta. Villages of huts, where children bathed naked on the muddy banks, exotic palm trees and grasslands, buffaloes wallowing in the mud, and rice paddies stretching as far as the eye could see.

At last the ship arrived at the city docks and moored up with much fanfare and blasting of its horn, and we were free to go ashore. There was so much clamour on the quayside that we were overwhelmed at first. Porters surrounded us, wanting to carry our luggage, to take us to whichever hotel would pay the most commission. In the end we found a rickshaw to take us to the Great Eastern Hotel, where the Darjeeling Tea company were putting us up for a night before we caught the train north to Darjeeling.

So here we are in Calcutta, in a sumptuous hotel, in a beautiful room with high ceilings and potted palms. This evening we will dine in the palm court, before catching the train tomorrow morning. It feels strange, and a little disloyal, to be indulging in such luxury when we're mourning our devastating loss. But things are not all so wonderful either. I'm still concerned about John's chest. He is still coughing quite a bit, but I'm hoping that the mountain air will help him recover completely.

I am rushing to finish this letter, Mrs Hutchings, so the concierge will mail it tomorrow morning after we've left the Great Eastern for the early train from Sealdah station. So much has happened since we said goodbye to you, and I apologise for the length of this letter, but I needed to get everything down, to let you know everything that has happened to us since we left.

Please put some flowers on Mother's grave for me, and when you do that, say a prayer for all the others I have lost. I know I can count on you to keep my secrets. You have been such a support to us both, I am eternally grateful. I will write again once we are in Darjeeling.

Your loving Daisy.

Helen finished the letter and passed it to Laura to read. They were on the train back to Devon. They were powering along the sea wall at Dawlish and she glanced at the darkening sky over the slate-grey, choppy waters and at the seabirds wheeling over the breakers. She'd always loved this stretch of the journey; the ever-changing views, the wild, unpredictable sea and the way it meant that she was almost home. Today she thought of how Daisy and John must have made this journey in reverse, nursing their terrible grief as they went, but hoping that it would signal the start of a better future.

She looked down at her lap and took up the next envelope. This letter was thinner, the postmark was Darjeeling and it was posted around a fortnight after the first one.

July 15th 1945

Dear Mrs Hutchings,

I am writing once again with more sadness than I can describe. It is almost as if my heart is so full of grief that it will burst. My darling John has gone from this world. There — I have written the words. I have grieved for him once before and it was a miracle that he came back to me, but he did return and I should have been more grateful than I was. I had no idea that we would have such a short time together or that he would be taken from me once again so quickly. As I write, I can't stop the tears flowing.

When we arrived, John's illness worsened, and he was admitted to hospital. I went there every day to visit him. And each day I could see that he was getting worse. He was slipping away before my eyes.

So this morning I buried the only boy I've ever loved. The one I'd intended to spend the rest of my life with. The one who'd risked everything to come back to the farm and save me; who'd been my constant companion and rock these past months: my lover, my friend and my soulmate . But I will always have a reminder of him, until the end of my days; the unborn child that is growing inside me, made from our love.

Please pray for us both, Mrs Hutchings,

Your loving Daisy.

Laura was silent for several minutes, again staring out of the window. Helen opened her mouth to say something, then decided to leave her to think. How could it be that the person she'd thought of as her sister her whole life didn't actually share her father? And how could her mother have lived a lie for so long, never told Laura the truth? She knew it would be even more of a shock to her sister. She knew it would take Laura time to process it.

The train rumbled over the River Dart and slowed as it pulled into Totnes station.

Laura turned back to Helen, her face composed now.

'You know, Dad will always be Dad to me, whether he was my biological father or not. And you're right: Mum did the right thing in marrying him. He was a fantastic father to us and husband to her. She couldn't have chosen better.'

Chapter Twenty-Eight

Helen

The next morning, Helen and Laura had agreed to go to the care home again to let their mother know that they'd tracked down her letters and that from them, they'd discovered the truth about Laura's birth. Helen was surprised at how well Laura seemed to be taking the news so far. She wondered whether her sister was hiding her true feelings. But it didn't feel as though anything had changed between them; if anything, it seemed to have brought them closer, united in their quest for the truth.

Before going to the home that morning, they'd arranged to meet at the cemetery at North Brent. It was the nearest one to the farm, and they had agreed that if there were any Reeves' graves in the area, this is where they'd be.

As Helen drove through the winding Devon lanes to North Brent from Totnes, she thought about the photograph of John and how she'd been drawn to those enigmatic eyes, had been desperate to find out more about him. The journal had confirmed that he'd been on board HMS *Berkeley* when she went down during the Dieppe raid, and that his life had been so cruelly cut short by the injuries he sustained that day. Now she knew why his face had struck such a chord with her; it was a familiar face, with the same high cheekbones and determined look that her sister had. How hadn't she spotted that when it was right under her nose? It all made sense now and she was grateful to her mother for having been so frank in her journal. It had made everything so clear.

Helen was entering the village of North Brent now. She drove carefully along the quiet village street and pulled up outside the cemetery. There was no sign of Laura's car. Late as usual, Helen thought, but with the sort of acceptance and affection that she wouldn't have felt a few weeks ago.

She got out of her car and walked through the wrought-iron gates into the cemetery. It suddenly came back to her how she used to creep in here with her schoolfriends, to smoke and to listen to pop music on a portable cassette player. They'd never taken any interest in the cemetery itself. In fact, they'd never actually looked at the names on the graves, just taunted each other with stories of what might happen if you walked over a grave by mistake; how the soul of the dead person would rise up and come to haunt you as you were sleeping.

She stood for a moment just inside the gate, taking in the atmosphere of the place, letting go of the tension that had built up in her body while she was reliving the unpleasant discussion with Jago. It was raining gently, a soft Devon rain that cast a mist over this tranquil, sacred place. The graveyard was enclosed by high stone walls and embedded in them at intervals were memorial plaques with inscriptions dedicated to those who'd passed away. The grass was overgrown, but a narrow path had been mown through the middle between the gravestones and around the outer edge.

There were benches placed around in front of the wall that looked neglected, with mossy, broken slats. Helen smiled, remembering how they would sit on those benches as teenagers. They were falling apart even then. Her name might well be carved into one of them.

Helen went to the other side of the graveyard and started walking slowly around the outer path, reading the inscriptions on the plaques mounted in the walls. She also paced up and down between the graves, examining the headstones, checking names. It was a good fifteen minutes before she spotted something: a plaque on the back wall. It gave her a start to see what was written there in black and white:

> *Here lie the remains of Joseph Reeves, born April 10th 1880, his daughter Elsie Freda Reeves, born 1st September 1927, baby, Joe Reeves, born 11th June 1942, together with three unknown and unnamed souls. All died tragically on 6th September 1944. God Rest Their Souls.*

Helen stood, transfixed, hardly noticing the rain soaking through her thin mac. She felt someone touch her shoulder and jumped.

'Sorry I'm late, Helen.' Laura was smiling, her cheeks flushed and she was out of breath. 'Had to drop Paul off at his constituency office. The traffic was murder…' Her eyes widened and colour drained from her face as she followed Helen's gaze and read the writing on the plaque.

'Oh, my goodness! Is this it?'

'Looks like it,' murmured Helen. 'And to think, we lived a few miles from here for years not even knowing it was there.'

'I know. It beggars belief. Look, they called him Joe. After Farmer Reeves,' said Laura. 'Mum would have hated that.'

'I wonder what he would have been like if he'd lived,' mused Helen.

'I always hankered after a brother,' said Laura.

They stood in silence for a while, contemplating the inscription on the wall and what might have been, as the rain got heavier, soaking into the ground, filling the air with the scent of wet soil and cut grass.

Later, at home, Helen logged onto her computer. There was something that was troubling her about all this. The newspaper report had suggested that only four bodies had been found; the rest had been presumed dead, but they hadn't recovered any remains. Perhaps there was just a chance that someone had survived?

She found a website where it was possible to view death certificates if you paid a fee. She started with Farmer Reeves. It didn't take too long. There it was in black and white, just as it was on the gravestone: Joseph Reeves, born 10 April 1880, died 6 June 1945. Cause of death: Asphyxiation by smoke inhalation.

Then she looked for Elsie. It took her a while, but what she found stopped her heart. There was a line through Elsie's entry in the register and a note: *Death recorded in error. Rectified in accordance with statutory declaration.*

Her hands trembling, she looked for Joe Edward Reeves. There it was again. A line through the entry and the same words beside it: *Death recorded in error. Rectified in accordance with statutory declaration of mother.*

She sat there, staring at the entry for a long time. So long that the letters began to blur before her eyes, the realisation of what it meant sinking in gradually. He had lived after all. Baby Edward had lived. He hadn't perished in the fire. That meant that her brother could be somewhere out there. She thought of her mother, her life slipping away in that care home, a life of guilt and regret that she hadn't been able to save her son. Helen knew that she owed it to her to find him. To put things right between them once and for all.

But if Edward had lived, how could she find out where he was now? Glancing at her watch, she realised there were a couple of hours before the register office in Newton Abbot closed for the afternoon. Gathering her notes and bag, she rushed out to her car and set off.

The woman behind the desk at the register office was very helpful. She assured Helen that they did keep records of all statutory declarations that had been made in support of amendments to the register of deaths.

'I'm sure we will have kept that one. It's very rare for a death to be rectified. Very rare indeed.'

Helen waited anxiously as the woman went to the basement of the building and searched in the archives. After twenty minutes or so she reappeared with a box file.

'It was hard to track down, but here it is…'

She handed Helen a dusty document. It was a sworn declaration by one Elsie Farmer née Reeves that she had survived the fire at Black Moor Farm and that her death, and that of her infant son, Joe, had been recorded in error. Helen scanned the typed paragraphs quickly. At the bottom was a scrawled signature – and, crucially, an address… *129 Crooksbury Road, Sheffield, South Yorkshire.*

The woman made a copy for her and, after thanking her profusely, Helen left the office.

The next day, Helen told Jago she wasn't available to work in the shop and drove to Sheffield. It was a long and boring drive up the motorway but on the way she did a lot of thinking about what she'd found out about her mother over the past few months, how it explained so much and how it had resolved the difficulties in their relationship that had been festering for so long. She also thought warmly about Laura, and how this quest had brought them closer than ever before.

Number 129 Crooksbury Road was a terraced house in south Sheffield that opened straight onto a busy road. There was a builders' van parked outside, and as Helen approached the door, she could hear the sound of hammers and drills inside and pop music playing on a radio. She knocked on the door and waited. After a few moments a builder opened it, wiping his hands on his overalls.

'I'm looking for someone who used to live here,' began Helen. He looked at her expectantly.

'An Elsie Farmer and her son Joe. They lived here in the forties. Not sure for how long.'

The man laughed, wiping his brow with the back of his arm.

'Long time ago! I've just bought the place myself. From an old lady. We're doing it up to let out to students. There's a big demand for student accommodation nowadays.'

'Perhaps she might know something about it?'

'Maybe. She's moved into a bungalow round the corner. Sheltered accommodation. Nice and modern and easy to look after. I'll give you her address, if you like.'

He went away, and a few minutes later, returned and handed Helen a piece of torn card with a name and address scrawled on one side. 'It's just a few streets away. Turn left after the pub, then third on the right. You can't miss it.'

Thanking him, Helen returned to her car and drove the half-mile or so to the bungalow. It was in a row of similar one-storey buildings with neat front gardens. An old woman opened the door.

'Mrs Prior? I'm doing some family research and was wondering if you knew an Elsie Farmer who used to live in your house? I'm looking for her son, Joe.'

The old lady broke into a broad smile and said, 'Oh yes, I knew Elsie. She lived in that house for fifty years until she sold up and went into a home. I bought the place from her.'

'That's wonderful news. And do you know what happened to her son?'

'Young Joe? Lovely lad he was. Clever too. Went off to university to study to be a doctor. Last I heard, he was working in Manchester. He must be in his seventies now though. He will have retired, I suppose. Would you like to come in and have a cup of tea, my dear?'

*

Helen did the long drive home buzzing with excitement. Joe was probably alive and living in Manchester. He'd qualified as a doctor! How amazing that he'd had that calling even though he hadn't known that his birth mother had done the very same thing.

That first, important discovery had led to yet more research, this time with Laura's help. They'd started in the obvious place: the British Medical Association. It had meant a trip to the archives in central London. Both Helen and Laura had gone, enjoying the outing together and finding the time to also take a shopping trip to the King's Road, where Laura persuaded Helen to buy a couple of smart new outfits in which to start the next chapter in her life.

But although the BMA archives were helpful, they didn't lead them to him. They did discover a Doctor Joe Reeves who'd qualified in London in 1968 and practised in hospitals all over the country, including in Sheffield, until around ten years ago. But the trail went cold once he'd retired so they both joined several family history websites and each day, when they met up to visit Daisy, compared notes of their findings. The search had taken weeks and brought the two sisters closer than ever before.

Eventually Helen had read an article about post-war rationing and discovered that if Elsie had changed her name, she would have had to make it official to be able to receive a ration book. After a lot of false starts, she eventually found an entry in the *London Gazette* dated December 1945 that made her scalp tingle.

> *I, Elsie Freda Farmer of 129 Crooksbury Road, Sheffield, South Yorkshire, widow, a natural-born British subject, heretofore called and known by the name of 'Elsie Freda Reeves', hereby give notice that I have renounced and abandoned the name of Elsie Freda Reeves and will henceforth be known as Elsie Freda Farmer and that my son, Joe Reeves, a minor, for whom I have sole parental responsibility, will be henceforth be known by the name Joe Farmer.*

Further searching for any information about either Joe or Elsie proved fruitless for a while. Then Helen joined a chat forum on one of the sites and posted a question asking if anyone knew either Elsie, Freda or Joe Farmer. She mentioned that they'd lived in Sheffield in the 1940s while Joe was a child, and that he'd qualified as a doctor at the London Hospital in 1968.

It had been a few days since she'd received the message online.

Dear Helen, I think I'm the person you're looking for. I've been trying to research my family history for a few years without much success. How can I help you?

Chapter Twenty-Nine

Three Months Later

Helen stood beside Laura on the concourse at Exeter station. They were watching the Departures and Arrivals board. Neither of them could take their eyes off the yellow flashing names. Helen already had a crick in her neck and her eyes were going fuzzy watching them. Laura was tapping her foot impatiently.

They had come there together in Laura's car. Helen had been staying with Laura and Paul for a couple of days a week over the last month or so, having enrolled to do an art degree at the university. She was juggling the course with working in the antiques shop part-time.

She'd been apprehensive about telling Daisy about the course – after all, it was the memory of her mother's disapproval that had stopped her from trying it for years, but in the new spirit of understanding, one day she'd broached the subject, telling her that she was starting her degree the following month and that she was going to stay with Laura and Paul while studying. Daisy had smiled and taken her hand.

'Bloody train's delayed,' Laura said now. 'Typical. An extra fifteen minutes. Shall we go for a coffee to kill some time?'

'If you like. I don't really mind,' said Helen mildly.

'It's so annoying. Mum will be expecting us. She'll begin to fret if we're late.'

Helen smiled at her sister. What was an extra fifteen minutes in the context of the lifetime that Daisy had waited for this day?

After all, she'd lived through the war, survived bombings and the most punishing of conditions.

'Come on then,' said Laura. 'There's a café over there.'

Helen followed in Laura's wake as she strode across the concourse. Laura was already queuing at the counter as Helen entered the café, and she pointed across at a table for her sister to sit at. Helen sat down obediently and waited, discreetly checking her make-up in the little mirror she carried in her bag – she wanted to look her best today. And now she and Laura drank their coffees in silence, each too nervous and excited to speak, waiting for Edward to arrive. To tell him all about Daisy, and introduce their mother to her son.

Laura was continually checking her watch and glancing out of the window at the Arrivals board. The fifteen minutes ticked by very slowly. Finally, they heard the announcement: 'The delayed 10.42 from Manchester is about to arrive on Platform 1.'

They gulped their drinks and left the café, walking quickly through the station and onto Platform 1. As they waited and the train finally pulled in, Laura said to Helen, 'I'm so glad we're close now, Helen. I can't believe how these last few months have changed everything between us.'

'I'm glad too,' Helen whispered.

They hugged, and then they turned their attention to the passengers getting off the train, straining their eyes to see him. As the other passengers drifted away, there was one man left standing there. He was tall, a little taller than Helen and Laura, with steel-grey hair, dressed smartly in a suit and dark overcoat. He walked towards them and as he drew close enough for them to see his face, they could tell without a shadow of a doubt that he was Daisy's son.

A Letter from Ann

I want to say a huge thank you for choosing to read *The Runaway Sisters*. If you did enjoy it, and want to keep up to date with all my latest releases, just sign up at the following link. Your email address will never be shared and you can unsubscribe at any time.

www.bookouture.com/ann-bennett

I hope you loved *The Runaway Sisters* and if you did, I would be very grateful if you could write a review. I'd love to hear what you think, and it makes such a difference helping new readers to discover one of my books for the first time.

I love hearing from my readers – you can get in touch on my Facebook page, through Twitter, Goodreads or my website.

Thanks,
Ann

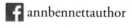 annbennettauthor

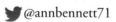 @annbennett71

Acknowledgements

This book was inspired by my mother's and aunt's wartime experience of being evacuated from Harrow-on-the-Hill to Plymouth at the start of WW2. Probably not the best place to be evacuated, I believe it became too unsafe for them to stay. But there the similarity ends. Other inspirations came from having lived in south Devon for several years and from continuing to visit family there. I love Totnes, the South Hams and the edge of Dartmoor, where the book is set.

Thanks go to my friend and writing buddy, Siobhan Daiko, for her constant support and encouragement for almost a decade, to my husband, Nick, for reading early drafts and to everyone who's supported me down the years by reading my books.

Made in United States
North Haven, CT
20 March 2024

50221695R00155